# Literary Reimaginings
# of Argentina's Independence

## History, Fiction, Politics

# Liverpool Latin American Studies

*Series Editor:* Matthew Brown, University of Bristol
*Emeritus Series Editor:* Professor John Fisher

Liverpool Latin American Studies, New Series 23

# Literary Reimaginings of Argentina's Independence
## History, Fiction, Politics

Catriona McAllister

LIVERPOOL UNIVERSITY PRESS

First published 2022 by
Liverpool University Press
4 Cambridge Street
Liverpool
L69 7ZU

British Library Cataloguing-in-Publication data
A British Library CIP record is available

ISBN 978-1-80034-845-5

Typeset by Carnegie Book Production, Lancaster

# Contents

# Acknowledgements

As with every book, this project would not have been possible without a small army of friends and colleagues supporting me along the way. I am extremely grateful to Joanna Page for her guidance, encouragement, and challenging questions in the first phase of this project, and to the many other colleagues who have read and commented on aspects of the work at various stages of the writing process, particularly Lucy Bell, Rory O'Bryen, Phil Swanson, Par Kumaraswami, and Cherilyn Elston. My weekly writing meetings with Eleanor Giraud have been invaluable during the editing process. I am also grateful for the support of a great many colleagues at the Centre of Latin American Studies, the University of Cambridge, and in the Department of Languages and Cultures at the University of Reading.

The first iteration of this project was made possible by the support of the Arts and Humanities Research Council, which funded my doctoral research, with additional support provided by both Emmanuel College, Cambridge, and the Simón Bolívar Fund at the Centre of Latin American Studies, Cambridge. I am also grateful for a period of study leave granted by my current institution, the University of Reading.

I would like to express my gratitude to Martín Kohan and Santiago Vega for stimulating discussions during my research trips to Buenos Aires, which proved instrumental in shaping the early stages of this project. I would also like to thank Manuel Santos Iñurrieta for providing me with a manuscript of his text prior to its publication, and to all the staff at the libraries and archives I visited in Buenos Aires.

Finally, I would like to thank my friends and family, who have supported and sustained me in so many ways. To my 'academic family', the friends and mentors who know the pressures of research and pick me up, dust me off, and put me back on track. To my friends outside the academy, who patiently listen to me talk about my projects and celebrate every achievement alongside me, while providing some much-needed perspective. And for my family, who have lived and breathed every moment of the project alongside me, and for whose love and support I will always be grateful.

# Introduction

## Writing and Rewriting Independence

Latin America has produced a vast array of fiction that could be described as 'historical', and the category of 'historical fiction' has attracted a substantial amount of critical attention over the last few decades. It would be hard to argue, therefore, that this branch of the region's literary output has been neglected: in fact, our ideas about contemporary Latin American historical fiction have consolidated into such a clear, recognizable critical position that our interpretations can be tinged with a sense of inevitability. While the novels themselves wrestle with a wide range of historical periods and narrative approaches, we frequently extract what they have in common under the umbrella of the 'Latin American Historical Novel'.

The current critical paradigm began to take shape in the late 1980s and early 1990s, when debates about the intersections between postmodernism, history, literature, and the shaping of knowledge found themselves in tune with the region's historical fiction. Through categories such as the 'new historical novel' and 'historiographic metafiction' (on which more below), we became familiar with the idea that self-reflexive historical fiction was performing a postmodern destabilizing of the past, reminding us that all history is a form of narrative and cautioning against absolutes. This reading can be applied to a significant proportion of Latin America's contemporary historical fiction, and therefore arguably became something of a victim of its own success, achieving a level of dominance that has created a feeling of circularity that could lead us to assume we have sufficient explanation of these texts.

This book, however, is born of a nagging sense that we might still be missing the point when it comes to these novels – that arguments foregrounding history and literature's shared reliance on narrative only begin to tap the potential of these texts, particularly in terms of their political arguments. What if the idea that history is narrative is not the final conclusion of these texts, but merely a starting point? If they seek to expose discursive foundations, is this the limit of their political critique? In fact, are abstract ideas of 'knowledge', 'fiction', and 'history' really the right starting place for interpreting these texts at all? My reading argues that, by departing from a different understanding of history, we can create much more satisfying and politically meaningful interpretations of these texts. Rather than speaking in abstract terms about 'history', my starting point recognizes the highly politicized function of particular historical discourses in the public sphere. By identifying what is at stake in the narration of a specific period, by mapping the ways in which these discourses have been appropriated by different actors and shaped within a particular national context, we can explore the diversity of critiques and alternative visions that emerge from literary rewritings of the past.

This introduction will therefore outline both the emergence of the still-dominant paradigm for reading Latin American historical fiction and the contribution I aim to make to this debate. My analysis focuses on texts that reimagine the period of Argentina's independence, a historical moment that offers a rich discursive landscape through which to explore the reading of historical fiction. This focus can be seen in some ways as a case study, illustrating my broader arguments about our reading of Latin American historical fiction, but it also maps out literary engagements with a period deeply connected to ideas of national origin and identity. As the moment of the birth of the *patria*, independence enjoys a privileged and unique role in the life of the nation. In Argentina, the long history of official and extra-official uses of this founding moment has transformed its narration into a site for the projection of conflicting political projects, and it is by understanding this trajectory that we can more fully unravel the ideological engagements of the texts that choose to re-imagine the period. My readings will therefore begin by outlining key narratives that underpin the independence tale, allowing new possibilities for interpreting literary rewritings to come to the fore. Through this approach, ideological nuances can be drawn out, parodic inversions can be detected and explored, and commentary on the present can be deciphered. Most significantly, however, we can reconsider how to frame our search for the political in these texts, ultimately re-evaluating what we consider to be the challenges posed by the playful, self-reflexive rewritings of contemporary Latin American historical fiction.

## Reading Latin American Historical Fiction

As mentioned above, the still-dominant approach to reading contempo-rary Latin American historical fiction emerged while postmodernism was enjoying a central position in cultural debate. This can be seen to have influenced our understanding of the genre in multiple ways, with Hayden White, Fredric Jameson, and Brian McHale being among those who have left their mark on our approach, but the theoretical formulation that provided the clearest direction for reading Latin American historical fiction is Linda Hutcheon's 'historiographic metafiction'. This contribution to postmodern theory examines literary engagements with history, mapping an interpretation that brings broader postmodern concerns to bear on this particular branch of fiction. For Hutcheon, 'historiographic metafiction' describes a category of texts whose questioning of history centres on 'the provisional, indeterminate nature of historical knowledge', 'the questioning of the ontological and epistemological status of historical "fact"' and 'the distrust of seeming neutrality and objectivity of recounting'.¹ 'Historiographic metafiction' is therefore profoundly concerned with epistemological provisionality and with exposing the processes by which systems of meaning are constructed and maintained.

Hutcheon's formulation has proved a persuasive and enduring model that has profoundly influenced the critical discourse surrounding contemporary Latin American historical fiction, even if her particular terminology is not always used. Writing in the late 1990s, Karl Kohut observed that 'la mayor parte de la crítica de la novela histórica' was taking its lead from Hutcheon.² The idea of epistemological scepticism so crucial to Hutcheon's historiographic metafiction is a recurring feature of important studies such as those by María Cristina Pons, Juan José Barrientos, Fernando Aínsa, and Magdalena Perkowska, and continues to be applied today.³ It is also present in the critical frameworks applied to single-text studies in a substantial range of literary criticism produced in the same period. Hayden White is also widely cited in this work, lending an idea of history as narrative that leads critics of historical fiction to contemplate an apparent collapse of the boundaries between literature and history. As a result of this influence of postmodern theory, the late twentieth-century paradigm for approaching Latin American historical fiction positions these novels as predominantly concerned with the problematization of stable truth and knowledge.

Another complementary strand of criticism that emerged at about the same time relates to the idea that something 'new' was happening in the Latin American historical novel in the mid-to-late twentieth century. Here, the most influential model was created by Seymour Menton, who outlined the defining features of the 'New Historical Novel'.⁴ These textual elements

---

1 Linda Hutcheon, *A Poetics of Postmodernism: History, Theory, Fiction* (New York: Routledge, 1988), p. 88.

2 Karl Kohut, 'Introducción', in *La invención del pasado: la novela histórica en el marco de la posmodernidad* (Frankfurt: Vervuert; Madrid: Iberoamericana, 1997), pp. 19–20.

3 María Cristina Pons, *Memorias del olvido: Del Paso, García Márquez, Saer y la novela histórica de fines del siglo XX* (Mexico City: Siglo Veintiuno, 1996); Juan Barrientos, *Ficción-historia: la nueva novela histórica hispanoamericana* (Mexico City: Universidad Nacional Autónoma de México, 2001); Fernando Aínsa, *Reescribir el pasado: historia y ficción en América Latina* (Mérida Venezuela: CELARG; El otro el mismo, 2003); Magdalena Perkowska, *Historias híbridas: La nueva novela histórica latinoamericana (1985–2000) ante las teorías posmodernas de la historia* (Madrid: Iberoamericana, 2008). For a more recent example of this approach, see Nancy Malaver Cruz, *Ficción y realidad: retos de la novela histórica (1992–2010)* (Bogotá: Universidad Central, 2018).

4 Seymour Menton, *Latin America's New Historical Novel* (Austin: University of Texas Press, 1993).

included the distortion of historical fact, metafiction, intertextuality, parody, the dialogic, heteroglossia, and the carnivalesque.[5] Significantly, this list bears a strong resemblance to the features Hutcheon ascribes to her historiographic metafictions, meaning that it is easy to read across both concepts and draw them together in textual analysis. Moreover, the presence of philosophical ideas concerning history that Menton considers as fundamental to the category ties in closely with the framing Hutcheon gives to history under postmodernism, as he asserts that 'the impossibility of ascertaining the true nature of reality or history' is a defining feature of New Historical Novels.[6] This foregrounds the epistemological instability present in Hutcheon's theorization, once more allowing for easy movement between a recognizable set of textual features and a particular understanding of historical fiction's purpose. While many critics have built upon Menton's model or disputed aspects of his characterization of the genre, current approaches to late twentieth-century Latin American historical fiction are still heavily indebted to this particular framing.

As the idea of a 'new' Latin American historical novel gained traction, a mode of reading this fiction became well established. The presence of metafictional devices and literary game-playing in a historical novel seemed inevitably to point to a warning that there can never be a single, definitive account of the past (or present), and that knowledge is inseparable from its discursive production. Their parodic play and self-reflexivity became apparently synonymous with a postmodern destabilizing of previous certainties, interrogating the construction of knowledge and revealing all meaning as indeterminate. It is the seeming ubiquity of this interpretation that has led to a feeling of critical exhaustion. Even several decades on from the most important theoretical advances in this field, and despite some significant further contributions (which will be discussed below), the core direction of travel in our interpretative frameworks has changed surprisingly little. The frustration at this strait-jacketed approach is neatly captured by Brian L. Price, who notes:

> se redujo el enfoque crítico al tomar en cuenta sólo ciertos aspectos que de un modo u otro todos tenían que ver con la autorreferencialidad literaria y la manera en que ésta problematiza de forma epistemológica aquello que solemos llamar realidad.[7]

---

5  Menton, *Latin America's New Historical Novel*, pp. 22–25.
6  Menton, *Latin America's New Historical Novel*, p. 23. Menton's assertion that 'the postmodern collapse of the "*grandes narrativas*" is unquestionably belied' by many of the 'New Historical Novels' refers to the continued prevalence of the tendency to construct 'totalizing' narratives that was characteristic of the Latin American Boom, rather than the continuation of the *grands récits* of modernity in the wider sense defined by Lyotard.
7  Brian L. Price (ed.). *Asaltos a la historia: reimaginando la ficción histórica hispanoamericana* (México DF, CP: Ediciones Eón, 2014), p. 10.

It seems clear, therefore, that we need to expand our interpretative possibilities for these texts if we hope to continue developing our understanding of what they have to offer.

In my view, part of the reason for this stalemate lies in our tendency to read 'the Latin American Historical Novel' as a genre. By reading historical fiction in this way, we are always dealing with interactions between abstract concepts of 'history' and 'literature' rather than interrogating any more specific discursive planes that may be at stake. The most prominent works on the Latin American historical novel are wide-ranging, spanning several countries and placing little emphasis on the historical period being rewritten (beyond discussion of whether treatments of the recent past should be included in the category).[8] This fuels the perception that the relationship between history and fiction is the primary focus of these texts, as comparing novels that dialogue with vastly different contexts ensures that their major points of contact are to be found at this general level. In seeking a unifying purpose behind such a rich and varied branch of Latin American literature a degree of 'flattening' is perhaps inevitable, and in the case of historical fiction it creates an important disconnect between the texts and the specific discourses they seek to reinvent or parody.

The consequences of this can be seen when we try to identify any more specific political purpose in these texts than the general questioning of epistemology noted above. According to Hutcheon's model, the unmasking of ideology is postmodernism's version of a political statement, as she argues that 'the self-reflexive, parodic art of the postmodern [underlines] in its ironic way the realization that all cultural forms of representation – literary, visual, aural – in high art or the mass media are ideologically grounded'.[9] Postmodernism therefore underlines, shows, or reveals the fact that all discourse has an ideological foundation, but this is the extent of its political potential. While this approach enables us to identify the shared characteristics of a wide range of texts, it creates a model that relies upon abstracting cultural products from their specific context. It is perhaps unsurprising, therefore, that a more concrete definition of these texts' political engagement does not emerge through the use of this framework. Despite the fact that the decontextualizing, 'universalizing impulses' of Hutcheon's framing of Latin American texts were criticized by Santiago Colás at an early stage of our debates on these novels,[10] this abstract vision of political engagement has proved influential for critical discourse on Latin American historical fiction,

---

8  See Menton, *Latin America's New Historical Novel*, pp. 18–19; Aínsa, *Reescribir el pasado*, p. 11; Pons, *Memorias del olvido*, pp. 15–23; Barrientos, *Ficción-historia*, pp. 13–14; and Daniel Balderston, 'Introduction', in *The Historical Novel in Latin America: A Symposium* (Gaithersburg: Hispamérica, 1986), p. 9.

9  Linda Hutcheon, *The Politics of Postmodernism* (New York: Routledge, 2002), p. 3.

10  Santiago Colás, *Postmodernity in Latin America: The Argentine Paradigm* (Durham, NC: Duke University Press, 1994), p. 4.

creating the impression that unmasking apparent neutrality or objectivity is the primary political contribution of these texts.

The other definition of the political that frequently emerges in relation to this genre is the idea of 'cultural resistance': Colás's Marxist-inspired discussion focuses on outlining the specific character of Latin American postmodernism as an 'oppositional politics';[11] Pons portrays the genre as a model of subaltern resistance; and Perkowska discusses the utopian spirit implicit in writing alternative versions of history.[12] However, ascribing a unified political position to these texts in the form of a generalized 'resistance' risks producing a misleading impression of ideological uniformity (on the basis of aesthetic similarity). Similarly, we often see observations that this branch of fiction is political through its focus on the marginal, particularly its embracing of marginal voices.[13] While this is often true, this is again only one dimension of the political explorations at stake in this fiction. My reading will respond to each of these familiar interpretations of the political in Latin American historical fiction by engaging with these texts as political articulations in a different sense: as distinct responses to a set of ideologically charged narratives that build layered and nuanced critiques responding to the pressing concerns of their time.

Over more recent years, there have been several acknowledgements of the fact that our interpretative paradigms for this genre have become tired, leading to attempts to generate new approaches. Some, such as Victoria Carpenter's 2010 edited volume, seek to move forward by refocusing the debate on different questions. In Carpenter's volume, the key theoretical focus is 'the non-linear nature of time' and its creation of multiple histories that affect 'the creation, destruction and recreation of collective memory and, consequently, national identities'.[14] This raises the important question of the ways in which literary reinterpretations of history can intervene in and alter the public discursive landscape, and also foregrounds the issue of time over knowledge construction, moving beyond the familiar critical position. This generates many interesting textual readings, but does not resolve the questions around historical discourse that are the focus of this book. My aim is to interrogate the long-standing framing of the genre, returning to familiar questions and providing different answers.

---

11  It is worth noting that Colás frames his argument around the question of postmodernity rather than the historical novel specifically, but his argument contains an important focus on literary uses of history in Latin America, and Argentina specifically.

12  Pons, *Memorias del olvido*, pp. 265–66; Perkowska, *Historias híbridas*, p. 104.

13  See, for example, Santiago Juan-Navarro, *Archival Reflections : Postmodern Fiction of the Americas (Self-reflexivity, Historical Revisionism, Utopia)* (Lewisburg: Bucknell University Press; London: Associated University Presses, 1999), p. 290.

14  Victoria Carpenter (ed.), *(Re)Collecting the Past: History and Collective Memory in Latin American Narrative* (Oxford: Peter Lang, 2010), p. 3.

Helene Carol Weldt-Basson proposes moving away from postmodernism and instead reading Latin American historical fiction through other theoretical paradigms: feminism and postcolonial studies.[15] This offers a possible route out of the impasse, moving away from the focus on the indeterminate status of knowledge and instead opening clearer paths to engagement with the political content of these texts. In her introduction to the edited volume, Weldt-Basson uses these frameworks to argue that there has been a shift in the focus of the Latin American historical novel, with feminist and postcolonial themes and representations gaining in prominence over recent decades. This helps to move us beyond the focus on the genre's formal evolution, which has created a sense of a 'before' and 'after' in the Latin American historical novel: a traditional manifestation that aligns with Lukács's reading of the genre,[16] and a 'new' version that deploys the features described above and undermines traditional epistemology (and ideas of historical progress). A reading such as Weldt-Basson's helps to unravel the multiple textures, priorities, and concerns of this diverse branch of fiction, and to lay claim to its ongoing evolution.

Weldt-Basson's approach is an important interpretative move as it implicitly highlights an important and understudied dimension of this historical fiction: its constantly changing nature in response to immediate contemporary political concerns. These novels cast the lens of the present over well-worn, traditional narratives, and we must imagine that these foundational tales will continue to be rewritten through fiction, through whatever significant political concerns emerge in the future. However, this 'side-stepping' of postmodernism does not acknowledge the synergistic relationship between the evolution of Latin American historical fiction and the postmodern ideas that have dominated our interpretations to date. These texts are consciously drawing on the climate of ideas generated by this critical turn, but our interpretations of the ways in which this paradigm is applied remain limited. Feminism and postcolonialism both hold potential for creating new readings, as Weldt-Basson demonstrates, but my approach instead focuses on addressing this gap by rebuilding our understanding of the relationship between literature and history in these novels. My bid for a way forward begins with recognizing the politicized content of the historical discourses that are parodied, upended, and reconstructed by fiction, in order to assert that it is not 'history' that is being challenged, but the specific political constructs associated with these recognizable, often national, narratives of the past.

One of the most frequently cited characteristics of Latin American contemporary historical fiction is its challenge to 'official history'.[17] The specific

---

15  Helene Carol Weldt-Basson (ed.), *Redefining the Latin American Historical Novel: The Impact of Feminism and Postcolonialism* (Basingstoke: Palgrave Macmillan, 2013).

16  Georg Lukács, *The Historical Novel* (London: Merlin Press, 1962).

17  See, for example, Pons, *Memorias del olvido*, pp. 16–17; Aínsa, *Reescribir el pasado*, pp. 11, 29; Perkowska, *Historias híbridas* pp. 37–38.

narratives of 'official history' are left unexplained, however, preventing us from engaging with the potential political implications of overturning this vision of the past. In this book, I will argue that by focusing on genre and grouping texts that engage with very different historical moments, we often fail to ask why authors are rewriting a specific historical period, or what the significance of that period is in the public imagination. This abstraction from the meanings attributed to the period in popular consciousness occurs much more frequently in relation to novels that tackle the 'distant past' than those that explore more recent history. Novels that deal with twentieth-century history are often considered in the context of their dialogue with political circumstances, with key examples in Argentina being the literary treatment of the Falklands/Malvinas conflict, fictional explorations of the figure of Evita, and literary approaches to the 1976–83 military dictatorship. However, the postmodern historical novel framework is often discarded in analysis of these texts, considered irrelevant to treatments of recent history, and as a result this framework is ignored instead of overtly challenged, and the lessons we could glean from the way we read texts that engage with recent history are therefore not applied to other literary treatments of the past. Where novels dealing with twentieth-century history are treated as examples of historical fiction, the existing paradigm is usually invoked in order to highlight a generalized epistemological questioning within the text, therefore reinforcing dominant understandings of these Latin American texts.[18]

There are some studies that hone in on the representation of earlier periods, particularly treatments of the conquest, such as *A Twice-told Tale: Reinventing the Encounter in Iberian American Literature and Film*, edited by Santiago Juan-Navarro, Kimberle S. López's *Latin American Novels of the Conquest: Reinventing the New World* and Mark Hernández's *Figural Conquistadors: Rewriting the New World's Discovery and Conquest in Mexican and River Plate Novels of the 1980s and 1990s*.[19] Despite the more specific historical focus, López's work and Juan-Navarro's introduction to his volume

---

18  Compare Pamela Bacarisse, 'The Projection of Peronism in the Novels of Manuel Puig', in *The Historical Novel in Latin America: A Symposium*, ed. by Daniel Balderston (Gaithersburg: Hispamérica, 1986), which makes no reference to a postmodern context or the stability of historical knowledge in its consideration of the recent past, and Lloyd Hughes Davies, 'Portraits of a Lady: Postmodern Readings of Tomas Eloy Martinez's "Santa Evita"', *The Modern Language Review*, 95 (2000), 415–23, which takes the second approach highlighted above.

19  Santiago Juan-Navarro (ed.), *A Twice-told Tale: Reinventing the Encounter in Iberian American Literature and Film* (Newark: University of Delaware Press; London: Associated University Press, 2001); Kimberle S López, *Latin American Novels of the Conquest: Reinventing the New World* (Columbia: University of Missouri Press, 2002); Mark Hernández, *Figural Conquistadors: Rewriting the New World's Discovery and Conquest in Mexican and River Plate Novels of the 1980s and 1990s* (Lewisburg: Bucknell University Press, 2006).

are both framed within the concerns of the New Historical Novel, rather than as a theoretical challenge to this approach. Hernández, however, departs from an overview of the Chronicles of the Indies and the ways in which these have been read as literature as well as history, thereby pinpointing a distinct discursive tradition with which contemporary authors dialogue. This enables Hernández to unravel more concrete aims within these texts, such as their '[reflection] upon the way that institutional powers have invoked episodes from the discovery and conquest to explain and legitimate the present' and these novels' desire to 'critique the recent historical past'.[20] In her contribution to *A Twice-Told Tale*, Victoria E. Campos also departs from the Chronicles to explore rewritings of the past in Mexico, recognizing the need to situate our response to contemporary historical fiction in relation to broader cultural debates and the original historical narratives rewritten by the texts.[21] By employing the *crónica de Indias* rather than the historical novel as a locus for comparison, Campos identifies a cultural critique that does not present knowledge as 'indeterminate' but rather as a powerful political tool that must be dissected in order to establish an effective counter-position. These contributions reveal how moving beyond the tendency of historical novel criticism to treat history as an order of discourse, rather than engaging with the way that specific historical episodes have been configured, provides a necessary alternative focus for our consideration of the place of history in the texts. However, we still need to consciously turn these types of readings back on the dominance of the historical novel framework, using them to move away from abstract discussions of 'history', and home in further on what we mean by the historical challenges presented by these novels.

Literary treatments of independence have also garnered some dedicated critical attention, particularly in the wake of the bicentenary celebrations across Spanish America in the first decades of the twentieth-first century. Examples include *Escrituras y reescrituras de la Independencia* (eds. Camilla Cattarulla and Ilaria Magnani, 2012), *Representaciones literarias de las independencias iberoamericanas* (ed. Luisa Ballesteros Rosas, 2018), and an earlier volume dedicated specifically to Argentina: *El archivo de la independencia y la ficción contemporánea* (2004), edited by Alicia Chibán.[22] In terms of the literary theoretical framework, the analyses in these volumes again often draw on the new historical novel and a postmodern framing of literary engagements with history, therefore tending to lead to similar conclusions as

---

20  Hernández, *Figural Conquistadors*, p. 20.
21  Victoria E. Campos, 'Toward a New History: Twentieth-Century Debates in Mexico on Narrating the National Past', in Juan-Navarro, *A Twice-told Tale*, p. 48.
22  Camilla Cattarulla and Ilaria Magnani (eds.), *Escrituras y reescrituras de la independencia* (Buenos Aires: Corregidor, 2012); Luisa Ballesteros Rosas (ed.), *Representaciones literarias de las independencias iberoamericanas* (Madrid: SIAL Ediciones, 2018); Alicia Chibán (ed.), *El archivo de la independencia y la ficción contemporánea* (Salta: Universidad Nacional de Salta, 2004).

more general works on historical fiction. Many of these readings also seek to deepen the exploration of historical detail in literary texts, which can provide valuable insight but is a different proposal to the analysis I will undertake in this book. Although historical detail in itself will necessarily form part of my consideration of the texts, my main concern is to trace the ways in which independence has been signified by different political projects throughout Argentina's history, and to dissect the role allocated to this foundational period within nation-building projects in order to reconsider the idea of the political in the literary texts I will explore.

In the same way that the conquest is discursively produced by the *crónicas de Indias*, the writing of independence occupies its own discursive space that must be acknowledged and understood in order to progress beyond generalized statements regarding the production of knowledge that dominate the analysis of the region's historical fiction to date. I refer to a discursive space that exists in the public imaginary, shaped by the uses of independence as a nation-building discourse, rather than one that is the preserve of professional historians. What matters is the use of well-worn understandings of particular figures and events, the historical narratives familiar from readers' school days, the stories that are reproduced in public life, and the way that literary texts seek to intervene in this landscape. Carolina Pizarro Cortés provides some valuable insights into the ways in which literary texts engage with some aspects of this 'public life' of independence, focusing her analysis on the way that fiction seeks to decentre historical subjects.[23] My objective is a broader one, examining a wide range of narratives that underpin conventional tellings of the independence tale. I have also very deliberately selected a single-country focus as, despite commonalities between several Latin American countries in the narration and function of independence, there are important national specificities that are essential to any analysis of the political in these texts. This book therefore aims to intervene both in deepening our understanding of literary approaches to independence, a period with a crucial role in identity discourses and political debate, and also to establish a mode of reading that can deepen and extend our analysis of the political focus of self-reflexive Latin American historical fiction.

## Writing Independence, Envisaging the Nation

In order to understand the discursive space of independence, it is important to recognize that it is not merely a historical period like any other. As the designated origin of the nation, it holds a unique status in national mythology, filled with symbolic potential. As the first moment that the state can lay claim to its citizens, it houses the 'birth of the nation', and as such

23 Carolina Pizarro Cortés, 'The Decentring of the Historical Subject in the Contemporary Imaginary of the Independence Process', *Journal of Latin American Cultural Studies*, 20 (2011), 323–42.

represents the creation not only of a political reality, but also the *patria* as a discursive construct. It therefore also marks the beginning of the quest to *define* the nation, to fill this new, empty signifier with meaning. For nations that celebrate independence, the period occupies a unique position in shared rituals and self-construction, as outlined here by Anssi Paasi:

> Independence brings together material processes (e.g. construction and naturalization of national and military landscapes, symbols and maps) and events (e.g. independence/national days, flag days, commemorations of national 'heroes') that fuse various spatial and historical scales. It is thus a pivotal aspect of 'national meta-narratives' that define the key elements of the purported national identity (Morrisey, 2014) and conditions of the subjectification and consent of citizens as re-producers of such narratives.[24]

Independence therefore occupies a prominent and ongoing role as a site for projecting discourses on the nation, a role that is crucial to understanding its use in literature.

In Argentina, independence has been consciously employed in efforts of nation-building since its own beginning. The potential power of this symbolic origin was recognized even before full independence was achieved, with the state apparatus of commemoration set in motion almost immediately after the events of *la semana de mayo*, the week that saw the overthrow of the Spanish Viceroy in Buenos Aires in 1810. The *primer triunvirato* commemorated the first anniversary with the construction of a pyramid in the central square, while 25 May was declared 'día de fiesta cívica' in 1813.[25] These first governments showed a keen awareness of the importance of performing the nation as a way to establish and guarantee its continued existence. In his *Decreto de la supresión de honores* of 8 December 1810, Mariano Moreno offers an analysis of the role of the symbolic in granting authority to a power structure, highlighting the need for the new government to offer the *pueblo* 'la misma pompa del antiguo simulacro, hasta que repetidas lecciones lo dispusiesen a recibir sin riesgo de equivocarse el precioso presente de su libertad'.[26] Future governments proved no less alert to the potential of performance to create acceptance of a form of governance: under the *segundo triunvirato*, the *marcha patriótica* (the song that would become Argentina's national anthem) was rushed out to the provinces as soon as it was approved in Buenos Aires, as part of a conscious attempt to compete against rival identities (both provincial

---

24 Anssi Paasi, 'Dancing on the Graves: Independence, Hot/Banal Nationalism and the Mobilization of Memory', *Political Geography*, 54 (2016), pp. 21–31, at p. 22.

25 Esteban Buch, *O juremos con gloria morir: historia de una épica de estado* (Buenos Aires: Sudamericana, 1994), p. 29.

26 Quoted in Buch, *O juremos con gloria morir*, p. 32. While this decree was aimed at distancing new practices from the monarchic models of colonial times, it carves out a significant role for the symbolic in establishing a new legitimate authority (see Buch, pp. 31–33).

and continental).[27] These attempts to generate an apparatus for the worship of the *patria* consciously drew on models of ritual offered by Catholicism,[28] and Tulio Halperín Donghi notes that the 'años afiebrados' after May 1810 saw the creation of 'una nueva liturgia revolucionaria', which would prove an enduring means of performing national belonging.[29] The independence era produced the most recognizable patriotic symbols: the flag, the national anthem, the national coat of arms, the flag of the Andes. For Argentina's first governments, these represented means of creating and legitimizing a sense of nationhood in the face of an uncertain future for the incipient nation. They were the first attempts to perform Argentina into being, and these efforts created a basic toolkit of national symbolism that remains at the heart of official ritual to this day.

Independence has therefore been a locus for the projection of a unified Argentine nation since the very moment of the May Revolution in 1810, used to shape and underpin certain conceptions of national identity and allocated a crucial role in legitimizing the state as a political structure. The traditional narrative of Independence is composed of a dual epic: the *semana de mayo* in 1810 is the epic of democracy and the creation of the state, followed by a military epic that cements the nation's existence and its boundaries through the wars of independence. This vision of Argentina's independence, of course, places 1810 firmly as the date of the nation's inception. As Rebecca Earle highlights, this idea of 1810 as origin began during the independence war, was elaborated by the 1837 generation, and 'had by the late nineteenth century become standard among the Porteño intelligentsia'.[30] Earle notes that the 1837 generation present this moment as not only the birth date of the *patria* but 'the time when history began'.[31] Luis Alberto Romero reiterates this basic tenant of the traditional independence narrative, highlighting: 'Como decía un antiguo profesor de la Universidad de Buenos Aires, si se le pregunta de sopetón a un historiador graduado cuándo comienza la historia argentina, responderá sin vacilar: el 25 de Mayo de 1810.'[32]

---

27  Buch, *O juremos con gloria morir*, p. 17.
28  This is underscored by Mexican essayist Carlos Monsiváis, who notes, 'A lo largo de las guerras de Independencia, la creación de símbolos y paradigmas de las naciones obedece a un esquema inevitable: la traducción a la vida civil de los modelos impuestos por el catolicismo.' Monsiváis, 'Pero ¿Hubo alguna vez once mil héroes?: "Si desenvainas, ¿por qué no posas de una vez para el escultor?"', in *Aires de familia: cultura y sociedad en América Latina* (Barcelona: Anagrama, 2000), pp. 79–112, at p. 79.
29  Tulio Halperín Donghi, *Revolución y guerra: formación de una élite dirigente en la Argentina criolla* (Buenos Aires: Siglo Veintiuno, 1972), p. 182.
30  Rebecca Earle. '"Padres de La Patria" and the Ancestral Past: Commemorations of Independence in Nineteenth-Century Spanish America', *Journal of Latin American Studies*, 34(4) (November 2002), 775–805, at p. 793.
31  Earle, "Padres de la Patria", p. 799.
32  Luis Alberto Romero, *La Argentina en la escuela: la idea de nación en los textos escolares* (Buenos Aires: Siglo Veintiuno, 2004), p. 19.

These observations both confirm the central association of independence with (national and historical) origin and foreground the shaping of the traditional independence narrative in Argentina, which is closely bound up with the idea of 'official history'. In Argentina, the term is used to refer (frequently disparagingly) to a very specific set of discourses that have occupied a privileged position in the public sphere, filtered through the education system and other official channels over the course of the last century. This is often labelled as the 'liberal' version of history, where 'civilization' wins out over 'barbarism' as the nation-state sets itself on its modernizing path.[33] This narrative, and the challenges it has faced (termed 'historical revisionism', framed in a specific way as outlined below), have occupied a prominent role in national political life. These 'liberal' and 'revisionist' discourses came to be identified with different ideological projects and even became a political tool in their own right, as Silvia Sigal and Eliseo Verón describe:

> No debe olvidarse [...] que la cultura argentina se caracterizó, desde los alrededores de 1930 hasta nuestros días, por la presencia de la historia como política y de la política como historia, gracias a la fuerza del 'revisionismo histórico'.[34]

The narratives created by 'official history' formed a powerful and relatively stable vision of the nation's past. While the understanding of the period in professional historiography has moved forward over multiple decades, and historical revisionism has had a significant impact on public discourse, this vision managed to establish itself and remain as a fixed narrative in the education system throughout most of the twentieth century, changing very little over the course of the decades. This version is deeply indebted to the accounts of Bartolomé Mitre, the first historian of independence and, aptly, the founder of Argentine historiography as a professional discipline. The national epic he created around certain figures, particularly through his histories of the military hero José de San Martín and military leader and member of the *primera junta* Manuel Belgrano, remains the foundation of the 'official' version to the present day.

Mitre's two major histories of independence, *Historia de Belgrano y de la independencia argentina* and *Historia de San Martín y de la emancipación sudamericana*, provide a rich and detailed account of the period.[35] They also

---

33  On the use of the term 'liberalism' to characterize this 'official' history, see Michael Goebel, *Argentina's Partisan Past: Nationalism and the Politics of History* (Liverpool: Liverpool University Press, 2011), pp. 24–28.

34  Silvia Sigal and Eliseo Verón, *Perón o muerte: los fundamentos discursivos del fenómeno peronista* (Buenos Aires: Legasa, 1986), p. 182.

35  Bartolomé Mitre, *Historia de Belgrano y de la independencia argentina*, Biblioteca argentina, 23–26, 4 vols (Buenos Aires: J. Roldan y C.a, 1927) and Bartolomé Mitre, *Historia de San Martín y de la emancipación sudamericana*, 3 vols (Buenos Aires: Diario La Nación, 1950). The definitive versions of most of these works were not published

offer an image of Argentina's past that seeks to define the nation on a grand scale, providing detailed descriptions of national geography and population, and situating independence in a wider history dating back to the arrival of the Spanish. Alongside these two histories of independence, the *Galería de celebridades argentinas* (edited by Mitre with assistance from Domingo Faustino Sarmiento)[36] established a national pantheon of heroes, known as 'próceres', which is still recognizable today. Mitre's historical accounts began to be published in 1857, only five years after the defeat of Juan Manuel de Rosas at the Battle of Caseros in 1852, and just five years before Mitre would be inaugurated as president of Argentina in 1862. The fusion of history and politics in Argentina was therefore present from the origin of the nation's historiography: if Sarmiento embarked on an overtly political enterprise in his contribution to literature with *Facundo: civilización y barbarie*, Mitre performed the same task through historiography. These statesmen and authors enacted their political will through their official roles and intellectual contributions, creating a synergy between cultural and political life. Mitre's vision of history is therefore an unashamedly politicized project, targeted at affirming the legitimacy of the Unitarian cause after the defeat of the Federalist alternative.[37] This version of history is therefore sometimes referred to as 'la línea Mayo-Caseros', presenting the battle that brought about Rosas's defeat as the culmination of the democratic project embarked upon by the enlightened men of the 1810 revolution.

This historical vision encountered its crystallized form at the start of the twentieth century with the Nueva Escuela Histórica Argentina, which was responsible for producing the hugely influential collection of history textbooks that set the tone for school history for the entire century. As Luis Alberto Romero notes, 'a lo largo de varias décadas de intensa actividad, este grupo elaboró una imagen del pasado argentino tan consistente que se transformó en sentido común'.[38] For the Nueva Escuela, 'la nación era el principio organizativo y estructurador de todo relato o explicación del pasado'.[39] The period of independence was allocated a particularly prominent role in this objective, dominating the content of school history textbooks, and therefore for almost

---

until the 1880s, although Mitre's major historical writing took place from 1853 to 1859. Nicolas Shumway, *The Invention of Argentina* (Berkeley: University of California Press, 1991), p. 190.

36  Shumway, *The Invention of Argentina*, p. 191.

37  Shumway, *The Invention of Argentina*, p. 191.

38  Romero, *La Argentina en la escuela*, p. 40. Official channels of education were not the only forms of communication of this patriotic historical vision. For example, the popular children's magazine *Billiken*, founded in 1919, also played a role in providing visions of the *próceres* that supported the celebratory school narrative. See Mirta Varela, *Los hombres ilustres del* Billiken: *héroes en los medios y en la escuela* (Buenos Aires: Colihue, 1994).

39  Romero, *La Argentina en la escuela*, p. 41.

100 years, school stories of independence 'buscaban encender en el pecho de los estudiantes un orgullo nacional que les permitiera emular en el presente las lejanas epopeyas del pasado'.⁴⁰

The historical vision of the Nueva Escuela emerged during a time when education had been allocated an important role in the creation of national sentiment. In the decades following the 1880s, in a context in which the ability to inspire patriotic love in the hearts of the national population was a project of the utmost significance for Argentina's leaders, education was given a special, explicit mission to intervene in the creation of a national identity.⁴¹ Argentina was of course not alone in identifying primary education as an important site for the creation of patriotic feeling. Eric Hobsbawm notes this as a general characteristic of nationalism in the period of 1880–1914, when mass immigration and international rivalries led many nations to mobilize their symbolic apparatus to fuller effect.⁴² Carlos Monsiváis affirms the significance of education in the symbolic production of the new republics across Latin America, recognizing that 'Al servicio de los héroes se coloca ese formidable aparato de condolencias y homenajes de la República, los programas de historia escolar'.⁴³ Significantly, however, in Argentina the patriotic vision created in this foundational period remained intact for many decades.⁴⁴ In 1884, the government passed a reform so fundamental that the Argentine Ministry of Education still describes it as 'la piedra basal del sistema educativo nacional'.⁴⁵ The Ley de Educación Común made primary education compulsory, free, and universal. This was accompanied in 1887 by a reform of the syllabus to 'robustecer por medio de la educación común el principio de la nacionalidad', giving preference to 'los ramos referentes a la República: su geografía, tradiciones, historia y organización política'.⁴⁶ The combination of these reforms radically altered the relationship between the state and schooling, based on an instruction with the nation at its heart. In the words of Maristella Svampa, from this

40 Gonzalo de Amézola, 'Argentina', in *Los procesos independentistas iberoamericanos en los manuales de historia*, 3 vols (Madrid: Organización de Estados Iberoamericanos para la Educación, la Ciencia y la Cultura, 2005), I, pp. 17–80, at p. 17.

41 See Lilia Ana Bertoni, *Patriotas, cosmopolitas y nacionalistas: la construcción de la nacionalidad argentina a fines del siglo XIX* (Buenos Aires: Fondo de cultura económica, 2001), pp. 24–36.

42 E. J Hobsbawm, *Nations and Nationalism since 1780: Programme, Myth, Reality* (Cambridge: Cambridge University Press, 1992), p. 90.

43 Monsiváis, 'Pero ¿Hubo alguna vez once mil héroes?', p. 85.

44 Luis Alberto Romero, *La Argentina en la escuela*, pp. 20–21.

45 Portal Oficial del Gobierno de la República Argentina, 'Sistema educativo', Ley 1420.

46 'Reforma del Reglamento y Plan de Estudios', in *El Monitor*, tomo VIII, no. 122, 1887, pp. 50, 53, cited in Bertoni, *Patriotas, cosmopolitas y nacionalistas*, p. 47. *El Monitor* is an official publication that communicates education news to teachers across Argentina.

point to the Centenary 'es la época en la cual el Estado argentino va a asumir, mediante el monopolio de la educación y el adoctrinamiento escolar, la función de productor de la nación'.[47] History (along with language) was given particular importance as a tool to shape these future citizens and house the essence of the nation.[48] The version of independence history that became familiar to generations of Argentine school children throughout much of the twentieth century was therefore forged in harmony with this vision of education as a route to national belonging and patriotic pride.[49]

Significantly, this apparently static 'official history' of school textbooks has been subject to revision since the return to democracy in 1983. Following the substantial educational reform of 1993, the old conception of these discourses – the epic mode of history designed to inspire patriotic allegiance in future generations – was replaced with a more subdued narrative with less focus on military exploits. Since these reforms, the *revolución de mayo* and wars of independence have lost their previous centrality in school history, leading to greater focus on social and economic transformations rather than merely the actions of the national heroes.[50] Further, the possibility of maintaining one unified vision of school history has been fundamentally challenged by the changes of the past decades, as changes to the textbook market have meant that there is greater diversity of perspectives and a much faster turnover of books.[51] The twenty-first century has seen still further changes, both in terms of attempting to represent a more inclusive history and finding ways to narrate the more recent past.[52] Yet the concept of official history in Argentina is still understood and invoked, usually critically, as was particularly the case during the revisionist resurgence of the 2000s. The teaching of the history of independence also remains an important part of the school curriculum, even though its framing has changed.

'La historia oficial' of independence is therefore far from an abstract notion. It is a patriotic vision of the past associated with *mitrismo*, shaped by the priorities of the Centenary Generation and the Nueva Escuela, and profoundly linked with the teaching of school history into the late twentieth century. The following sections of this introduction will sketch different

---

47 Maristella Svampa, *El dilema argentino: civilización o barbarie: de Sarmiento al revisionismo peronista* (Buenos Aires: El cielo por asalto, 1994), p. 87. On the broader context here, see Bertoni, *Patriotas, cosmopolitas y nacionalistas*.

48 Jean H. Delaney, 'Imagining "El Ser Argentino": Cultural Nationalism and Romantic Concepts of Nationhood in Early Twentieth-Century Argentina', *Journal of Latin American Studies*, 34 (2002), 625–58, at pp. 629, 640–41.

49 For more detail on the shaping of this historical vision under the Nueva Escuela and the Centenary Generation, see Goebel, *Argentina's Partisan Past*, Chapter 1.

50 Delaney, 'Imagining "El Ser Argentino"', pp. 28, 56.

51 Romero, *La Argentina en la escuela*, p. 221.

52 Elizabeth Jelin and Federico Lorenz (comps.), *Educación y memoria: la escuela elabora el pasado* (Madrid: Siglo XXI : Social Science Research Council, 2004).

strands of this narrative – its representation of heroism in the *semana de mayo*, the military epic that underpins it, and the vision of the nation it sustains – and outline the significance of these threads of 'official' history for the textual readings I will undertake in the main part of this book. It will also provide an initial sketch of the relevance of historical revisionism to my analysis. Rather than undertaking a linear account of independence, I have chosen these themes as important elements that are picked up in the literary texts studied, as 'narrative units' that can help us to understand the particular implications of reworking this period and its appeal as a site for literary reinvention. Each of my chapters will engage with more detailed aspects of the 'discursive space' of independence, but here I take a broader thematic approach to explore familiar ways in which the period has been encoded in its traditional telling.

## May 1810 and the mitrista Narrative

A key component of the traditional independence tale is a celebration of 25 May 1810 and its surrounding events, which culminated in the creation of the *primera junta*. The events of the *semana de mayo* are encoded as a heroic revolution that overthrew the tyranny of colonial rule and brought the wonders of freedom and democracy to the nation. Despite the differing political positions of *los hombres de mayo*, the major figures of the events leading to 25 May, the narrative of this event relayed in the education system throughout much of the twentieth century posits the foundational moment of the *patria* as one of harmony, with disagreements between different factions minimized. As Luis Alberto Romero indicates, 'se trata de explicar que cada grupo buscaba el bien de la patria por caminos que eran apenas un poco diferentes'.[53] This forms part of the transformation of 'chance' into 'destiny' that Benedict Anderson describes as characteristic of nationalism:[54] the creation of a unified republic is presented as the only possible outcome, and the construction of the nation is asserted as an undisputed common goal. Through this presentation of *la semana de mayo*, independence becomes fused with the idea of the nation as an ultimate good, a unifying principle with an unquestionable moral foundation. Moreover, the 'official' account of 25 May, beginning with the writings of Mitre, is presented as an 'epic of democracy', a necessary revolution that gave expression to the Argentine people's inalienable right to freedom. Within this framework, the *hombres de mayo* become visionaries who were able to follow the courage of their convictions in pursuit of their utopian ideals.

This 'official' depiction of 25 May therefore presents a series of key concepts that will prove fundamental to the rewritings undertaken by the two texts that form the basis of my first chapter, Martín Caparrós's *Ansay ó*

---

53 Romero, *La Argentina en la escuela*, p. 59.
54 Benedict Anderson, *Imagined Communities: Reflections on the Origin and Spread of Nationalism*, p. 11.

*los infortunios de la gloria* and Andrés Rivera's *La revolución es un sueño eterno*. These are the ideas of moral righteousness, utopian idealism, and the fusion of revolution and democracy at the heart of this tale. The merging of the ideologically distinct positions of the historical actors of this moment is also unpicked by these texts, which reassert the importance of the political points at stake as the first steps towards independence took place. My readings will explore the way that both authors bring events of the twentieth century, particularly the crisis of utopia following the defeat of the left-wing revolutionary projects of the late 1960s and early 1970s in Argentina, to bear upon this celebratory discourse that promises a glorious national future and in relation to some alternative historiographical representations of the period. In my first chapter, I will discuss the treatment of this element of 'liberal' historiography by historians on the Left, and particularly the historical narrative constructed by the country's major Communist Party, in order to draw out the deeply politicized nature of the critique presented by Andrés Rivera's *La revolución es un sueño eterno*. These themes also resurge in a very different context in one of the texts dealt with in my final chapter: Manuel Santos Iñurrieta's play *Mariano Moreno y un teatro de operaciones* (2012). This much more recent text draws on the cultural context surrounding the Bicentenary in Argentina, and offers a very different perspective on these basic themes of the independence tale.

## The Military Epic

By narrating independence through celebratory histories with a strong focus on the battlefield, Mitre (a general as well as a statesman) created a tale of military heroism that has proved one of 'official' history's most lasting legacies. The most significant figure in this aspect of the narrative is José de San Martín, crowned by Mitre as the *padre de la patria* and framed as an international liberator (alongside Bolívar) due to his involvement in the Independence struggle beyond Argentina.[55] In his analysis of the figure of San Martín in Argentine culture, Martín Kohan, one of the authors included in my corpus, argues that the *padre de la patria* functions as cultural capital that can be appropriated in order to lend authority to any political project: 'San Martín se coloca más allá, *es* un más allá, y de esa manera desactiva toda oposición entre argentinos, habilita un limbo de fraternidades y reconciliación.'[56] While Mayo 1810 was subject to debate and re-signification

---

55  Specifically, Chile and Peru. This characterization of Argentina as the second cradle of South American Independence largely stems from the historical writings of Bartolomé Mitre, which will be discussed in detail below.

56  Kohan, *Narrar a San Martín*, p. 16. This appeal to the nation as a higher value beyond the petty conflicts of day-to-day politics has been a significant feature of Argentine political discourse, perhaps most significantly being employed extensively by Perón. Silvia Sigal and Eliseo Verón, *Perón o muerte: los fundamentos discursivos del fenómeno peronista* (Buenos Aires: Legasa, 1986), pp. 50–53.

within Argentina's twentieth-century historiographical battles, the wars of independence themselves emerged relatively unscathed, avoiding becoming a site of contestation. In an article tracing the historiography of independence in Argentina, Gabriel Di Meglio notes that throughout most of the century 'de hecho es uno de los escasos terrenos de relativo consenso con los cuales contó el campo historiográfico en un período cargado de batallas entre distintas formas de interpretar el pasado, que tenían un correlato directo en la forma de pensar la acción sobre el presente'.[57]

Significantly, the specific narrative that surrounds these events was not only relatively stable, but had a consistently close relationship with the military in its re-telling. Di Meglio describes how throughout much of the twentieth century, the narrative of independence retained the strong military focus first established by Mitre, and was more often than not in the hands of members of the military themselves, noting that, from the Academia Nacional de la Historia's 1930s state-commissioned *Historia de la Nación Argentina* to the recent update of this work at the close of the twentieth century, the chapters dedicated to the wars of independence were almost exclusively written by military men.[58] Di Meglio observes that, until recent decades, the wars elicited little interest from historians outside of this paradigm, leaving this as a stable narrative limited almost exclusively to the 'aspectos operacionales y técnicos' of the war.[59]

This technical military focus also carried through to schools, with Luis Alberto Romero noting that 'hasta la reforma curricular de 1979, las campañas de San Martín merecen un capítulo especial en los textos, dedicados a detallar hasta las menores cuestiones militares'.[60] Romero notes that the importance of the military focus of independence in school history built gradually until finding its fixed form in the 1930s.[61] Martín Kohan expresses this military focus as a defining feature of the system, referring to the 'culto militarista del sistema escolar argentino'.[62] Rouquié goes even further in this respect, claiming that in the late twentieth century 'la mayoría de los ciudadanos argentinos no está lejos de pensar que su país es una creación de sus generales. En efecto, es lo que enseña la 'historia-batalla' de las escuelas, no sin fundamento'.[63] The narrative of the independence wars therefore changed relatively little throughout most

---

57 Gabriel Di Meglio, 'La guerra de independencia en la historiografía argentina', in *Debates sobre las independencias iberoamericanas*, ed. by Manuel Chust and José Antonio Serrano (Madrid: Iberoamericana; Frankfurt: Vervuert, 2007), p. 37.

58 Di Meglio, 'La guerra de independencia en la historiografía argentina', pp. 33–37.

59 Di Meglio, 'La guerra de independencia en la historiografía argentina', p. 35.

60 Romero, *La Argentina en la escuela*, p. 64.

61 Romero, *La Argentina en la escuela*, p. 60.

62 Kohan, *Narrar a San Martín*, p. 14.

63 Alain Rouquié, *Poder militar y sociedad política en la Argentina* (Buenos Aires: Emecé, 1981), p. 73.

of the last century, being strongly focused on the military aspects of the conflict rather than on its social or political consequences. This discourse can be seen to position the military as essential to state formation, which echoes the narrative that has underpinned the actions of the military in every coup of Argentina's twentieth-century history: that the military are the saviours of the nation, ready to step in to protect the *patria* whenever it is required of them.[64]

As already noted, both the role and framing of this military narrative have shifted in school history in recent decades, but the traditional vision remains an important departure point for the texts in my corpus as a means of reflecting on the construction and purpose of the nation-state. My second chapter draws out the significance of the rewriting of this military epic in two texts, Martín Kohan's *El informe: San Martín y el otro cruce de los Andes* (1997) and Osvaldo Soriano's *El ojo de la patria* (1992). Both of these texts utilize independence to establish a reflection on the military epic as a discourse of Argentine nation-building, invoking both the consequences of military defeat in the Falklands/Malvinas conflict and the impact of the state violence inflicted by the military regime of 1976–83. The significance of these two events for the presentation of independence in Kohan's and Soriano's novels will be explored in detail in this chapter, focused on the construction of the idea of *patria* in both texts.

### Vision of the Nation

Mitre's sweeping account of Argentina's past in the *Historia de Belgrano* also lays down some of the most important founding narratives of national identity in the sense of defining the 'Argentine people'. This is partly constructed as a racial narrative, with Argentina's 'whiteness' given a starring role in her purported superiority. The indigenous peoples of the River Plate region are characterized completely differently to those of other Latin American countries, notably Chile, where Mitre tells of 'la varonil raza indígena que defendía su suelo'.[65] By contrast, River Plate indigenous peoples are presented as passive and weak, 'giving in' to colonization: 'los indígenas ocupantes del suelo, obedeciendo a su índole nativa, se plegaban mansamente; los más belicosos intentaban disputar el dominio de las costas, pero a los primeros choques cedían el terreno' (21–22). This narrative of passivity is carried forth in the way that Mitre describes Argentine *mestizaje*. He celebrates the creation of 'una nueva y hermosa raza' born out of the union of the European and indigenous population, but constructs this as European blood winning out over the 'inferior race':

> De su fusión, resultó ese tipo original, en que la sangre europea ha prevalecido por su superioridad, regenerándose constantemente por la inmigración, y a cuyo lado ha crecido mejorándose esa otra raza mixta del

---

64  Goebel, *Argentina's Partisan Past*, p. 182.
65  Mitre, *Historia de Belgrano*, I, p. 21.

negro y del blanco, que se ha asimilado las cualidades físicas y morales de la raza superior.[66]

Argentina's indigenous population is therefore consistently characterized as a passive element that will eventually fade away, retreating into the desert and ceding to white racial 'superiority'.

Michael Goebel highlights that a conference to commemorate the Conquest of the Desert held by the military junta in 1979 repeated several of these identity narratives, fused with the idea of the military duty to protect the land:

> The understanding of Argentine nationality that underpinned the conference combined various elements. On the one hand, what was celebrated was a territorial definition of the nation-state that stressed the military extension of the state's reach and the civic virtues that were necessary to accompany this. On the other hand, the indigenous peoples south of the frontier were often cast as 'foreigners', revealing an underlying identification of Argentine nationality with whiteness.[67]

The founding of Argentina's ideas of national identity in whiteness has received substantial critical attention, particularly recently,[68] but the framing above helps to illustrate the visible 'dotted line' from the founding historical discourses of independence through to a specific nationalistic view. Luis Alberto Romero is forthright on the implications of the traditional school narrative framing in this sense:

> Un sentido común instalado en los manuales escolares que en muchos aspectos es incompatible con un régimen político democrático, y con los valores de los derechos humanos y el pluralismo: un cierto tipo de nacionalismo traumático, que combina la soberbia con la paranoia y que ha alimentado algunas de las peores experiencias de la sociedad argentina.[69]

The *mitrista* combination of the 'military epic' mode and a narrative of uncontested greatness, fused with specific constructions of race, clearly offers up a necessity of rewriting in a contemporary context, which has been performed by historiography but also in literature.

What is at stake in the vision of independence that is communicated through public channels is therefore of the utmost significance. The fact that the fossilized 'official' narrative of the past appears no longer to reflect

---

66  *Historia de* Belgrano, p. 43. Argentina is the only nation that Mitre characterizes in this way, stating, for example, that the indigenous population dominated in Peru's racial make-up. *Historia de Belgrano*, I, p. 23.

67  Goebel, *Argentina's Partisan Past*, p. 193.

68  Relevant examples include Ignacio Aguiló, *The Darkening Nation: Race, Neoliberalism and Crisis in Argentina* (Cardiff: University of Wales Press, 2018) and Erika Denise Edwards, *Hiding in Plain Sight: Black Women, the Law, and the Making of a White Argentine Republic* (Tuscaloosa, AL: The University of Alabama Press, 2020).

69  Romero, *La Argentina en la escuela*, p. 215.

and promote values considered desirable for the instruction of tomorrow's citizens is an important point of dialogue for the texts I will explore, which take it upon themselves to offer up alternative visions. The racial narrative that accompanies the writing of independence is of particular importance for my analysis of Washington Cucurto's *1810: la Revolución de Mayo vivida por los negros* (2008) and these discourses are therefore explored in more depth in Chapter 3. The texts of my corpus as a whole create a dialogue between the idea of the nation contained in the discourses of independence and a contemporary context that has altered radically since the initial shaping of this past, a shifting context that will be explored in detail through the chapters of my book.

### The 'Unofficial Line': Alternatives to the Dominant Narrative

As already alluded to, the rigidity of the traditional, school-history discourse on independence does not mean that this narrative remained unchallenged in public consciousness until recent decades. From the 1930s on, revisionist historians sought to oppose this liberal version and provide alternatives. In its origins, this 'rebellion' was linked to the incipient Argentine Nationalist movement, as a reaction to the outcomes of the 1930 coup, and over time revisionism became intrinsically associated with the Peronist cause (despite Perón's ambivalent initial response to comparisons with previously maligned historical figures).[70] These alternatives stemmed from different parts of the political spectrum, from historians who sought to recover the Spanish legacy in America as part of a drive to assert the Catholic values of the nation, to an emphasis on the popular aspect of leaders such as Rosas as opposed to the Europhile *próceres*, seen as imposing the will of Buenos Aires on the nation.[71] This rejection of the '*extranjerizante*' perspective of political figures such as Sarmiento and Mitre was picked up in left-wing discourse of the 1960s, with its focus on anti-imperialism and the need for 'true' revolution. It also became key to the discourse of the Juventud Peronista, for whom history became an explicitly political battleground. Several independence heroes were incorporated into this narrative, as part of what Sigal and Verón describe as 'una historia *inmóvil* cuyos episodios son meras repeticiones de un mismo acontecimiento: la lucha del bloque Pueblo-Patria contra el Imperialismo, una sucesión de 17 de octubres y de septiembres de 1955'.[72] These figures were therefore recruited for a cause once more based in the national, but with a

---

70   Tulio Halperín Donghi, *El revisionismo histórico argentino* (Mexico City: Siglo Veintiuno, 1970), p. 29.

71   Donghi, *El revisionismo histórico argentino*, pp. 30–33. See also Shumway's discussion of Argentine nationalism in *The Invention of Argentina*, pp. 214–49.

72   Sigal and Verón, *Perón o muerte*, p. 182. The date 17 October 1945 saw a mass protest in favour of Perón's release from prison, marking a crucial turning point in the history of Peronism. In September 1955, the *revolución libertadora* ousted Perón from power.

rhetoric focused on social change, the popular, and support for the working classes. This discourse was repeated by the Montoneros, who posited Rosas as a truly national hero whose defeat by the oligarchy had opened the country to English imperialism.[73] This revisionist rhetoric of resistance found renewed vigour under Kirchnerism in the early twenty-first century, as I will explore in greater detail in Chapter 3.

Despite the range of ideological positions encompassed under the 'revisionist' umbrella, significant features recur, particularly the desire to challenge the traditional national pantheon, usually through the addition of federalist *caudillos* (particularly Rosas), and a combative rhetoric promising the revelation of a 'truth' hidden until now. The nature of this narrative offers a tantalizing notion of 'truth finally uncovered'. As well as a challenge to the ideological content of 'official' history, therefore, revisionism represents an attack on the academic norms sanctioned by the lettered city. In this sense, independence evokes both a monolithic, state-imposed discourse that has changed little over the past century, and a dynamic site of contestation and resignification, inseparably linked to pivotal moments of Argentina's twentieth-century history. My analysis will explore the intersections between not only the texts and the traditional narrative, but also some of these key alternative visions that are part of the public imaginary of the period in their own right.

*Independence as a Site of Discursive Reinscription*
It is clear from the discussion above that the role allocated to independence as a force to 'civilize' the national population, to teach citizens how to 'be Argentine' through the inculcation of patriotic sentiment, marks this period out as a very particular moment of history within national discourse, inseparable from the definition of the nation and its values. Moreover, the seductive appeal of independence as a site for the inscription of political discourse and legitimacy renders it ripe for reinterpretation, as noted by Alexander Betancourt Mendieta:

> la Independencia ha sido una materia inagotable en la escritura de la historia en América Latina ya que en cualquier momento los episodios de aquellas gestas pueden usarse para articular interpretaciones desde las más variadas posiciones ideológicas y para las más disímiles coyunturas políticas.[74]

This observation also holds true for literature: the independence period is frequently revisited, offering the opportunity to explore multiple interpretations and resignifications. The narrative appeal of independence as a site for

---

73 Goebel, *Argentina's Partisan Past*, p. 191.
74 Alexander Betancourt Mendieta (ed.), *Escritura de la historia y política: el sesquicentenario de la Independencia en América Latina* (Lima: IFEA, Instituto Francés de Estudios Andinos, 2016), p. 10.

potential rewriting is, of course, not unique to Argentina (either in histori-ography or in literature), but as argued above the particular representation of the period in a national context has significant bearing on the political points of contact between the literary texts and the 'original' they seek to modify. Importantly, rewriting relies on the fact that Argentine readers have familiarity with not only key figures and events from the period, but also the way these have been represented in traditional tellings and publicly visible alternatives, and this offers writers wide scope to subvert existing narratives.

In its 'official' incarnation, independence in Argentina is narrated as a morality tale with an educational purpose, as a triumph of good over evil aimed at uniting the national community in shared celebration of moral and military victory. In this sense, the narration of this foundational period can be conceived of as a parable or even as a national 'fairy tale'. In his study on the subversion of fairy tales, Jack Zipes highlights the intimate association between fairy tales and a civilizing discourse that instructs readers in society's vision of correct behaviour:

> Almost all critics who have studied the emergence of the literary fairy tale in Europe agree that educated writers purposely appropriated the oral folktale and converted it into a type of literary discourse about mores, values, and manners so that children and adults would become civilized according to the social code of that time.[75]

Independence fulfils this same function for the establishment of the *patria* as a shared value essential to the 'social code' of a unified nation, representing part of what holds the national 'imagined community' together. Zipes notes that it is due to this link between social codes and the morality communicated through fairy tale that 'in each new stage of civilization, in each new historical epoch, the symbols and configurations of the tales were endowed with new meaning, transformed, or eliminated in reaction to the needs and conflicts of the people within the social order'.[76] The ways in which independence has been signified and resignified over time creates a series of 'codes' at work in this particular narrative. The idea that rewriting a fairy tale can represent a conscious attempt to expose and confront these 'codes' is highly significant for the light it sheds on the impulse behind the literary reconfiguration of narratives ordained with an explicit 'civilizing' purpose within a society. If the subversion of fairy tale represents an attempt to confront the mores and values endorsed by a community, then the subversion of the well-worn tale of independence can be considered as a similar attack on the social (and political) code enshrined in its traditional narrative form. In her essay on the fictionalization of history in the literature of the early 1980s in Argentina, Marta Morello-Frosch considers this mission behind the communication of

---

75 Jack Zipes, *Fairy Tales and the Art of Subversion: The Classical Genre for Children and the Process of Civilization* (London: Heinemann, 1983), p. 3.
76 Zipes, *Fairy Tales and the Art of Subversion*, p. 6.

historical experience to have reached its end point in contemporary literature, stating:

> Ya no se piensa en la validez de la narratividad como proyecto ético, historias con fin (moral y social) sino que se trata de traer al público narraciones privadas, testimonios personales, de retomar espacios discursivos comunales, y de socializar una vez más la función de la cultura.[77]

My exploration of contemporary fictional accounts of independence will seek to problematize the assumption that the presence of plurality and self-reflexivity in these texts indicates a departure from attempts to construct a 'social and moral' vision. In analysing the subversion of independence discourse, I will argue that it is precisely the ongoing function of this period as an unparalleled locus for the idea of the nation that renders these reconfigurations significant, and that allows us to consider them as potential alternative constructions of the values of the national community rather than a move away from this purpose.

## Rewriting Independence: Texts and Contexts

The literary texts that make up my corpus represent self-conscious engagements with the framings of the independence narrative outlined above, establishing a critical dialogue with the specific forms taken by Argentine nationalism and the vision of the nation created since the declaration of Argentina's 'birth'. They interrogate historical discourses and explore well-known stories and figures that (Argentine) readers will have encountered, often extensively, during their school studies or in public discourse on the nation's past. As noted above, this is crucial to my argument: it is this play with pre-existing knowledge that determines the political impact of these texts. Moreover, these texts interpellate a historical vision widely acknowledged as not only outdated, but also deeply connected to some of the most problematic framings of Argentina's self-conception, particularly in terms of the centrality of the military epic and the representation of the relationship between race and the nation.

As is also clear from the preliminary mapping of the narrative components of independence above, the traditional discourses invoked by these texts are tales of history performed and written by men. The texts of my corpus call upon and reimagine this discursive tradition, dwelling particularly on the militaristic shaping of this narrative and the heroism it celebrates. I have therefore selected texts that focus on these male heroes, questioning and reconfiguring their role in shaping patriotic discourse and the ways in which the nation can be defined. The authors of my corpus are also all male, and

---

77 Marta Morello-Frosch, 'La ficción de la historia en la narrativa argentina reciente', in *The Historical Novel in Latin America: A Symposium*, ed. by Daniel Balderston (Gaithersburg: Hispamérica, 1986), pp. 201–8, at p. 203.

this study therefore delves into a world originally created by men, being rewritten by male authors who engage with these masculinist narratives and their meaning in their contemporary historical circumstances.

There is also important, politicised work happening in historical fiction which tells female-centred stories of the independence period, often framed as filling in 'gaps' in the official record of this part of the nation's past and frequently written by women authors. Many of these texts either foreground alternative heroines or engage with historical women associated with the *próceres*, such as their wives, using these stories to both highlight exclusionary shapings of the past and provide comment on the male figures central to the 'official' version.[78] In narrative terms, these texts often take a more traditional approach to the genre of the historical novel, although many still reflect on the construction of historical discourses and the voices that are represented.[79] These novels offer interesting interventions into the politicized landscape of independence discourse and would warrant detailed study in their own right, as demonstrated for example by the work of Weldt-Basson discussed above. The texts of my corpus instead centre our gaze on the male-constructed world of this national past, unravelling its foundations, internal contradictions and implications for *patria* and heroic narratives in the present.

My corpus is made up of six texts that provide a fictional retelling of an aspect of independence. Four of the novels in my corpus display the characteristics associated with postmodern historical fiction: Martín Caparrós's *Ansay ó los infortunios de la gloria*, Andrés Rivera's *La revolución es un sueño eterno*, Martín Kohan's *El informe: San Martín y el otro cruce de los Andes*, and Washington Cucurto's *1810: la Revolución de Mayo vivida por los negros*. By comparing and contrasting these texts, I aim to demonstrate the need to delve into the historical discourses that they rework in order to establish a meaningful discussion of their interaction with 'the political'. This is targeted at moving beyond the critical suppositions outlined above about the indeterminate nature of knowledge and systems of meaning-making in novels that can be described as stylistically 'new historical novels' or 'historiographic metafictions'. One of the other two texts is a novel by Osvaldo Soriano, *El ojo de la patria*, which does not display the same self-reflexive narrative style as the four texts above, and is a spy novel rather than an example of 'historical' fiction, but engages in a self-aware reflection on the figure of the *prócer* in the

---

78 Examples of the latter include *Pasión y traición* by Florencia Canale and *Lupe* by Silvia Miguens.

79 It is important to note that there are female-authored Argentine historical novels that take a more overtly self-reflexive approach, although the best-known examples often engage with a slightly different period, such as *Juanamanuela, mucha mujer* (Martha Mercader) and *Río de las congojas* (Libertad Demitrópulos). A detailed analysis of the editorial landscape for female-authored historical fiction would also be an interesting prism on the topic, given the importance of some more commercial collections relating to the genre.

novel's contemporary context. The novel's function within my corpus is to question the assumption that a text must display new historical novel/historiographic metafiction technical features if we are to consider it as interrogating the foundation of historical discourses. My final text is a play that engages in self-reflexive historical game-playing, Manuel Santos's *Mariano Moreno y un teatro de operaciones*. By introducing a theatrical work into my discussion, I aim to demonstrate that wider cultural debates surrounding independence provide a more significant framework for the consideration of my whole corpus than a focus on genre that cannot take these specific articulations into account.

The texts are paired in order to reflect their engagement with specific themes intrinsic to the independence narrative and the relationship this bears to contemporary political debates. The first chapter examines *Ansay ó los infortunios de la gloria* and *La revolución es un sueño eterno* through the theme of revolution and democracy, read in relation to the crisis of the Argentine Left in the late 1970s. The second chapter contrasts Kohan's *El informe: San Martín y el otro cruce de los Andes* and Soriano's *El ojo de la patria*, exploring the idea of nationhood and *patria* in relation to the post-dictatorship and post-Malvinas context. The final chapter pairs *1810: la Revolución de Mayo vivida por los negros* and *Mariano Moreno y un teatro de operaciones* through their engagement with the popular in relation to the moment of the Bicentenary.

To choose to re-write independence is to engage in specific debates about the meaning of Argentine history, to explore the political projects that have led to the present day, and also to delve into the mythic time of the nation in which 'nationality' is based. Evaluating the use of these politicized historical discourses within the texts of my corpus offers the opportunity, therefore, to reassert the crucial link between the public function of independence as a discourse of nation-building and patriotism and the way the period is imaginatively reconfigured through literature. In this way, we can reconsider whether these texts ask us merely to reflect on the processes by which discourses are created and sustained, and begin to uncover their questions (and answers) about the political past and future of the nation. This will provide an insight into how Argentine literature has approached important national origin narratives, but also offer a mode of reading that can allow us to more fully recognize the political articulations of Latin American historical fiction.

CHAPTER 1

# Revolution and Democracy

## Martín Caparrós's *Ansay ó los infortunios de la gloria* and Andrés Rivera's *La revolución es un sueño eterno*

The traditional account of independence celebrates the success of a revolution, an uprising against an oppressive power in order to bring about a glorious new form of governance. The two texts that will form the basis of this chapter – Andrés Rivera's *La revolución es un sueño eterno* (1987) and Martín Caparrós's *Ansay ó los infortunios de la gloria* (1984) – both take this heroic, revolutionary thread as the focus for their re-casting of the independence narrative, presenting it from a radically disenchanted perspective. I will argue that their inversion of revolutionary rhetoric represents an engagement with the crisis of the militant certainties of the early 1970s in Argentina, using the specific meanings attributed to independence to explore the use of revolutionary violence in defence of a cause within the texts.

Reading the texts in this way contrasts with the treatment they have received in literary criticism to date. Neither text has received much detailed attention, but both have been predominantly considered within broader trends of historical fiction. As a result, their self-reflexive use of the past has been interpreted as part of the postmodern interrogation of historical discourse outlined in my Introduction. In the case of *La revolución es un sueño eterno*, this has focused predominantly on themes of memory, the unstable nature of history, oral versus written sources, and a general challenge to 'official' history, without engaging with the specific discourses this entails.[1]

---

1  See Edgardo Berg, *Poéticas en suspenso: migraciones narrativas en Ricardo Piglia, Andrés Rivera y Juan José Saer* (Buenos Aires: Biblos, 2002), pp. 110–25; Claudia Gilman, 'Historia, poder y poética del padecimiento en las novelas de Andrés Rivera', in *La novela argentina de los años 80*, ed. by Roland Spiller (Frankfurt: Vervuert, 1991), pp. 47–64; Sabrina Riva, '*La revolución es un sueño eterno*, de Andrés Rivera: una subjetiva genealogía del poder', *Espéculo*, 37 (2007) <http://www.ucm.es/info/especulo/numero037/suetern.html> [accessed 26 September 2019].

While these are significant elements of the novel, I will argue that extricating their potential implications from the political context invoked by the text fails to address its most important concerns. My reading, therefore, will privilege the political manipulations of the independence narrative that Rivera is undertaking, grounded in the significance of his treatment of the themes of failed utopia and revolution in the context of 1980s Argentina. This reading will locate the text's palpable sense of disenchantment, fragmentation of individual subjectivity, and reworking of historical discourse within a more concrete framework than the dominant mode for reading this type of fiction, aiming to explain the dual process of questioning and re-affirmation within the text.

Caparrós's novel has received even less academic attention, and has also been predominantly considered in terms of a general questioning of history, and particularly under the banner of new engagements with the historical novel. Emblematic of this is Pons's characterization of the novel within a broad approach to recent historical fiction, which slots Caparrós's use of a Spanish *Comandante*'s memoirs within a turn towards secondary or little-known events, and describes it as an example of a recent tendency to include characters that write memoirs.[2] However, this ignores the fact that Caparrós's use of Ansay's memoirs has a very specific and politically targeted function within the novel, as I will explore in this chapter, rather than simply 'retelling' the period through a lesser-known perspective. Comparing *Ansay* with Tomás Eloy Martínez's *La novela de Perón* through their shared focus on memoir, as Pons does, privileges a formal similarity over the very different political situation that each text invokes. Similarly, Elena Altuna's analysis of the novel, despite alluding to its contemporary context in general terms, perceives *Ansay* as primarily concerned with the familiar postmodern desire to present alternative versions to counteract the existence of one discernible 'truth', using what she describes as an 'estética del fragmento' in order to attack the epistemological status of the historical document.[3] By perceiving the text as an attempt to recover hidden aspects of the past, particularly the voice of 'los perdedores', Altuna sidesteps the implications of exploiting the specific non-canonical narrative Caparrós chooses as the basis for his rewriting, thus leaving aside any deeper conclusions about the political relevance of the text. While a broader approach to considering these rewritings of history offers the potential to establish trends, the use of the 'historical novel' critical framework obfuscates the implications of the particular rewritings they produce. The bringing together of a detailed reading of both authors' specific manipulation

---

2  María Cristina Pons, 'El secreto de la historia y el regreso de la novela histórica', in *Historia crítica de la literatura argentina Vol. 11, La narración gana la partida*, ed. by Elsa Drucaroff (Buenos Aires: Emecé, 2000), pp. 97–116, at pp. 108–11.

3  Elena Altuna, 'Las gestas imaginarias: Ansay revisitado', in *El archivo de la independencia y la ficción contemporánea*, ed. by Alicia Chibán (Salta: Universidad Nacional de Salta, 2004), pp. 263–76, at p. 268.

of the independence narrative with the often overt parallels with Argentina's recent past in this chapter will foreground the politicized commentary present in the texts and provide a more detailed and nuanced analysis of their engagement with history. This approach also disputes the assumption that interpellating certain postmodern ideas of history – particularly its status as narrative rather than objective fact – represents a blurring of boundaries between literature and history in order to assert the constructed nature of the past, as is often asserted in criticism on the genre. My analysis will suggest a different outcome of the meeting of literature and history in these texts, one that is grounded in an interrogation of independence as a legitimizing discourse rather than an abstract idea of historical knowledge.

## Revolution: Victory, Death, and Critique

Both *Ansay* and *La revolución* rely upon a parallel between the revolutionary epic of independence and the atmosphere of hope and faith in revolution in 1960s and 1970s Argentina to develop their questioning and critique. The analogy is not purely a construction of the texts, but can be seen to evoke the way in which the rhetoric of victory surrounding the independence tale was actively used by militant groups to carve out similarities between these historical heroic exploits and their own projects, seeking to insert their fight within a national historical context.[4] The national anthem, a ritual celebration of the original national revolutionary victory, was used by both Peronist and non-Peronist groups in public acts, with a conscious appeal to its 'death or victory' call to arms. Esteban Buch notes that 'en los actos del Ejército Revolucionario, junto a *La internacional* y una marcha partidaria, el *"o juremos con gloria morir"* será seguido del rítmico grito *"ERP, ERP, morir o vencer"'.*[5] José Pablo Feinmann recalls the use of the anthem in Peronist acts, describing how 'el verso *Coronados de gloria vivamos* se canta con dulce musicalidad, en tanto que *o juremos con gloria morir* se entona con vehemencia, convicción, furia, es decir, como un *juramento de guerra*'.[6] The imperative to fight for a cause to the death underpins this direct connection, as Feinmann poignantly expresses:

> Quienes, sí, aceptaron y eligieron vivir bajo la gravedad del mandato heroico fundacional de nuestro Himno fueron los militantes de la izquierda peronista. Asumiendo que protagonizaban una guerra de liberación nacional encontraron en esas estrofas una *singularidad patria* para entonar su concepción heroica de la vida. (66)

4 On the use of nineteenth-century history by the *Juventud Peronista* see Sigal and Verón, *Perón o muerte*, pp. 181–83.
5 Buch, *O juremos con gloria morir*, p. 126.
6 José Pablo Feinmann, *La sangre derramada: ensayo sobre la violencia política* (Buenos Aires: Ariel, 1998), p. 67.

This characterization recognizes the function of independence as a potent symbol of heroism, sacrifice for the greater good, and the creation of a glorious future for the nation, underscoring the affinity between this heroic depiction of revolution and the self-presentation of the militant projects of the late 1960s and early 1970s. It also stresses the significance of independence as a source of authority that can be used to validate political projects and ideas: if independence represents the 'ultimate good' of the *patria*, then an appeal to this period as a parallel for events in the present can furnish them with a sense of legitimacy. By employing the rhetoric of glory embodied in the national anthem's celebration of the independence fight, these revolutionary movements connected their struggle to this previous triumph of 'good' over 'evil' through their shared conception of heroism.

The experience of defeat these projects suffered in Argentina fundamentally undermined the clarity offered by this revolutionary vision, however. The beauty of a mantra that contemplates only victory or death was contaminated by the complexities of lived experience and the compromised realities of the organizations themselves, as Richard Gillespie highlights in his celebrated history of the Montoneros when discussing the unflinchingly absolute revolutionary commitment the Montonero chiefs expected of the guerilla fighters taken prisoner:

> Prompted by pain, Montoneros talked because of the political bankruptcy of their organization and its military decline; they talked because they knew their friends were talking; because their leaders had taken off and abandoned them. Far too much was expected of these prisoners by guerrilla chiefs who demanded heroism and solidarity as the norms of conduct and who refused to tolerate the less glorious aspects of human nature.[7]

This insight illustrates how the revolutionary 'contract' demanding complete commitment was compromised by the realities of guerrilla warfare and the harsh repression it faced, and how departure from this contract represented a shattering of a fundamental aspect of revolutionary identity. This ideal required an individual to subjugate their personal desires entirely to the good of the cause, to have, in the words of Pilar Calveiro, 'una vida sacrificada, de renuncia de la plenitud personal para obtener un fin superior y colectivo'.[8] Those who survived the repression of the 1970s were beyond the scope of the options dictated by this revolutionary mantra, and had to face both the defeat of this ideal and the necessity of constructing some form of alternative identity. Hugo Vezzetti, in his study of the revolutionary organizations of the 1970s, notes that both surviving militants and sympathizers with their

---

7 Richard Gillespie, *Soldiers of Peron: Argentina's Montoneros* (Oxford: Clarendon, 1982), pp. 247–48.
8 Pilar Calveiro, *Política y/o violencia: una aproximación a la guerrilla de los años 70* (Buenos Aires: Norma, 2005), pp. 16–17.

cause had no choice but to re-define their horizons, and after their defeat 'se reinsertaron como pudieron en las nuevas coordenadas'.[9]

This transition from revolutionary idealism to the search for an alternative was accompanied by a process of disillusionment and self-critique from those involved in these organizations and their supporters. This process was overshadowed in public discourse by the characterization of these individuals as victims of repression in the immediate return to democracy, paradigmatically in the 1984 *Nunca más* report, which sought to document the fate of the disappeared. However, the context of these internal debates provides a crucial backdrop for the treatment of revolution in both of the texts that I will explore in this chapter. One of the most visible sources of dissent was the response to the Montoneros's failed 'counteroffensive' strategy in 1979, where the organization attempted to launch a renewed attack on the military regime, resulting in significant loss of life among its fighters. This counteroffensive led to very public critique of the organization's actions from prominent Montonero members, most notably resulting in the departure of two splinter groups: 'Peronismo en la resistencia' and 'Montoneros 17 de octubre'. Rodolfo Galimberti and Juan Gelman's open letter of resignation as they formed the first of these groups cited the organization's militarism, elitist structure, 'mad sectarianism', and lack of internal democratic culture, which they blamed for stifling critical reflection, as the reasons for their departure.[10] Post-1979, the organization closed whole departments abroad to silence internal critique.[11] Those in exile gradually drifted away from their organizational allegiances as the process of disillusionment set in and the military defeat of these organizations became increasingly clear.[12]

The testimonies of ex-guerrilla fighters provide valuable insights into the internal critique of this period. *La voluntad: una historia de la militancia revolucionaria en la Argentina* compiled by Martín Caparrós and Eduardo Anguita, represents one of the most significant attempts to 'capture' the functioning of the guerrilla organizations through the perspective of those who participated in them. This detailed history formed part of attempts in the 1990s to recover the experiences of those who fought for a cause they believed in, rather than portraying the defeated militants exclusively as victims of the military regime. The final volume of the history concludes with an opportunity for the informants to reflect upon their participation

9 Hugo Vezzetti, *Sobre la violencia revolucionaria: memorias y olvidos* (Buenos Aires: Siglo Veintiuno, 2009), p. 138.

10 Gillespie, *Soldiers of Perón*, p. 266, citing Galimberti and Gelman's open letter of 22 February 1979.

11 Gillespie, *Soldiers of Perón*, pp. 268–69.

12 Marina Franco and Pilar González Bernaldo, 'Cuando el sujeto deviene objeto: la construcción del exilio argentino en Francia', in *Represión y destierro: itinerarios del exilio argentino*, ed. by Pablo Yankelevich (La Plata: Al Margen, 2004), pp. 17–48, at p. 27.

from the perspective of the present (the mid-1990s). Alongside more positive valuations of the objectives the organizations had in their sights, these testimonies contain reflections on the reasons individuals chose to distance themselves from their organizations. While the severity of criticism varies significantly, authoritarian organizational structures (particularly regarding the Montoneros), the impossibility of internal critique, and tactics leading to unnecessary deaths are common threads. One of the harshest judgements is that offered by Nicolás Casullo, an ex-Montonero who left Argentina in 1975, and condemns:

> Los autoritarismos de conducción, la verticalidad de funcionamiento, las jefaturas de corte despótico, los alineamientos forzados con las cadenas de mando, la arbitrariedad de las decisiones, la extinción de toda individu-alidad genuinamente pensante, la obligatoriedad de los acatamientos, los dispositivos cercenadores de las discrepancias, la penalización del que disentía, el recelo sobre el que ponía en duda las cosas, la gimnasia del pacto con el propio poder del aparato, la imposibilidad de modificar los cursos.[13]

The strength of feeling behind this bitter reflection poignantly demonstrates the fracturing of high-minded ideals through internal dissent and conflict that formed part of the process of disillusionment described above. The experience of defeat therefore included the shock and horror at the harsh repression suffered at the hands of the military regime, but also a process of soul-searching that led to a reassessment of the rhetoric of victory through armed uprising that had characterized the previous years.

In her study of the Argentine Left from the days of revolutionary idealism to the return to democracy, María Matilde Ollier emphasizes the shift in critique in about 1980, from discussion of the choice of tactics employed to an outright rejection of armed struggle as the way of bringing about change.[14] Vezzetti also highlights this transformation, stating: 'En el exilio, después de la derrota, las revisiones personales y políticas llevaron a la mayor parte de los militantes y los simpatizantes de la causa revolucionaria a distanciarse de la fe en el poder supremo de las armas.'[15] The combination of incontrovertible military defeat and disenchantment with the functioning of the revolutionary organizations played a key role in this process, as Ollier describes:

> Este pasaje se lleva a cabo a partir de la contundencia de distintas realidades políticas —aparte de la sufrida en la Argentina— que muestran

---

13  Cited in Eduardo Anguita and Martín Caparrós, *La voluntad: una historia de la militancia revolucionaria en la Argentina*, 3rd edn, 3 vols (Buenos Aires: Norma, 1997), III, p. 468. Pilar Calveiro also records similar criticisms in *Política y/o violencia*, p. 125.
14  María Matilde Ollier, *De la revolución a la democracia: cambios privados, públicos y políticos de la izquierda argentina* (Buenos Aires: Siglo Veintiuno, 2009), p. 189.
15  Vezzetti, *Sobre la violencia revolucionaria*, p. 70.

la ineficacia del camino armado, por un lado, y de la observación sobre los comportamientos y los supuestos que acompañaban la militancia —el determinismo, el absolutismo de las ideologías, la concepción de que el fin justifica los medios, el dogmatismo y la rigidez grupal y personal—, por el otro. (189)

The critique of armed struggle led to a reassessment of the revolutionary mentality that underpinned the actions of the guerrilla organizations. The faith in change through taking up arms is at odds with the democratic principle of achieving change through the ballot box, and these democratic forms had been dismissed as 'burgués' and 'liberal' at the height of revolutionary fervour.[16] Juan Carlos Portantiero captured this change of sentiment in his contribution to the first issue of *Controversia*, the magazine that provided a vital focal point for debates among Argentine exiles in Mexico, stating that after 1976 'la democracia formal ya no aparece como un puro reclamo liberal'.[17] In their study on Argentine exiles in Paris, Marina Franco and Pilar González Bernaldo go as far as to describe democracy as 'un valor ausente del imaginario político de los años setenta'.[18] This shift from revolutionary to democratic discourse among many left-wing groups in Argentina represented a fundamental change in their rhetoric and political practice, which owed much to the strategies of resistance developed by organizations formed in exile. Pablo Yankelevich argues that perhaps the most significant common denominator among all the groups in exile was their construction of an identity around the principles of denouncing the crimes of the military dictatorship and the defence of human rights.[19] Franco and González Bernaldo highlight that among exiles in Paris, the emergence of a new political language and practice, grounded in the defence of democratic principles, gradually replaced the language of political militancy of the early 1970s (36). Significantly, these authors demonstrate how the conception of democracy promoted by these organizations emphasized its role as a guarantee of individual liberties and human rights, a significant shift in discourse that brought these formal aspects of democracy to the fore (33–34).

Caparrós spent his time in exile in Paris and Madrid, both places where significant human rights groups were formed.[20] As I will explore through

16  Ollier, *De la revolución a la democracia*, pp. 197, 200. Vezzetti, *Sobre la violencia revolucionaria*, p. 96.

17  *Controversia* no. 1, quoted in Vezzetti, *Sobre la violencia revolucionaria*, p. 96. This belief in violence was not exclusive to the guerrilla, but was shared by other groups and individuals, including politicians, intellectuals, and artists. Calveiro, *Política y/o violencia*, p. 127.

18  Franco and González Bernaldo, 'Cuando el sujeto deviene objeto', p. 44.

19  Pablo Yankelevich, 'Tras las huellas del exilio: a manera de presentación', in *Represión y destierro*, p. 12.

20  For France, see Franco and González Bernaldo, 'Cuando el sujeto deviene objeto'. Regarding the situation in Spain, see Guillermo Mira Delli-Zotti, 'La singularidad

my analysis, *Ansay*'s denunciation of violence and human rights abuses can be clearly read against this context. The democratic aspects explored by Caparrós's text are those attacked by the military dictatorship, with a particular focus on censorship and human rights. Caparrós's text straddles these two threads of response, sustaining a strongly pro-democratic discourse that equally denounces state terror and the violent imposition of revolutionary change. The revolutionary (or counter-revolutionary) subject is therefore constructed both as the perpetrator of violence and its victim, as the text asks at what point 'revolution' becomes 'authoritarianism' by inverting the power relationships of conventional narratives.

The texts take completely divergent lines of argument on this point, however, with Rivera's novel maintaining a clear critique of the bourgeois nature of liberal democracy. By the time Rivera's text is published, the desired-for return to democracy has been achieved, and Alfonsín's government has already created controversy by moving from establishing CONADEP (National Commission on the Disappearance of Persons) to passing the *Punto Final* law of 1985. The two texts are therefore responding to slightly different political moments, and different aspects of left-wing political traditions in Argentina. As a result, the two novels' widely differing reflections on the nature of revolution, filtered through the narrative of independence, reveal a very different 'moral' to be drawn from the fable-like use of the nation's myth of origin in these two texts.

## *Ansay ó los infortunios de la gloria*: The Violence of the Absolute

Martín Caparrós's first published novel, *Ansay ó los infortunios de la gloria*, tells the tale of Faustino Ansay, a Spanish *Comandante de armas* at the time of the May Revolution in 1810. The text incorporates fragments of the memoir that the real-life Ansay left behind,[21] interwoven with third-person narration, other documents from the independence period, and an 'imagined' memoir situated at the time of the Spanish Conquest. Caparrós pits the perspective of Ansay against the writings of the more familiar figure of Mariano Moreno, the Jacobin revolutionary celebrated primarily for his role as secretary of the

---

del exilio argentino en Madrid: entre las respuestas a la represión de los '70 y la interpelación a la Argentina postdictatorial', in *Represión y destierro: itinerarios del exilio argentino*, ed. by Pablo Yankelevich (La Plata: Al Margen, 2004), pp. 87–112.

21  Faustino Ansay, 'Relación de los acontecimientos ocurridos en la ciudad de Mendoza en los meses de junio y julio de 1810', in *Biblioteca de Mayo, Tomo IV: Diarios y Crónicas* (Buenos Aires: Senado de la Nación, 1960), pp. 3314–64 and 'Relación de los padecimientos y ocurrencias acaecidas al coronel de caballería don Faustino Ansay desde el mes de mayo de 1810, que se hallaba en la ciudad de Mendoza en la América del Sud hasta el 23 de octubre de 1822 que llegó a Zaragoza, su patria, escrita por él mismo, año de 1822', in *Biblioteca de Mayo, Tomo IV: Diarios y Crónicas* (Buenos Aires: Senado de la Nación, 1960), pp. 3365–94.

*primera junta*, Argentina's first government created on 25 May 1810. The novel charts Ansay's decline as Moreno rises, focusing on the Spaniard's experience of defeat and Moreno's discursive projections of a new political order.

The text is certainly far from a traditional historical novel, and displays many of the characteristics most closely associated with self-reflexive ('postmodern') historical fiction. It is intensely self-reflexive, as will be discussed below, and brings together a vast range of voices and sources in a display of both intertextuality and heteroglossia. Significantly, many of these voices are drawn from extracts of real documents rather than being presented through original fictional writing: in a sense the novel is more of a (pointedly edited) compendium of excerpts from documents surrounding independence than an entirely fictional creation. The process of selection and compilation therefore becomes one of the text's most significant narrative interventions, which can be seen as a metafictional commentary on the process of writing itself, constantly drawing our attention to the position from which each text is written and the seductive persuasiveness underlying the techniques of rhetorical mastery. By consistently presenting conflicting discursive configurations of the past, the text embraces the postmodern idea of history as a series of narratives, shaped according to the priorities and outlook of the writer. Rather than analysing this as a blurring of the boundaries between the literary and the historical, as a conventional postmodern reading might, however, my reading will examine the specific reconfigurations undertaken by Caparrós's text in order to draw out its searing political critique and reframe its metafictional retelling of the past.

The narrator provides an indication of the novel's purpose and intentions in the off-hand comment that 'si ésta fuese, en lugar de un tratado o intentona sobre el poder y la impotencia, una novela histórica, bronces más broncos deberían derribar de sus muros aquellas piedras cuya sola función es el ocultamiento obstinado de lo heroico, lo marmóreo'.[22] This disdainful dismissal of historical novels asserts that their function is to reveal the heroic hidden behind the ordinary, rather than to truly subject the past to rigorous re-examination. By overtly distancing itself from this celebration of the pantheon, the text proclaims its right to appropriate history for its own self-defined purposes. Caparrós therefore sidesteps the rhetoric of revisionist challenges to the 'historia oficial' of independence, which relies on revealing 'hidden' facts about the nation's past and its heroes. Instead, *Ansay* confronts the public function of independence as a celebration of the heroic and an unambiguous tale of moral victory. By dissecting the primordial narrative function of the independence tale, the novel provides a disquieting critique of the idea of unflinching ideological commitment, rather than simply attempting to offer an 'alternative' perspective on a well-known period of the past.

---

22 Martín Caparrós, *Ansay ó los infortunios de la Gloria* (Buenos Aires: Seix Barral, 2005), p. 177. Further references to this edition of *Ansay* are given after quotations in the text.

*Democratic Discourse: The Strategy of Ideals*

Caparrós's re-telling of independence through the experiences of a man imprisoned at the hands of Argentina's first governments represents a dramatic inversion of the heroic status of this narrative. Epic is transformed into a tale of defeat and repression, disrupting the clear-cut morality of the independence fight. The 'official' narrative of independence, which I explored in my Introduction, condenses the complex political landscape of 1810 into a morally unambiguous tale of 'right' (the *porteño* revolution) versus 'wrong' (the Spaniards clinging to an 'incorrect' belief system). Through its careful selection of real historical documents, *Ansay* retains the presentation of the 1810 revolution as a shattering of the existing political order, but detaches it from any guarantee of the glory of this act.

This subversion of the familiar narrative is primarily achieved through the juxtaposition of excerpts from historical documents that offer radically different perspectives. The first of the novel's two parts is composed of three parallel plot structures that provide contrasting inscriptions of independence: the experiences of the *realista* Ansay, the writings of Moreno, and the letters of Moreno's wife, María Guadalupe, sent to her husband on his 1811 voyage before discovering his death. Moreno's writings convey the perspective of the *primera junta*, presented through a 'public' and 'private' face that communicate radically different visions. The public writings are predominantly taken from Moreno's real contributions to *La Gazeta de Buenos Aires*, the newspaper established to communicate the *primera junta*'s actions and ideas, and the 'behind the scenes' scheming is revealed through extracts from his controversial *Plan revolucionario de operaciones*, a secret report advocating extreme measures to ensure the success of Argentina's independence process.[23] Each quotation from the *Gazeta* is immediately preceded or followed by an excerpt from the *Plan* that directly undermines the grandiose ideals of the public discourse. This strategy transforms the *junta*'s glorious democratic role into an apparently deliberate attempt to manipulate and control the very *pueblo* upon whom the legitimacy of independence depends. While the Moreno of the *Gazeta* promises the public 'una exacta noticia de los procedimientos de la Junta', the *Plan* stresses the need to hide any actions that could be negatively perceived, stating that 'los pueblos nunca saben, ni ven, sino lo que se les enseña y muestra, ni oyen más que se les dice' (30–31). Similarly, an excerpt from the *Gazeta* that celebrates the 'esplendor y brillo' of truth is immediately followed by an extract from the Plan that shrouds this proclamation in irony and reveals the manipulative intent behind this public discourse. In a tone of extreme pragmatism far removed from the impassioned pleas of the preceding extract, Moreno describes the need to '[hacer] elogios los más elevados de la felicidad, libertad, igualdad y benevolencia del nuevo sistema'

---

23  Although the authorship of the *Plan* has been disputed, Caparrós's text offers no ambiguity in this respect, openly attributing the citations from the *Plan* to Moreno.

(34), thus exposing the Enlightenment discourse that permeates every public speech-act of the *primera junta* as nothing but a mechanism of rhetorical persuasion designed to shore up this new power structure. Furthermore, Moreno concludes:

> estos y otros discursos políticos deben ser el sistema y orden del entable de este negocio, figurándolos en las Gazetas no como publicados por las autoridades, sino como dictados por algunos ciudadanos, [...] y este ejemplo excitará más los ánimos y los prevendrá con mayor entusiasmo. (34–35)

This duplicitous, dishonest presentation of government propaganda undercuts the lofty rhetoric seen in the public proclamations.

These acute contrasts between public and private discourse reveal that the transcendent ideals of independence may represent little more than a politically expedient strategy of manipulation. The new government's public praise for those who have taken up arms in the name of the independence struggle is conveyed in a suitably eulogizing tone: Moreno celebrates the 'mártires' of the independence cause, promising 'la gratitud y la ternura' of those who will reap the benefits of their sacrifice (158). This laudatory portrayal of personal sacrifice connects suffering to a higher cause, counter-acting the void of death with the comforting promise of moral righteousness and a better life for those who remain. However, an extract from the secret *Plan* immediately juxtaposed with this grandiose rhetoric communicates a sinister intention behind this show of gratitude. Once the people have been persuaded into betraying the monarch, Moreno reasons, they will have no choice but to submit to the will of the revolutionary authorities, as they will be traitors to the crown, rendering themselves 'ya tan comprometidos que a nada podrán oponerse' (159). The people's choice to take up arms therefore becomes a way of enforcing their loyalty to the new government, rather than a means of serving a higher cause as portrayed in public discourse. This cynical manipulation is echoed in Moreno's public proposal that soldiers be given medals in recognition of their bravery, as 'la Patria quedará reconocida a esos guerreros infatigables' (156), with an extract of the *Plan* that posits the creation of a meaningless honours system to avoid the need to promote the middle tiers of the new regime. These juxtapositions therefore strip the heart-swelling promises of Moreno's public declarations of all their transcendent potential, and the deployment of the rhetoric of heroism reveals itself to be nothing more than a tool of persuasion, serving a set of vested interests and seeking to exercise control over the lower ranks of the new system.

Through these juxtapositions of public discourse and private scheming, Caparrós builds a picture of hypocrisy that portrays the primera junta as an astute and self-aware political entity rather than the guardian of a truly noble cause. This deflation of the transcendent potential of the revolutionary rhetoric of liberty and equality rewrites the most basic function of the independence tale: its association with glory, truth, and 'right'. The expression of worthy concepts is exposed as little more than a rhetorical convention that draws us in, but that ultimately offers no guarantee of moral validity. Rather than a straightforwardly postmodern attack on epistemological certainty, however, this unravelling of rhetorical codes represents a critique of the relationship between discourse and action in overtly politicized terms. It suggests that an appeal to the idea of 'right' is a necessary component of any political project, and builds a provocative vision of the discursive similarities between the projection of political visions that are, in ideological terms, completely opposed.

### Legitimizing Discourse and the Repressive State

The most significant comparison that the text establishes is between Argentina's first government and the 1976–83 military *junta*. Caparrós's novel rewrites independence as a narrative with a repressive state at its centre rather than a glorious new democratic regime ushered in by the flag-waving crowds of schoolbook narratives, creating a troubling vision of the *primera junta* as a powerful new state actor capable of inflicting violence. This provocatively re-positions Argentina's foundational moment as a form of military coup, excluding any mention of popular will and focusing exclusively on the seizing of power by a small, self-appointed group. The state epic is torn apart primarily through the presentation of this foundational period as a violent process seeking to impose itself by any means, hidden behind the veneer of high-flown, heart-swelling patriotic rhetoric discussed above. The almost unrecognizable narrative of repression that the text generates produces a re-inscription of the violence present in this radical political change, a violence all but absent in the 'official' narrative of 1810, and presented as unremittingly heroic in the ensuing wars. This violence is depicted both from 'above' – the discourse and actions of the revolutionary government – and 'below' – the experience of the victim through the figure of Ansay, generating a provocative re-reading of independence as a period of state violence.

The democratic credentials of independence are gradually eroded through Moreno's promotion of overtly anti-democratic practices in the extracts of the *Plan revolucionario de operaciones* cited in the novel. He advocates the manipulation of the legal system to privilege supporters of the independence cause, advises capital punishment for those opposed to 'la causa' and offers justification for state censorship, always counterposed with Enlightenment rhetoric on free speech, truth, and justice. His public lamentation over the deaths in the 'conspiración de Córdoba', the counter-revolutionary uprising led by Santiago de Liniers, is followed by a blood-thirsty insistence on the need to kill enemies, as 'de este modo se establecerá la santa libertad de la Patria' (70). The attempt to stamp out opposition is presented as a badge of honour that demonstrates the revolutionary commitment of the new political order:

Jamás, en ningún tiempo de revolución, se vio adoptada por los gobernantes la moderación ni la tolerancia; el menor pensamiento de un hombre que sea contrario a un nuevo sistema es un delito por la influencia y por el estrago que puede causar con su ejemplo, y su castigo es irremediable. (73)

Ultimately, we discover that the *primera junta* has established prisons to torture and murder its political enemies.

These anti-democratic practices at the heart of Argentina's democratic origin portray themselves as necessary tools to achieve a higher aim – an end that justifies the means – but this rationale is shattered within the text. At a discursive level, there are clear parallels with the justifications offered by the military *junta* of the *proceso* for their actions to curb 'subversion', a correlation that is pointed up by the text's ironic reference to the war of independence as 'aquella guerra por excelencia "limpia" y modélica' (278). The text's aim in evoking this context is not to emphasize the repressive nature of the *proceso*, however, but to use this threatening shadow to destabilize the narrative of independence: to deny the possibility that war can ever be 'clean', or that any ideological discourse can ever guarantee its status as 'right'.

While all the repressive practices advocated by Moreno can be seen as evoking those put in place by the *junta*, the disquieting presentation of 1810 as a form of military coup is completed through powerful discursive parallels. Among the documents from independence reproduced in the novel is the 'Proclama' issued by the *primera junta* on 26 May 1810, announcing the arrival in power of Argentina's first independent government. The presence of this text instantly evokes the most famous 'Proclama' of recent Argentine history: that issued by the military junta of the *proceso* on 24 March 1976.[24] Although the 1976 document is not reproduced in the text, the strikingly similar rhetorical pattern between both 'Proclamas' leaves little doubt about the implied reference for an informed reader. Both documents begin by noting the presence of instability ('incertidumbre de las opiniones'/'vacío de poder') and insisting upon the new authorities' obligation to take control (responding to 'las aclamaciones generales'/'una obligación irrenunciable'); they promise efficacy in their task ('un deseo eficaz, un zelo activo'/'absoluta firmeza y vocación de servicio'); plead repeatedly for unity in working towards this goal ('todos debemos cooperar á la consolidación de esta importante obra'/'se convoca en un esfuerzo común a los hombres y mujeres, sin exclusiones, que habitan este suelo', etc.); and conclude by insisting on the 'common good' and a positive eventual outcome ('Ella afianzará de un modo estable la tranquilidad y bien general á que aspiramos'/'esta empresa que, persiguiendo el bien común, alcanzará —con la ayuda de Dios— la

---

24 Proclama, 24 March 1976. Cited in República Argentina, Junta Militar, *Documentos básicos y bases políticas de las Fuerzas Armadas para el Proceso de Reorganización Nacional* (Buenos Aires: Imprenta del Congreso de la Nación, 1980), pp. 11–12.

plena recuperación nacional').[25] The appeals to 'nuestra Religion Santa', 'la comun prosperidad', and the observance of the rule of Law in the 1810 proclamation all also find their echo in the 'Acta' the *proceso* junta also issued on 24 March 1976: moral, economic, and judicial imperatives occupy centre stage among the aims that are established, in equally general but rhetorically elevated terms.[26]

The almost eerie similarity in the construction of these two documents offers a disturbing vision of the national past, whereby its most celebrated, glorious moment becomes analogous to its darkest experience of violence. Again, the rhetorical means by which the *primera junta* establishes itself as a revolutionary force rescuing the nation from 'evil' are revealed as discursive attempts to assert legitimacy rather than ideologically sound expressions of the victory of 'las luces' over obscurantism and oppression. If both these regimes justify their actions through the same rhetoric, this becomes nothing more than a hollow shell designed to further a set of political aims. Moreover, the text's insistence on the violent actions of the independence government provides a stark and sobering reflection on our willingness to accept violence in the name of a cause we believe is 'right'. Rather than confirming this as a valid revolutionary position, the text proclaims us complicit in acts of repression through the parallels it establishes: in accepting independence as a moral imperative, it seems that we too proclaim this violence as 'necessary' and 'justified', but the reality of what this implies is made all too clear through the figure of the victim that the text forces us to confront.

*Reinstating the Victim: Inversion and Anachronisms*
The clear-cut heroism of independence relies heavily on its presentation as resistance, the uprising of the oppressed against the powerful, and therefore 'official history' offers no construction of the defeated enemy as 'victim'. *Ansay* reinserts the victim at the heart of what the violence of independence can signify: the second part of the text leaves behind the revolutionary government's processes of self-construction and represents the experience of independence exclusively from this victimary perspective. Throughout the first part of the text, the sections that focus on Ansay are the most novelistic of the three plot strands, with extracts from the original memoirs seamlessly incorporated into the narrator's prose or rewritten as description and dialogue. However, at this point the narrator takes great pains to extract Ansay from his function as character within the novel and re-locate him as a real historical figure, insisting that he existed and 'sufrió las cárceles de la Revolución de

---

25  Citations from *Ansay* (the first of the two in each set of parentheses), all p. 13, retaining original nineteenth-century spelling. Citations from the 1976 'Proclama', all in *Documentos básicos*, pp. 11–12.

26  Acta para el Proceso de Reorganización Nacional, Buenos Aires, 24 March 1976. Cited in República Argentina, Junta Militar, *Documentos básicos*, pp. 9–10. Citations from *Ansay*, all p. 13, again preserving original spelling.

Mayo' (228). Ansay's account is dramatically re-positioned through this sudden shift: the narrator's imaginative speculations are suddenly replaced by a pitiful testimony of abuse inflicted on a political prisoner, taken from a real historical document. This shift in tone is accompanied by the inclusion of quotation marks around Ansay's prose and an acknowledgement of the source after each fragment from his *memorias*, which up until this point have been woven into the narrative with no explicit indications or separation from Caparrós's imaginative contributions. The extracts from Ansay's memoirs take the form of a prisoner's testimony within this setting, as he details the poor conditions, forced labour, and killing of prisoners by the guards, in a tale filled with pathos. This is accompanied by a new insistence on factual detail by the narrator, who (with palpable irony) informs us that he was greatly surprised to discover that in 1817, 'en plena edad de los intachables padres fundadores', Pueyrredón kept more than 500 Spanish prisoners 'en condiciones dudosamente reivindicables' (278).

This pared-down narrative approach, which the narrator says will be written 'con las características de un informe', evokes the discursive conventions of denunciations of abuses of human rights. This connection is explicitly evoked in the insistence that in the independence wars, 'había reclusos que ya, adelantándose aparentemente a su tiempo, pedían el respeto de sus "derechos del hombre"' (278). As *Ansay* was published in 1984, the year that CONADEP presented the *Nunca más* report detailing the abuses of the military *junta*, these references invoke the full weight of the politically urgent task of uncovering and punishing the dictatorship's atrocities. The use of first-person testimony of the abuse suffered in captivity had already long been employed as a strategy of political activism in the strategy of opposition to the dictatorship from exile. As early as 1977, the Spanish branch of CADHU (Comisión Argentina de Derechos Humanos) published a report entitled *Argentina: proceso al genocidio*, described by Guillermo Mira Delli-Zotti as one of the earliest and most complete reports on the actions of the dictatorship, including testimonies of victims who had survived imprisonment and torture.[27] The event of the World Cup had seen 'la proliferación de testimonios y denuncias sobre la barbarie de la dictadura [argentina]' in Spain, while prison testimonies had also been published in France, the other base used by Caparrós while in exile.[28] The novel's appeals to prison testimonies and reports of human rights abuses therefore directly evoke a very active political context in order to create a stark parallel between the methods of Argentina's first 'heroic' governments and the nation's recent traumatic past.

27  Mira Delli-Zotti, 'La singularidad del exilio argentino en Madrid', p. 94.
28  Mira Delli-Zotti, 'La singularidad', p. 96. Regarding France, see Franco and González Bernaldo, who cite testimonies such as M. Benasayag's *Malgré tout. Contes à voix basse des prisions argentines* and CADHU's *Témoignage du génocide en Argentine*, both published in 1980. 'Cuando el sujeto deviene objeto', p. 33.

Crucially, this strategy reveals that the text's use of real documents to destabilize the 'official' narrative of 1810 does not put their validity as historical sources in doubt, as argued in Altuna's reading described above. Rather than asserting the provisional nature of historical knowledge, the text positions these documents as incontrovertible proof of the existence of repressive violence in Argentina's most heroic period by presenting them as testimony. The status of historical documentation as 'fact' is therefore reconfirmed, and used as the basis for the denunciation of violence.

The anachronistic application of twentieth-century terminology for acts of state violence represented by this evocation of the discourse of human rights is continued throughout the section. The prison, 'el depósito de Las Bruscas', is referred to as 'un campo de concentración' (277). The application of this term, so intimately associated with the most extreme forms of twentieth-century state violence, establishes an explicit affinity between these universally condemned atrocities and the mechanisms employed by Argentina's founding fathers. The reference to the concentration camp of las Bruscas as 'la solución' to the overcrowding of the prisons in the provinces conveys both an alarming practicality and connotations of the Nazi 'final solution', a parallel that is emphasized through the use of a quotation from Hitler's *Mein Kampf* as the epigraph to the novel's epilogue. The parallel between the prisons of Argentina's first governments, the Nazi concentration camps, and, implicitly, the abuses of the *proceso*, juxtaposed with the pathos-filled descriptions of Ansay's suffering, deny any argument for the exceptionalism of the methods and aims of Argentina's independence process.

*Parallel Processes and Circular Time*
This layering of experiences of state violence in the text is underpinned by its play with the idea of history and historical time. Caparrós provides one of the most significant keys to the novel in his narrator's presentation of the concentration camp as both 'metáfora de los tiempos que corren' and a demonstration of the fact that 'en todos los tiempos se cuecen habas' (278). These two apparently contradictory statements, evoking state violence as both something uniquely contemporary and omnipresent throughout history, combine to explode both the conventional understanding of chronological historical time and the 'exceptional' status of the modern-day repression denounced by the text. Through this blending of present and a cyclical vision of history, the perpetration of atrocities is presented as both the defining characteristic of the contemporary age and the expression of an underlying pattern, erupting with catastrophic intensity in the historical processes of the recent past.

The interweaving, overlapping, and fragmenting structure of the text explodes our conventional apprehension of time in order to draw out more deep-seated, essential similarities between the processes at work. The significance of this approach is drawn to the fore in the text's conceptualization of imprisonment. Rather than dwelling on the deprivation of liberty Ansay experiences as a prisoner, the narrator explores his abstraction from standard conceptions of space and time. Through his captivity, Ansay is portrayed as cut off from the illusion of chronological progression, what the narrator terms 'el tiempo histórico', and is instead plunged into 'ese tiempo sin espacio, el tiempo de la cárcel, tiempo detenido, donde cada día es el eterno recomenzar del anterior' (262). This Nietzschean reference renders teleological conceptions of history irrelevant, frustrating the sense of progress implicit in a linear conception of historical time and replacing it with what the narrator terms 'el tiempo del mito' (260). Chronological time is presented as a construction, a human invention encapsulated in the mechanical object of the clock: 'Es el reloj quien nos ha hecho ilusorios señores del tiempo y su decurso' (261). This suggests that Ansay's experience of time in captivity exposes the true nature of time, usually masked with an illusion of meaning. The repetition and echoes that constantly appear throughout the text suggest that the time of the novel is this 'tiempo de la cárcel', the non-space of 'fantasía' and 'delirio' that Ansay inhabits, where events are no longer tied to temporal circumstances but instead are free to establish alternative patterns and logics. This invites us to read the overlapping time periods in the novel as a series of repeating patterns that will continue to recur, rather than individual moments that have been overcome by the inexorable progress of history. This depiction of time represents a direct and self-conscious challenge to the Marxist view of historical development, which relies upon a linear vision of history to underpin its vision of progression towards revolution. It is precisely the compulsion to impose 'progress' that is under attack, presented as a logic that masks similarities between historical processes that could provide an essential means of reflecting on our present.

The text's disruption of time is translated into a questioning of the consequences of ideological certainty. *Ansay* draws together different historical events that have been assigned fixed positions on the scale of morality within 'official history' in Argentina (and beyond): the Spanish Conquest and the abuses of Nazi Germany, examples of colonial empire and genocide, and the Argentine independence process, inscribed as a process of liberation. By creating this complex web of parallels between the different threads, Caparrós prises them from their specific historical circumstances to show the similar functioning of their discursive structures and mechanisms of physical repression. Without the incorporation of the founding fathers of independence, this narrative strategy could represent an indictment of specific historical processes that represent widely acknowledged abuses of power. By introducing a heroic tale of national liberation alongside these other frameworks, however, the moral exemption granted to the violence of independence is shattered, and instead we are left with an interrogation of the relationship between ideology and the enactment of violence. The text's exploration of how different ideological systems justify the 'necessity' of their violence is deliberately constructed through the medium of independence in order to fragment traditional ideas of heroism as acting (often violently) in the name of some evident 'right'. This disruption brings the text's critique to bear on all forms of violence undertaken in the name of a cause – a fact that troubles the militant certainties of 1970s Argentina as well as tearing down the justifications for state repression.

The particular repeating narrative that Caparrós traces is the creation of a thought system – an ideology – that presents itself as the truth and whose inevitable outcome is the perpetration of violence. The illusion of certainty that ideological systems create is challenged through the play with time that Caparrós undertakes. The novel's second part is composed of alternating sections entitled 'los infortunios' and 'la gloria'. 'Los infortunios' recounts the experiences of the captive Ansay as detailed above, but the sections entitled 'la gloria' follow an unnamed Spanish conquistador in a style that parodies the *crónicas de Indias*. Although never explicitly named, this conquistador has the same basic life experiences and worldview as nineteenth-century Ansay. They share the same birthplace and have inherited the same framework of ideas, encapsulated in the formula 'ReyPatriaDiosEspañaHonra' (17). These sections therefore re-imagine Ansay's experiences as part of the Spanish Conquest, the heroic narrative instilled in the *comandante* as a child.

This direct paralleling is used to produce a reflection on the contrasting fates of the same man born into two very different centuries. The same discursive formulations, the same system of ideas, produce radically different outcomes in each case. The sustaining structures that allow conquistador Ansay to operate with such a glorious sense of righteous certainty are not available to him in 1810. This earlier Ansay reveals a staggering capacity to uphold his belief system in the face of adversity. He lives among a group known as the Tutula, but this radical confrontation with an alternative worldview produces no alteration in his ideas or beliefs; he neither learns from them nor attempts to understand the worth of any of their customs, but instead immediately condemns their difference. The misfortunes that befall him are interpreted as acts of God that further validate his unshakeable convictions: when the child he fathers by a Tutula girl is stillborn, he interprets this as God protecting the child from living among the depravity of the Tutula's cross-dressing gay men. This plot detail recurs in the life of nineteenth-century Ansay when his slave lover falls pregnant and undergoes a secret abortion. However, the Ansay of 1810, whose certainties are falling apart before his eyes, makes no attempt to imbue the events of his life with divine significance. Without a framework of belief, this becomes merely another human tragedy, just another event in the life of an individual.

This radically different fate based on the same actions by the protagonist suggests the almost arbitrary nature of these victories and defeats: the victorious outcome is due to the response offered by the indigenous and *patriota* 'other' rather than the intrinsic truth of the beliefs held. When the ideology of the conquest is replaced with that of independence, a worldview that seemed invincible comes crashing down. Ansay's attempts to characterize the uprising of Argentine revolutionaries as a temporary interference in the 'correct' political order by referring to the *patriotas* as 'insurgentes' and 'rebeldes' are ultimately futile: a pointed reminder that language is the projection of a desired reality rather than a guarantee of incontrovertible truth. This shattered stability is replaced by another structure that sees itself in exactly the same way: the bringer of a truth so transcendent that it justifies the perpetration of violence and the loss of life. In the same way, the text repeatedly underlines the similarity between religious belief and the other belief systems held in the novel. The extracts from documents by the *primera junta* frequently reference God; Ansay invokes God as part of his colonial belief system; and the quotation from *Mein Kampf* asserts that 'obro conforme a la voluntad del Creador omnipotente. Lucho por la obra de Dios' (299). This confirms the problematization of strong belief as a justification for violence that characterizes the interweaving of different historical periods throughout the text: if Hitler, the Argentine military dictatorship and conquistadors can all appeal to the same logic to justify their actions, then the absolute belief of ideological fanaticism is no longer a guarantee of 'right'.

This interweaving of historical moments gradually dismantles the exceptional status that can be granted to the violence perpetrated in the name of 'revolution'. In *La voluntad*, Caparrós and Anguita provide the following comment on the self-styled *revolución argentina*, the military coup that propelled General Onganía into power in 1966:

> Compartía con otro tipo de revoluciones esa característica de creer y proclamar que la grandeza de sus fines alcanzaba para justificar el empleo de cualquier medio. En realidad, era una idea muy difundida en esos días —no sólo entre la izquierda—, como cada vez que un sector social supone que aquello que propone es tan importante, está tan de acuerdo con el sentido de la historia, o las verdades últimas de la religión o la filosofía, que hay que ponerlo en marcha como sea.[29]

This statement provides a reflection on the idea that 'the end justifies the means' with clear implications for the interweaving of different political projects described above. Rather than associating revolution purely with projects on the Left, the authors acknowledge the idea of revolution as a discursive construct that relies on the same mechanisms of self-presentation no matter the political project that lies beneath this framework. This throws into sharp relief the critique outlined above. In challenging us to acknowledge the similarity of the legitimizing discourse employed by these sharply contrasting moments of history, *Ansay* does not assert the provisional nature of any form of judgement, but instead demands that we hold acts of violence to account regardless of the system of meaning that lies behind them.

29 Anguita and Caparrós, *La voluntad*, I, p. 22.

Rather than a challenge to the ideals of 'liberal humanism',[30] therefore, this represents an indictment of the relationship between discursive constructions of the political and the actions that we carry out in their name.

Despite the bitter irony the text employs to tear down conventional rhetorical presentations of the revolutionary hero, and its illustration of the dangers of the rigidity of thought underpinning a committed ideological stance, a glimmer of pathos emerges. This complexity is indicated in the following reflection by the narrator:

> ¿Qué lector no ha sentido alguna vez el deseo o la necesidad de unir sus esfuerzos a una causa cualquiera, de hacer de su vida un paseo militar a través de fortificaciones enemigas desertadas ante la fuerza de la idea —o las armas— triunfantes? (212–13)

This depiction of ideological commitment acknowledges the seductive appeal of certainty, conveyed with a certain sense of nostalgia and loss. This sense of longing is also present in the pathos underpinning the portrayal of Ansay as a victim, marking it as a significant theme of the novel. Although unequivocal belief is shown to lead to potentially extreme consequences, the human desire to contribute to a higher purpose is acknowledged as a powerful and even natural impulse that makes sense of an individual's existence. The reassuring simplicity of the denunciation that characterizes much of the text is profoundly troubled by this presentation of the dilemma of the individual. It acknowledges that in renouncing the possibility of violence, the Manichean call to 'death or victory', we must also sacrifice the heady euphoria of certainty and commitment that accompanies it. This can be read against the destruction of the strength of conviction and idealism of the Argentina of the 1960s and 1970s, which was crushed not only by the horror of the brutality of state repression, but also by the trauma of witnessing a heroic ideal converted into suffering, grief, and wasted sacrifice, as the testimonies from *La voluntad*, cited at the opening of this chapter, reveal. The text can therefore be seen as both a denunciation of state terrorism and a critique of the organization and methods of the militant groups, but also a poignant reminder that an era in which the ability to change the world seemed a possibility has come to a close.

To read *Ansay* as a dismantling of abstract concepts such as epistemological stability risks performing a serious misreading of the political point at stake, therefore. Postmodern ideas of history are certainly called into play, but they are employed with a far more specific purpose, where a complex and nuanced discussion of the relationship between the individual and ideology, strength of conviction and action, and the discursive strategies of political regimes comes to the fore. The text's use of the independence narrative can be interpreted as an attempt to draw an alternative lesson from this paradigmatically didactic tale: rather than learning to love the *patria*, we are challenged to reassess

---

30 See Hutcheon, *A Poetics of Postmodernism*, p. 57.

the schoolbook history of valiant struggle and sacrifice in the light of the recent past. By subverting this 'civilizing' narrative, therefore, *Ansay* seizes the opportunity to reveal the constructed nature of history, but deploys this narrative approach as a means of overtly politicized critique with a clearly defined focus, not an abstract engagement with 'unravelling' past framings. The text reminds us of the power of discursive projections and the role they play in constructing political realities, ultimately reconfirming the 'national myth' of independence as a compelling site for the continual reconfiguration of collective goals and values.

### *La revolución es un sueño eterno*: From the Ideal to the Real

Rivera's *La revolución es un sueño eterno* dialogues with the same context of utopian defeat evoked by Caparrós's text. The novel rewrites independence through the figure of Juan José Castelli, one of the more radical leaders of the May Revolution who occupies a secondary role in most accounts of independence (both traditional and revisionist), overshadowed by the more powerful figure of Mariano Moreno. Rivera presents Castelli at the end of his life: the defeated and outcast revolutionary who was once known as the 'orator of the Revolution' and now approaches his death from cancer of the tongue. The text relates a series of meetings that capture defining moments of the past, from the 'English Invasions' of 1806 and 1807, through to 1812, the year of Castelli's death, interspersed with philosophical reflections and often grotesque depictions of Castelli's rapidly deteriorating physical condition. This plot structure combines a narrative thread focused on mortality and transience with an overtly politicized reading of the May Revolution, weaving them together to provide an image of the relationship between revolution and democracy that displays crucial differences with the vision constructed in *Ansay*.

Once again, Rivera's novel represents a highly self-reflexive engagement with the past that displays many of the formal characteristics associated with the new historical novel or historiographic metafiction. Its play with history is largely concerned with the selective capturing of information about the past, drawn to our attention through frequent metafictional reflection. The text is predominantly made up of two 'notebooks' authored by Rivera's Castelli that create a fragmented, episodic, and partial account of the events they describe. Written documentation reveals itself as an inadequate factual source: we are told how easy it is to falsify documents, we witness threats that papers will be destroyed, and Castelli draws our attention to all that is being excluded from his written account, describing 'los silencios de esa escritura apretada y firme'.[31] Most significantly, the greatest work of the ex-revolutionary's life has been the spoken word, which we are frequently reminded is an ephemeral

---

31 Andrés Rivera, *La revolución es un sueño eterno* (Buenos Aires: Alfaguara, 2000), p. 49. Further references to this edition are given after quotations in the text.

part of historical experience. Castelli often refuses to confirm that he spoke any words at all, with the caveat of 'si algo dijo' left to hang over many of his supposed utterances as orator. The fragmented narrative and 'heteroglossia' of the text – shifting between discourses including revolutionary speeches, legal courtroom speak, and intimate diary writing – are coupled with the extensive use of irony and parody, particularly in two key episodes that I will discuss in my analysis: the courtroom scene and the depiction of negotiations between the Argentines and the British. These stylistic features combine to create a fictional account of the past that places the process of the text's own construction at the heart of its thematic concerns.

However, I will argue that this metafictional 'destabilizing' of written sources and meditation on the transience of spoken language does not represent a comment on the discursive plurality of the past, but a reflection on political commitment and utopian failure. These seemingly unstable written and oral sources are positioned as contributions made by individuals to a wider political process, rather than historical records from which we might hope to construct an accurate vision of the past. The text's reflections on their precarious nature are almost exclusively filtered through the figure of Castelli, whose defeat as a revolutionary has shattered the world of idealistic certainty he cultivated in his youth. The concern with evidence in the text is therefore much more profoundly connected to the idea of personal legacy than the possibility of establishing a fixed historical position, representing a crucial intersection of the individual and historical process. Framing the text's obsession with the fragility of documentation within this concern with permanence and fear of futility reshapes our reading of its metafictional treatment of history. My analysis will therefore draw out the highly politicized re-reading of the past produced by the text in order to re-situate its metafictional reflection within this context of defeated utopian ideals.

### Recasting Revolution: Democracy and Defeat

*La revolución es un sueño eterno* develops two major strands of political critique, linked through the theme of revolution. The first of these is its ideological reshaping of the 'official' independence narrative, which becomes a means of denouncing the insufficiency of the present. The narrative on the 1810 revolution that Rivera produces follows neither the *mitrista* line (where May 1810 represents the glorious birth of democracy) nor the revisionist defence of the *caudillos* as an alternative to power falling into the hands of a *porteño* elite. The text elaborates a framework that presents May 1810 as a defeated revolution, resulting in a nominal transfer of power rather than a democratic sea change.

This particular challenge establishes a dialogue with a less well-known but significant vision of the Argentine past: the narrative constructed by the country's Communist Party (Partido Comunista de la Argentina (PCA)), of which Rivera was a member for several years. Omar Acha, in his study of historiographies of the Left in Argentina, provides a detailed account of the evolution of the Communist Party's narrative and the main arguments it sustains, analysed through the use of history in the Party's official publications and those of the most prominent historians associated with the Party.[32] Acha's outline of this narrative reveals how Marxist ideas were mapped onto a reading of Argentina's past and deployed as part of the PCA's process of self-construction. He describes how the Party's prevailing vision throughout most of the twentieth century confirms the heroic status of *Mayo*, particularly through the figure of Mariano Moreno, but presents it as an incomplete process, characterized as a bourgeois revolution that did not fully succeed. Rather than attacking the bourgeois nature of 1810, from the 1930s onwards the Party's official publications portray it as a form of progress: Argentina at the point of the Revolution is presented as a feudal society in need of capitalist development before a true popular revolution can take place. Within this narrative, 1810 therefore becomes a necessary but incomplete stage of development. As a result, this Communist Party vision of the past concludes that, due to the incomplete nature of the 1810 revolution, Argentina has not fully passed through its capitalist phase of modernization and is being held back by residual feudal structures. While 1810 is praised, therefore, it is not presented as a clean break with the past as in the *mitrista* liberal version, nor as giving birth to Argentina's true destiny. Instead, it is constructed as a heroic endeavour that was frustrated in its more radical aims, but that ultimately brought positive change for the nation.[33]

The vision of the May Revolution detailed above is vital to situating Rivera's presentation of history in *La revolución es un sueño eterno*. The text establishes a tension between the revolutionary potential of this decisive historical moment and the reality of its outcomes, offering a more pessimistic reading of the 'incomplete revolution' thread established by the PCA. The potential internal contradiction that this tension creates, simultaneously praising and condemning the revolution, can be read with greater clarity against the backdrop of this Communist narrative. The revolution that Rivera casts in a positive light is the 'unrealized revolution' of the more radical wing, portrayed through the figure of Castelli. This is the same ideological branch that receives the greatest praise in the narrative detailed above, as having the potential to inspire the popular classes to fight for freedom. Reading the text in relation to this narrative enables us to go beyond the generalizations about a 'challenge to official history' in postmodern historical fiction. *La revolución es un sueño eterno* does not provide a challenge to the dominant narrative in abstract terms, but presents a rewriting with a clear ideological positioning that can be considered a directly political intervention.

---

32 Omar Acha, *Historia crítica de la historiografía argentina. Vol 1: Las izquierdas en el siglo XX* (Buenos Aires: Prometeo Libros, 2009).

33 See Acha, *Historia crítica*, p. 147–67.

*Dissecting Democracy: Structures of Power and Ideological Critique*

By presenting 1810 as an incomplete revolution, the text dismantles the right of this narrative to occupy the position of 'national epic'. It constructs instead a catalogue of failures with an overtly Marxist ideological focus, transforming a tale of 'revolution' into an indictment of bourgeois liberal democracy and thereby severing the harmonious fusion of revolution and democracy that underpins the traditional version of the tale. The novel depicts the form of democracy that emerges from May 1810 as serving the interests of the elites rather than representing a truly popular form of government, thus rendering revolution an unrealized future necessity rather than a completed glorious act. The text can therefore be seen as an attempt to map out the power structures concealed behind the narrative of democracy celebrated in the liberal version of the nation's founding moment. It builds a definition of revolution as something much deeper than overthrowing a political leader, which it presents as nothing more than a change of figurehead while the real sources of power remain unaltered. This is stressed repeatedly in the text, such as in the reflection, 'Castelli sabe, ahora, que el poder no se deshace con un desplante de orillero' and 'Cambiaron las máscaras [...]. No cambió a Buenos Aires ni al país' (33, 97). The susceptibility of revolution to succumb to the existing structures of power is a source of bitter reflection for Castelli, epitomized in the following quotation that he recalls: '*el movimiento revolucionario resulta, a la postre, vencido: le faltan, siempre, conocimientos, habilidad, medios, armas, jefes, un plan de acción fijo, y cae indefenso, ante los conspiradores, que disponen de experiencia, habilidad y astucia*' (84). The revolution Castelli depicts is built upon youth and idealism and has no defence against this wealth of experience and the political astuteness of the ruling classes. The creation of liberal democracy is therefore denied its traditional status as a revolutionary act, illustrating the need for a new surge of political reform.

Rivera's choice of Castelli as protagonist rather than the more famous figure of Moreno represents a significant attempt to carve out a space for the more radical idea of revolution foregrounded by the text. The novel's distinctly unsympathetic portrayal of Moreno casts him as a 'sell out', kowtowing to the imperialist British and supporting the powerful church, a sentiment summarized in the novel's assertion: 'Moreno, que tenía fe, creía en Dios y pactaba con el Diablo' (74). Far from a radical revolutionary, Moreno is cast as a staunch supporter of the structures of power and privilege that underpin Argentine society at the moment of the Revolution. His class allegiances are made clear when Castelli notes that the wealthy 'caballeros' who formed part of the Alto Perú army were 'personas, según el señor Mariano Moreno, porque eran blancos y vestían de frac o levita en sus salones o en los salones de sus amigos' (51). Rivera chooses to present his perspective through an 'alternative' figure, therefore, one that can embody the idea of unfulfilled revolutionary commitment that drives the ideological focus of the text.

In the text's analysis of the 'true' power structures underpinning the supposedly democratic government, two major nuclei of control are exposed: the land-owning classes and imperial powers. Criticism of these political forces has clear origins in left-wing discourse of the 1960s and 1970s in Argentina, with particular relevance to the construction of nineteenth-century history by historians involved in the Communist Party. As noted above, the Marxist view of the historical development of modes of production is essential to the positioning of independence in this left-wing vision of the national past. The arrival of independence is roughly equated to the transition from feudalism to capitalism, which represents an essential precursor to the creation of socialism in Marxist thought. However, Communist historian Rodolfo Puiggrós's influential writings posit that this transition is incomplete, and the nation is still held back by the continued existence of feudal structures.[34] Puiggrós establishes the two major obstacles to progression as foreign intervention and the *criollo* landowners, stating: 'El feudalismo se habría preservado en la combinación de latifundio y monopolio extranjero, los verdaderos enemigos de la nación.'[35] The importance of feudal remnants as a hindrance to development is a prominent narrative strand of *La revolución*, combining critique of Argentina's economic elite with a harsh indictment of the influence of foreign powers, conveyed through the role of the British in the text. The anti-imperialist rhetoric present in the text unites fierce criticism of these structural obstacles to progress with both an illustration of the oppression that this economic system generates and an indictment of the web of personal interest that underlies the revolutionary 'failure' of 1810.

The negative effects of both foreign intervention and the power wielded by the land-owning classes are primarily explored through two key scenes in the novel: the meeting between the British General William Carr Beresford and Argentine revolutionary leaders (including Moreno and Castelli), and Castelli's conversation with his ex-lover, Irene Orellano Stark, a member of the *latifundista* oligarchy. Beresford's major role in Argentine history is as leader of the 1806 'English Invasion', in which the people of Buenos Aires rose up against the foreign invaders and successfully retained control of the city (inscribed in Argentine 'official' history as a heroic precursor to the independence struggle). Beresford is therefore closely associated with an event that is commonly depicted as an act of imperial aggression, and it is this connotation that is drawn to the fore through his presence in the text. The willingness of Argentina's early governments to establish trade links with the British is well known, as the glowing praise for Britain's liberal economic model in Mitre's accounts of the period attests. The meeting that Rivera portrays between the Argentine authorities and the British General combines

34 Acha, *Historia crítica de la historiografía argentina*, p. 157. Acha describes Puiggrós' *De la colonia a la revolución* as 'el estudio que organizará buena parte de la agenda historiográfica de las izquierdas en la Argentina del resto del siglo' (ibid.).

35 Cited in Acha, *Historia crítica*.

this strong connotation of imperial expansionism with the introduction of liberal economics, thus equating the establishment of these trade links with the surrender of political control to a foreign power.

The meeting with Beresford is presented through a disconcerting process of translation, whereby the Argentine Agrelo misinterprets, twists, and edits the speeches of both parties to the point that any meaningful communication breaks down. The translation process rarely produces anything that resembles the original enunciation, but instead draws out the underlying power relations of the scene, such as when Beresford welcomes the Argentines with the words 'Caballeros, están en su casa' and Agrelo translates that 'el general Beresford se pregunta si es nuestro huésped o nuestro anfitrión' (69). This destroys the veneer of courtesy masking Beresford's words and exposes the assumption of the position of dominance underlying this formulaic welcome. Towards the end of the discussion, Agrelo translates Beresford's rambling speech about the benefits he can offer the Argentine leaders with the aggressive: '¿Quiénes son ustedes, caballeros? ¿En nombre de qué, caballeros, invaden el retiro, temporalmente forzoso, de un rudo soldado, y le proponen tratos que avergonzarían a un salteador de caminos?' (74). The text therefore ironically undercuts Beresford's show of courtesy by directly communicating the underlying attitude behind the pact he offers, which is based on providing these men with personal benefits, a comfortable life, perhaps a statue in London, in exchange for becoming subjects of the British crown. By transforming Beresford's subtle original enunciation into an expression of outrage, Agrelo's translation exposes the General's complete unwillingness to work together as an equal partner, instead interpreting any attempt by the Argentines to negotiate as an insult to his power and status.

Beresford, like Irene Orellano Stark later in the novel, is an undeveloped character who functions as an almost allegorical symbol of imperialism, appearing purely as an emissary of the foreign power he represents. He outlines a capitalist economic programme that promises to respect private property and 'los derechos, privilegios y costumbres de las personas decentes de Buenos Aires' (70), ensure the continuation of slavery, and institute a free trade policy. His innocuous-sounding reasoning behind this free trade strategy, that 'el pueblo podría disfrutar de la producción de otros países a un precio moderado', is filtered through several layers of irony. This solitary mention of the 'pueblo' is surrounded by clear concessions to the dominant classes, or 'las personas decentes' as Beresford's euphemistic language describes them. The Englishman also betrays the unspoken aims of his proposal as his apparently meandering prose moves from the free trade agreement to a reflection on power, culminating in the assertion that 'Inglaterra es el poder': a bald statement that unravels the niceties of his previous speech. The exploitative structure underpinning the proposal is also made explicit through his detached, matter-of-fact description of the violence created by the ideology he represents:

Inglaterra es un imperio gracias a los niños que mueren en sus minas, y que mueren como moscas por caprichosos, necios o maleducados. Curiosamente, los negros y los indios también mueren como moscas en las minas de la América española. Son datos estadísticos. (72)

The absurdly illogical nature of Beresford's argumentation contributes to the intensely ironic tone of the scene, exposing imperialism as requiring violent exploitation and devoid of any sense of humanity.

The *latifundista* counterpart to this scene in the novel is Castelli's meeting with Irene Orellano Stark, which presents a similarly objectionable character and an equally explicit ideological foundation to the scene. Castelli finds Irene:

En una vasta casa, con colgaduras de damasco y oro, capilla propia, y símbolos de un poder —grillos y cadenas, un tráfico de cincuenta mil mulas al año, y mil o dos mil carretas, vaya uno a saber, a nombre de las familias que dictan la ley, y el despiadado aborrecimiento por el indio y el mestizo— que la Primera Junta y su ejército no supieron doblegar. (78)

The association between wealth, power, the land-owning class, and oppression that Irene represents is made extremely clear through this listing of her privileges and their consequences, as is the failure of independence to overthrow this cosy oligarchical system.

The novel's repudiation of this system is emphasized throughout the scene through the unpalatable character of Irene, who spends the majority of the conversation lamenting the 'ungrateful' behaviour of her slave Belén, whom Castelli has come to find. Irene expresses her dissatisfaction in language that portrays her owning slaves as a gracious act of charity, insisting on her generosity as she has fed, clothed, and educated them, and '[los] apartó, hasta donde pudo, de ritos horrendos y africanos' (83). The overt racism and paternalistic attitude she displays here imbue her attempt to portray her actions as saintly charity with an intense irony which denies her protestations any validity. Moreover, her focus on the financial return of selling Belén betrays the purely economic motivation behind her complaints, as she bemoans the fact that the price she sold Belén for does not come close to recovering 'lo que invirtió' (82). The language she uses also offers significant parallels with that of the imperialist Beresford, such as her descriptions of Belén as 'insoportable', 'descarriada', 'alguien que nació insolente y presumida' (82), which echo his explanation of exploited children's propensity to die in droves on their own failings ('por caprichosos, necios o maleducados') (83). Both evade any recognition of exploitation by attributing all problems to personality failings in those they abuse, normalizing their own behaviour and transforming structural inequality into a question of the individual, thus neutralizing its political implications. Like Beresford's use of 'las personas decentes', Irene's appeal to 'cualquier persona honorable' is a thinly veiled class reference, which once again shows bourgeois language covering exploitation with a veneer of respectability. These linguistic parallels reveal shared underlying attitudes between these embodiments of imperialism and the landed classes, exposing an entrenched connection between them that responds to the same set of interests.

The economic control that the *latifundistas* maintain over the other classes is translated into the sexual commerce between them. The disillusioned Castelli provides a graphic depiction of these relationships and their consequences, stating that men of all social classes 'introducen sus miembros en un agujero tibio y húmedo y, a veces, infernal' (78). He insists upon the disjuncture between the hidden nature of this interaction and its political effects, exposing the crucial discrepancy between what is written publicly about the national economy (citing Moreno's famous *Representación de los hacendados*) and the true power structures that control the flow of wealth. Individual relationships are therefore portrayed as underpinning the outcome of major political questions, stressed in Castelli's claim that 'un país de revolucionarios sin revolución se lee en aquello que no se escribe' (78). Personal behaviour is exposed as a political tool that the ruling classes consciously exploit to their own advantage, and revolutionary ideals are frittered away in the daily complexities of individual lives.

Castelli serves as an important 'cautionary tale' in this respect; despite the strength of his beliefs, he, along with his fellow revolutionaries, has become caught up in relations with this landed class. The text underscores this sexual/economic betrayal in a striking image: 'Juan José Castelli chupó plata en la punta olorosa de las tetas que se erguían en la helada noche altoperuana' (79). Despite his complicity in this surreptitious form of power as a young man, the older Castelli is able to perceive the political significance of these sexual relationships and is repulsed by the woman who was once his lover. In a gesture of defiance, when he leaves Irene after their meeting, he spits the putrid phlegm from his cancerous mouth into his hand and rubs it in her face – a futile but significant rebellion that reinforces his rejection of the economic status quo and confirms the novel's rejection of the crippling political intimacy between sectors of power.

The denunciation of corrupt power structures is also conveyed through the depiction of a third 'counterrevolutionary' force: the Catholic Church. This once again forms part of the text's Marxist-inspired denunciation of the forces governing society, portraying the Church as hypocritical and colluding in the oppression created by the economic system. This is a major theme of the trial scenes, which depict Castelli's prosecution by Saavedra's First Triunvirate: the event that led to the 'orator of the revolution' becoming an outcast from the newly created political system. In the text's construction of this episode, the revolutionary Castelli is prosecuted on spurious moral charges, which are revealed to be nothing more than a convenient means of clipping his political wings in order to rein in his more radical revolutionary project. The courtroom scenes depict a legal system controlled by the political and economic elites, who exploit the rhetoric of Catholic morality for their own gain. Rather than a direct narration of the scene, the trial is largely communicated through quotation of the prosecutor's questions and caustic monologues by Castelli, in which he lambasts the hypocrisy of his prosecutors and their exploitation of the supposedly impartial legal system in heavily ironic prose. The monologues take the form of an imagined defence, and while they ostensibly adopt the codes and value system of the courtroom, they simultaneously expose its hypocritical nature and irrelevance of the charges to the political point that is really at stake. The allegations against Castelli are founded on questions of sexual morality but the text exposes their hidden intent with biting irony, comparing the link between his sexual conduct and the fate of the nation in the ridiculous hyperbolic image of the connection between an umbilical cord and a foetus, and bombastically overstating the 'evident' link between his personal behaviour and the tranquillity of polite society.

This vision of morality is consistently portrayed as punitive, meaningless, and perverse in itself, as Castelli lists the public Catholic practices of members of the court (including punishing activities such as self-flagellation) and their own indulgence in the sexual crimes he is accused of committing. The unrelenting intense irony running through all these descriptions shows mock deference to these moral codes but delivers a clear and unforgiving message, denouncing the subjugation of legal impartiality to undemocratic power structures that serve one another's interests under a guise of abstract concepts of 'decency'. The space of the court itself is desanctified and delegitimized through this politicized use of sexual morality. Hidden power structures rooted in class are once again to the fore, as Castelli describes the court as '[un] espacio legitimado por el poder, donde acusadores y reos, como si no fueran acusadores y reos, como si no simbolizaran, unos y otros, un mundo y otro, deben dirimir qué es lo justo y qué lo arbitrario, qué lo perverso y qué lo digno' (22). The fusion of Church morality and legal practice undermines the ostensible moral role of both institutions, transforming them into part of the wider structures characterized as oppressive within the text.

The text's denunciation of corrupt power structures, united in the 'unholy trinity' of church, imperialism, and feudalism, therefore provides a retelling of the past with an explicitly Marxist ideological focus. By problematizing the traditional independence narrative's claim to revolutionary status, the novel reasserts the need for profound institutional change in order to bring about the radical reform that remains 'unfinished' by the fight for liberation from Spanish rule. Reading *La revolución* in relation to left-wing rewritings of independence, particularly the historical vision of intellectuals involved in the PCA, therefore brings the text's political critique into sharp focus. Beyond merely highlighting the ideological background to the text, this allows us to consider its configuration of the relationship between politics and literature. The vision of history produced by the PCA represents an explicitly didactic attempt to narrate the national past in relation to the Party's ideological beliefs, thereby marking out the structural change that this organization aims to translate into political reality. This use of history represents an attempt to intervene directly in the political sphere, and can therefore be considered a form of political action. By demonstrating the close relationship between this narrative and the vision of the national past that Rivera presents, my reading underscores the didactic nature of *La revolución es un sueño eterno*, which similarly seeks to adapt the nation's foundational narrative to a set of ideological values that run counter to the liberal narrative. This allows us to perceive the text as political far beyond the usual characterization of self-reflexive historical fiction, positioning it as an attempt to exploit literature as a means of raising ideological consciousness, rather than merely an attempt to underscore the constructed nature of knowledge about the past.

*Utopia and Revolution*
Alongside its ideological denunciation of political structures, the text develops a second narrative line that provides a more nuanced reflection on the idea of revolution. Although the text portrays a need for radical political reform, the heroism of the revolutionary ideal is subject to profound questioning. By presenting independence through the figure of a dying man whose dreams have failed to become reality, Rivera explores a traditionally heroic vision through the prism of defeat. This provides a crucial context for the idea of personal legacy that I alluded to at the beginning of my discussion of the novel. The shadow of mortality hangs over the text from the start, threatening futility in the place of any lasting contribution. This reflection on mortality is suggested in the text's title, a word play that encompasses the full range of meaning of 'sueño' as eternal dream/sleep. As 'dream', its meaning is unstably positioned on the fault line between revolution as a constant desire and an impossibility. For the dream to remain 'eternal', revolution must be both a utopia in the etymological sense of a 'non-place', an unrealizable ideal, and a desire that will always be fought for. But as an 'eternal sleep', revolution promises the finality of death. This evokes an atheist slogan from eighteenth-century revolutionary France that was popular among the more radical wing of the Argentine independence movement, which stated that 'death is an eternal sleep' in opposition to the Christian concept of eternal life.[36] By replacing 'death' with 'revolution', Rivera hints at the potential for revolution to result in empty oblivion rather than the glory of eternal paradise.

    Rather than solely exploring this theme at the level of historical and political process, the text positions Castelli as the embodiment of the consequences of defeat at a personal level. Through the notebooks that make up the majority of the text, the ex-revolutionary struggles to come to terms with the failure of the project that previously gave meaning to his life. This is coupled with reflection on the responsibility he bears for the suffering of those who were

---

36  See Osvaldo Soriano, *Cuentos de los años felices* (Buenos Aires: Sudamericana, 1994), p. 123.

prepared to fight for him, to whom he promised a glorious future that has not been delivered. This reflection on the experience of utopian defeat has clear echoes with the process of disillusionment suffered by the Left in Argentina from the mid-1970s. In his analysis of the militant violence of the 1970s, Feinmann offers a poignant reflection on the reality behind the rhetoric of revolutionary martyrdom:

> Así, el triste día del sepelio de Rodolfo Ortega Peña, asesinado por las ráfagas fascistas de la Triple A, la izquierda peronista entonó una consigna destinada a exaltar la belleza de la muerte militante: *Vea, vea, vea, qué cosa más bonita, Ortega dio la vida por la patria socialista.* Se equivocaban: no existe la muerte bonita, no hay belleza en la muerte. Hubieran debido exaltar otra cosa: que Ortega había vivido por la patria socialista, que esa elección había entregado un sentido a todos los actos de su vida y que su muerte, lejos de ser bonita, era terriblemente dolorosa, fea, y no bella, cruel.[37]

This critique of the heroic conception of death sustained by the revolutionary organizations conveys a profound sense of sadness and loss, but does not correspond to the alternative characterization of the militants as 'victims'. Instead, it recognizes the celebration of commitment to political ideals, but creates a space for mourning. In his testimony in *La voluntad*, Emiliano Costa, an ex-Montonero, conveys a similar sense of wasted sacrifice, partly laying the blame at the door of the leaders of these organizations when he states that 'creo que tienen una enorme responsabilidad en haber llevado al abismo, al fracaso y a la esterilidad [...] el sacrificio de una generación'.[38] In the same volume, Susana Sanz echoes this combined sense of responsibility and loss in her description of her feeling of 'la obligación de continuar para que tantas muertes tuvieran sentido, para que tanto sacrificio no fuera en vano' (494). This sheds light on Rivera's presentation of Castelli's experience of defeat, particularly the orator's recurring guilt regarding '[los] que murieron por haberlo escuchado' and his statement that 'los sueños que omiten la sangre son de inasible belleza' (33). The figure of Segundo Reyes, a black freed slave who served under Castelli in the Ejército del Alto Perú, provides the most poignant example of this in the text (other than Castelli himself). Reyes narrates his recollections of Castelli in his revolutionary days, recalling how he was entranced by the hypnotic prose and entrancing vision of equality promised by the 'orator of the revolution' in his speeches and declaring himself 'un perfecto idiota' for having believed the orator's word 'como se cree en la palabra del Mesías' (111). The outcome of this intoxicating vision is painful for Castelli to witness: for Reyes, it resulted in losing a leg in battle and accepting discrimination rather than a world of equality. These

37 Feinmann, *La sangre derramada*, p. 68.
38 Anguita and Caparrós, *La voluntad*, III, p. 470.

characters are therefore facing the dilemma of living beyond the demise of the ideal that gave their lives purpose – another clear point of contact with the militant experience in Argentina, as illustrated by comparison with the following reflection by ex-militant Mercedes Depino:

> Hace poco más de veinte años creíamos estar a punto de tocar el cielo con las manos, de alcanzar la utopía de construir una sociedad más justa. Un mundo mejor. De hacer la Revolución. Sin embargo, en pocos años el mundo se nos vino encima. Todo comenzó a desaparecer. [...] Y entonces los sobrevivientes tuvimos que aprender nuevamente a vivir...[39]

This parallels the whole plot structure of *La revolución*, encapsulating the dilemma faced by the surviving ex-revolutionaries who have to find a way to reconstruct their identity. It also provides a sharper focus for the recurring theme of mortality within the text. The dying Castelli wrestles with defining the contribution he has made through his own life, lamenting: 'No planté un árbol, no escribí un libro, escribe Castelli. Sólo hablé. ¿Dónde están mis palabras? No escribí un libro, no planté un árbol: sólo hablé. Y maté' (45–46). His attempts to forge a glorious new future through revolutionary change have failed, and as a result his certainty in the value of his individual contribution has been eroded.

'La disolución del sujeto' that Martha Barboza notes as a feature of the text can therefore also be constituted as a political reflection through this context of defeated utopia.[40] At several points in the musings of his notebooks, Castelli contemplates the idea of individual subjectivity as presenting a deceptive illusion of stability. He returns obsessively to the idea of his own name, attempting to understand the link between the Castelli who stood before his troops, promising a brave new world, and the wasted invalid he has become, referring to his past self as an actor, or 'eso que llaman Castelli' (102), and asks whether all his past selves can possibly be contained within this single signifier. This is not merely an abstract reflection upon the idea of the individual, however: Castelli's precarious subjectivity is fundamentally bound up with the fragmentation of his revolutionary identity. His public persona is fused with a commitment to a collective goal that disappears in the wake of defeat. This loss of a collective spirit of hope is found in the testimony of many of those who recall their militancy in *La voluntad*, but is perhaps most poignantly expressed by ex-Montonera Graciela Daleo:

> El 'nosotros' predominando sobre el 'yo'. Ni totalitarismos ni despersonalización, sino compromiso y ser parte de una identidad colectiva. (Así lo contamos desde fines de los 60 hasta gran parte de los 70. El 'yo' en los relatos reaparece cuando la dictadura había pulverizado parte de las

---

39  Anguita and Caparrós, *La voluntad*, III, p. 475.
40  Martha Barboza 'La escritura como desplazamiento de la oralidad en *La revolución es un sueño eterno*, de Andrés Rivera', *Espéculo*, 42 (2009).

organizaciones populares. El 'nosotros' se mantuvo en quienes resistieron escapando al cerco del miedo.)[41]

Castelli's transition from public orator to personal diary-writer symbolizes this withdrawal from the certainty of collective revolutionary belonging. *La revolución* represents the reintroduction of this 'yo', a recovering of subjectivity without the single feature that once rooted this identity in the solidity of purpose. The text's reflection on individual choice, contribution, and sacrifice is filtered through this politicized framework, and the transient nature of the spoken word highlighted above acquires further meaning through this context. Rather than being a statement of the impossibility of attaining reliable historical knowledge, it becomes a profound concern with this dissolution of individual meaning and communal purpose.

Despite this predominant concern with defeat, the text appeals to the unresolved need for revolution and confides faith in traditional conceptions of the role of history as a source of lessons to be learned for the present. This is made explicit in Castelli's warning, *'La historia no nos dio la espalda: habla a nuestras espaldas'* (24).[42] The text refuses to accept the 'end' of history presented as a *fait accompli*, to deny conventional ideas of historical progress, and to ignore lessons of the past. The final and most significant question asked in Castelli's notebooks is, *'¿qué revolución compensará las penas de los hombres?'* (172), encapsulating the need to continue utopian thought alongside recognition of the weighty responsibility of sacrifice that this brings.

## Conclusion: Defining the Political

*La revolución es un sueño eterno* and *Ansay ó los infortunios de la gloria* both employ the period of independence in order to elaborate a vision of the relationship between revolution and democracy, translated through the experiences of the Argentine Left from the late 1960s to the end of military rule. Both texts problematize the way in which revolution and democracy are characterized by the traditional narrative, disputing the unquestioning union of the two concepts in 'official' history, in order to elaborate their own politicized critique. The political focus of *Ansay* is a condemnation of the perpetration of violence in the name of a cause, constructed by interlacing contrasting historical periods in order to reveal disturbing underlying similarities beneath apparently antithetical ideological projects. By establishing these alarming parallels, the text denies the right of revolution to justify its use of violence, and troubles the idealistic certainty underpinning its rhetoric of heroism. The text also privileges a view of democracy as the institutional means of protecting civil liberties. This offers a less grandiose representation than the *mitrista* narrative of independence, and also departs from the dominant

---

41 Anguita and Caparrós, *La voluntad*, III, p. 472.
42 Italics in quotations from this text present in the original.

left-wing characterizations of democracy prior to the 1976–83 dictatorship in Argentina, which posited 'true' democracy as a popular system of government that would supplant the class oppression underpinning liberal democracy. In this way, *Ansay* explicitly appeals to human rights as a universal ideal beyond the reach of conflicting ideological aims.

While Caparrós's text embraces the shift towards the discourse of democracy and human rights that occurred in response to the atrocities of the military dictatorship, *La revolución* does not follow this redefinition. Rivera's text casts 1810 as a triumph of the bourgeoisie and therefore a failed revolution, ending in mediocre conformity rather than radical change. This characterization follows the idea of liberal democracy as a stage of historical development prior to the arrival of true revolution, and the text wrestles with the means of bringing this necessary change to fruition following the failure of the utopian project of 1810, which can be read as an allegorical recasting of the recent past.

Both texts are united, however, in the pathos of their portrayal of the individual who has lost the worldview that sustained their sense of identity and provided a foundation for their sense of purpose. Through the depiction of figures who have fought for an ideal that has failed, both novels explore the theme of personal disenchantment following the demise of utopian projects. It is this shared focus that throws into sharpest relief the significance of the political context invoked by the texts' rewriting of independence. By reading these works in relation to the crisis of the Argentine Left, we can perceive an underlying commentary on the relationship between the individual and ideology in a way that is quite different to seemingly abstract notions associated with the use of history in this genre. The attack on abstract concepts that Hutcheon positions at the heart of postmodern textual strategies does not contemplate this more introspective frame of critique, which seeks to understand the consequences of the dissolution of ideological certainty not only for the individual, but for a generation that believed in the possibility of radical change.

At the same time, these texts' political engagement also extends beyond other commonly applied definitions of the political in Latin American historical fiction. To frame them as acts of 'resistance' is to overlook both the complexity of their responses and the significant differences between the two texts (if anything, they are reflecting on the failure of resistance, at least in the terms conceived by the Argentine Left in the 1970s). Their engagements with the marginal are not embarked upon with the intention of broadening historical narratives, but instead to generate the narrative potential to reflect upon defeat and failure. The texts' use of postmodern ideas of history does not point to the illustration of the 'provisional, indeterminate nature of historical knowledge',[43] therefore, but to an altogether more concrete political

---

43 Hutcheon, *A Poetics of Postmodernism*, p. 88.

intervention. Their adaptations of the nation's founding narrative exploit and subvert the discourses that have been used to establish a symbolic foundation for the construction of the nation-state. This strategy represents both an attempt to overturn the political ideas underpinned by the conventional celebration of the period, and an appeal to the primordial role of independence as a period with a didactic function.

Rather than challenging the conventional role of history, these texts are, in fact, exploiting the didactic function of this origin narrative in order to produce a highly politicized critique. The freedom offered by postmodernism's linking of the discourses of literature and history represents an opportunity to construct a reading of the past that is as politically focused as a Peronist revisionist narrative or an interpretation offered by a Communist historian might be, but filtered through the specific features of art as a means of translating this critique through a memorable and nuanced act of storytelling. These texts are both 'political' in a very different way to the epistemological unravelling proposed by the postmodern historical novel framework. They provide reflection on the recent past by rewriting an extremely familiar narrative, not to undermine or even underscore methods of meaning-making, but with the intent of offering a provocative reading with direct implications for our judgement of contemporary political processes.

# CHAPTER 2

# Fragmenting the Nation

## Martín Kohan's *El informe: San Martín y el otro cruce de los Andes* and Osvaldo Soriano's *El ojo de la patria*

Reconsidering what we mean by 'the political' in relation to self-reflexive literary rewritings of history, as proposed in the previous chapter, raises a new set of questions regarding the engagement with epistemology in these texts. If, as I have argued, their dismantling of foundational historical narratives does not have abstract engagements with systems of knowledge production in its sights, then we must consider where the target of their critique lies. Understanding the unravelling of specific aspects of the independence tale that they undertake is therefore crucial to identifying these alternative sites of critique.

The tools provided by the postmodern theoretical turn offer more than an opportunity to dismantle the presentation of systems of thought as 'natural', and to assess the relationship between thought, language, and power. They can represent a recognition of the values inscribed by a particular historical narrative in a way that provides explicit praise, critique, or condemnation, making an intervention into highly politicized terrain in order to assert different values. This chapter will therefore seek to challenge the assumption that a self-reflexive destabilizing of the past in historical novels must represent a problematization of epistemology, as it is this connection which fuels the notion that late twentieth-century historical fiction is concerned with foregrounding instability and a narrativity that underscores different framings rather than mounting positions more easily identifiable as 'political'. Instead, through my exploration of Martín Kohan's *El informe: San Martín y el otro cruce de los Andes* (1997), I will analyse the specific critique that emerges from the text when considered as a reworking of one particular vision of the nation's past, and the presence of a clear set of values that emerges from this comparison. As a counterpoint to this, I will explore Osvaldo Soriano's *El ojo de la patria* (1992), a text that does *not* exhibit the playful parody and self-reflexivity associated with postmodern historical fiction, in order to discuss interactions between history and postmodernism beyond a specific set of formal textual features. My analysis therefore compares two texts that are stylistically very different in order to draw out how their use of history feeds into a debate centred on the meaning of the *patria* in post-dictatorship Argentina. I seek to show how this debate is masked by the dominant understandings of the Latin American historical novel, which encourages textual comparisons based on stylistic similarity rather than shared historical or political concerns. I also aim to problematize the supposition that a novel's self-reflexive play with history must represent a challenge to our processes of constructing knowledge (and, conversely, the implicit assumption that texts that do not display these characteristics are not engaged in challenging the stability of epistemology). Through my readings in this chapter, my purpose is therefore both to reconsider the presumed link between a self-reflexive treatment of history and postmodern epistemological questioning, and to demonstrate how using a thematic and contextualized approach can open up texts that use history to new comparisons that can allow for more nuanced interpretations, in this case focusing on interventions into the representation of the nation.

## Malvinas, Militarism, and Democracy: Questioning the *Patria*

The challenge to Argentina's traditional patriotic epic that Kohan's and Soriano's texts present draws on national debates that formed part of the process of reconstruction in the wake of the 1976–83 military dictatorship.[1] The return to democracy was accompanied by a process of evaluation and soul-searching, focused predominantly on the need to address the human rights abuses of the military regime. One aspect of this was the re-appraisal of the expected role of the military in civil society, as its traditional self-defined role as protector of the nation and guardian of the values of the *patria* had been fundamentally cast into doubt.[2]

The Falklands/Malvinas war played a significant role in this process, as the public response to the invasion raised uncomfortable questions about society's willingness to sanction the actions of a repressive regime in the name of a nationalist cause. The *junta*'s 1982 invasion of the islands had received widespread public support, but following defeat and the collapse of the military regime the conflict was quickly re-cast as a policy of the regime and associated with its human rights abuses, rather than perceived as a conflict in the name of civil society.[3] Yet the uncomfortable fact of the public

---

1  Short sections of the introduction to this chapter were included in the following: Catriona McAllister, 'Flying the Flag: Questions of Patriotism and the Malvinas Conflict', in G. Mira and F. Pedrosa (eds.), *Revisiting the Falklands-Malvinas Question: Transnational and Interdisciplinary Perspectives* (London: Institute of Latin American Studies, 2021), pp. 161–71. These sections are included here with permission from University of London Press.

2  See Federico Lorenz, *Las guerras por Malvinas* (Buenos Aires: Edhasa, 2006), p. 17.

3  Rosana Gúber, *Por qué Malvinas?: de la causa nacional a la guerra absurda* (Buenos Aires: Antropofagia, 2004), p. 147.

support for the invasion remained, and Vicente Palermo notes the significant challenge this presented to the powerful emerging narrative that positioned society exclusively as a victim of the military regime.[4] Federico Lorenz argues that as a result of this ambiguity the conflict 'fue considerada como un síntoma de una sociedad que había militarizado sus formas de relacionarse, y que debía ser reeducada', and cites Alain Rouquié's verdict that Malvinas (and the public support the conflict received) revealed a 'militarización muy profunda de la vida política y a la vez una politización de los militares que no es fácil de eliminar'.[5] Rouquié provides an insight into the central role of ingrained national narratives in this relationship when he states that 'pese al antimilitarismo táctico de los últimos tiempos, en abril de 1982 otra vez hubo quienes sacralizaron el ejército. Otra vez con "San Martín, el santo de la espada" y todo eso'.[6] The previous relationship between the military and patriotism had become intrinsically problematic and had to be redefined by the new democratic regime.

This process of restructuring led to significant institutional changes: the Armed Forces swore allegiance to Argentina's Constitution for the first time on 25 May 1987, fundamentally altering their relationship to the state.[7] Crucially, this need for change was enacted at a symbolic level as well as an institutional one. The shift in the model of patriotism had significant ramifications within education, which I have taken as a valuable indicator of official interventions in models of patriotism throughout this book. After the return to democracy, the need to construct a different type of citizen came to the fore, and the newly defined school subject of 'Educación cívica' marked a shift away from 'un discurso dogmático y definitivo sobre la identidad nacional' to a new focus on the formal aspects of democracy and the creation of citizens, re-orienting the concept of democracy from being an 'estilo de vida', as the military *junta* had posited, to being once more based in institutions and the political system.[8] Since 'official' history relies heavily on an epic military tale, it was perhaps inevitable that the new educational focus on the

---

4  Vicente Palermo, *Sal en las heridas: las Malvinas en la cultura argentina contemporánea* (Buenos Aires: Sudamericana, 2007), p. 282.

5  Lorenz, *Las guerras por Malvinas*, pp. 192, 190.

6  Rouquié cited in Lorenz, *Las guerras por Malvinas*, p. 190.

7  Alejandro Grimson, Mirta Amati, and Kaori Kodama, 'La nación escenificada por el Estado: una comparación de rituales patrios', in *Pasiones nacionales : política y cultura en Brasil y Argentina*, ed. by Alejandro Grimson, Mirta Amati, and José Nun (Buenos Aires: Edhasa, 2007), pp. 413–502, at p. 439.

8  Romero, *La Argentina en la escuela*, pp. 152–70. Romero describes how the *junta* reconfigured the idea of democracy as a 'way of life', separating it from the idea of democratic institutions and procedures, as this could not be reconciled with the military's undemocractic occupation of the country. Instead, the idea of Argentina as a 'democratic' and 'Christian' nation formed part of the *junta*'s positioning of the country as on the side of the West, particularly the US, within the Cold War context that coincided with their regime.

construction of democratic citizens rather than patriotic subjects would entail changes to this model. The historical narrative taught to school children became a subject of public debate in the early 1990s, considered as no longer fit for purpose for the demands of contemporary society: as Gonzalo de Amézola notes, 'el estudio del pasado en la escuela continuaba centrado en una exaltación patriótica que, si había tenido algún sentido en tiempos de la inmigración masiva, a fines del siglo XX carecía de toda significación'.[9] With the educational reforms of 1993, independence came to occupy a less dominant position, ceding ground to a new focus on twentieth-century history.[10] The role of the nation's military epic was questioned, and a school narrative that had remained largely unchanged for 100 years came under fire.

Federico Lorenz links this shift directly to the impact of the military dictatorship, stating that 'una de las consecuencias culturales profundas de la dictadura militar ha sido la destrucción del relato histórico nacional —total, abarcador, complaciente— como el que millares de argentinos se habituaron a recibir, compartir y transmitir en las escuelas'.[11] The meaning of the national itself had undergone redefinition through its appropriation by a repressive regime that had consistently defined the 'national interest' in terms of its own geopolitical worldview. In the words of Rosana Gúber, the dictatorship 'se arrogó la exclusiva y absoluta representación de la Nación'.[12] Alejandro Grimson, Mirta Amati, and Kaori Kodama argue that the military's use of the state's performative patriotic symbols had altered their potential meaning, creating a problematic association between markers of the national and the dictatorship:

> La dictadura militar produce efectos decisivos sobre la idea de nación. En la medida en que sustentaban su accionar en una retórica patriótica, consiguieron apoderarse de un conjunto de símbolos — como la bandera y la escarapela, el himno y otras canciones patrias.[13]

If the military epic no longer served as a guarantee of the solid foundation of the *patria*, then nor did the other most recognizable symbols of the nation. The trappings of patriotism had become tainted and their allocated role as symbols of unity and the nation-state had become corrupted. Lorenz underlines the political urgency of this dilemma for the newly instated democratic regime:

> ¿Cómo disputar a las Fuerzas Armadas o a la derecha reaccionaria elementos como los de 'soberanía' o 'patria'? El camino elegido fue el de

---

9  De Amézola, 'Argentina', pp. 26–28.
10  De Amézola, 'Argentina', pp. 17, 28.
11  Federico Lorenz, '¿Sueñan las ovejas con bicentenarios?', *El Monitor*, 23 (November 2009), p. 32.
12  Gúber, *Por qué Malvinas?* p. 229.
13  Grimson, Amati, and Kodama, 'La nación escenificada por el Estado', p. 431.

intentar quitarle el monopolio de símbolos [nacionales] a la institución militar, reinstalándolos en el altar republicano, lo que a la vez significaba subordinar simbólicamente a las Fuerzas Armadas al poder político civil.[14]

At the point of the return to democracy, the state was therefore faced with the task of reappropriating the nation's system of symbolic production in order to assert its own legitimacy. Redefining the concept of *patria* without its previously essential military component therefore represented an indispensable political task that was enacted, at least in part, through the restructuring of the symbolic. The military's role in the *ritos patrios* was minimized, including the notable absence of a military parade in the celebrations of 25 May for the decade from 1989 to 1999.[15]

The idea of the role of the state was also undergoing redefinition in the period in which both texts are published. The election of Menem in 1989 signalled the start of a neoliberal decade in Argentina, building on a process of economic change that had begun under the military dictatorship.[16] Maristella Svampa recognizes this not only as a shift in the economic model but also in the view of the state as 'agente y productor de la cohesión social', arguing:

> El país asistía a la crisis estructural del modelo nacional-popular, sin por ello descubrir la fórmula, a la vez económica y política, que permitiera reencontrar las claves perdidas de la integración social.[17]

Svampa perceives this as a radical change, whereby the previous model of society is replaced with 'un nuevo régimen, centrado en la primacía del mercado', and that therefore represents a hugely significant intervention in the definition of the relationship between the state and the nation (22). The transformation of Argentina's economy, therefore, represented another destabilization of the *patria* that had once been, the *patria* that had existed when the historical state epic and its attendant symbols had formed part of a stable narrative transmitted to every schoolboy and girl.

My reading of *El informe* and *El ojo de la patria* will therefore consider the use of independence in both texts as drawing on and contributing to this reconsideration of some of the most important founding pillars of Argentine national identity. Both re-imagine independence as a faltering state epic, unable to perform its original function of providing an ideal model for its citizens. Their differing responses to this perceived disintegration ultimately reveal opposing views of the role of history, which I will use to problematize the critical positions outlined at the start of the chapter.

---

14  Lorenz, *Las guerras por Malvinas*, pp. 189–90.
15  Grimson, Amati and Kodama, 'La nación escenificada por el Estado', pp. 435, 447.
16  Maristella Svampa, *La sociedad excluyente: la Argentina bajo el signo del neoliberalismo* (Buenos Aires: Taurus, 2005), p. 22.
17  Svampa, *La sociedad excluyente*, pp. 21–22, 25.

## *El informe: San Martín y el otro cruce de los Andes*: Myth and Military Epic

Martín Kohan's *El informe* reads almost as a catalogue of the literary techniques of postmodern historical play, self-consciously employed by a writer fluent in the discourses of literary theory. Metaliterary reflections on the nature of writing history abound, the mediated nature of historical knowledge is consistently drawn to our attention, and the text's humour relies heavily on parody and intertextuality. Although few critics have tackled the text, it is unsurprising that Alicia Chibán suggests that the novel lends itself to a reading 'en clave metahistórica', arguing that this opens it to comparison with a wide variety of texts from authors such as Alejo Carpentier, Carlos Fuentes, and Mario Vargas Llosa. Chibán's conclusion from the adoption of this framework is that the text exposes 'los límites y posibilidades del conocer y del construir la historia'.[18] My analysis will argue that this generalizing approach produces only a partial reading of the text, and that *El informe*'s metahistorical games can be more usefully read as a parodic engagement with Argentine identity narratives. This is not merely an attempt to shed light on a previously obscured theme, but to use this shift in perspective to reconsider the conclusions we draw about the text's play with history, and therefore to produce a more in-depth reading of the novel.

Kohan is best known for his fiction situated in periods of recent history, particularly *Dos veces junio* (2002) and *Ciencias morales* (2007), which both explore the context of the 1976 to 1983 military dictatorship. My reading of *El informe* is also, in part, targeted at drawing out a fundamental theme across the whole of Kohan's literary output: a critique of Argentina's self-image and self-construction, above all in relation to a militarized conception of the nation.[19] The concern with defining the 'historical novel' encourages us to read *El informe* as detached from these later works, as they deal with the very recent past. However, our reading of Kohan's later work could be significantly enriched by considering his literary output as a corpus. By highlighting this recurring critique within Kohan's work, I aim to stress that the reading of historical fiction I propose can enable more meaningful comparison across texts. My use of contextual grounding is targeted at identifying politicized concerns that can take us beyond considering disruption of 'the historical' as a challenge to generalized ideas about knowledge. By identifying Kohan's use of history in *El informe* as a

---

18  Alicia Chibán, 'Vivir, escribir, pensar la historia: *El informe: San Martín y el otro cruce de los Andes*, de Martín Kohan', in *El archivo de la independencia y la ficción contemporánea*, ed. by Alicia Chibán (Salta: Universidad Nacional de Salta, 2004), pp. 81–90, at p. 81.

19  I explore this in greater detail in relation to two more recent novels by Kohan in an article: 'Borders Inscribed on the Body: Geopolitics and the Everyday in the Work of Martín Kohan', *Bulletin of Latin American Research*, 39(4) (2020), pp. 453–65.

problematization of the nation rather than of our ability to access the past, the text's game-playing gains a purpose that would otherwise be lost in the circularity of apparent postmodern 'questioning'.

To interpret *El informe*'s play with history as questioning mechanisms of knowledge production is to miss the true target of the novel's parody. If we assume that History is what is at stake, we obscure the biting critique of specific historical codes and their role in Argentina's national imaginary within the text. Kohan's use of independence discourse in *El informe* is grounded in an intimate knowledge of the historical texts that shaped the national narrative about the period. His doctoral thesis, published as *Narrar a San Martín* (2005), charts the construction of the military hero as the *padre de la patria* and examines the myths and values surrounding this figure so intimately connected with national identity. This detailed exploration of how the 'historia oficial' of independence has emerged and the values it sustains has evident implications for a reading of *El informe*, and in a sense the works can be seen as two sides of the same literary project: the thesis traces the process of the period's mythification and identifies its specific narratives, while the novel performs a parodic operation on these same discourses. At the heart of both is a questioning of what it means to base a nation's *ritos patrios* around a celebration of war and military heroism, particularly in the wake of the disaster of Malvinas. In *Narrar*, Kohan makes this connection clear, describing a crisis in Argentina's patriotic model following the Malvinas conflict: 'los cimientos de la consagración sanmartiniana —el heroísmo bélico, la rectitud castrense, la evidencia de la verdad histórica, la transcendencia de los valores nacionales— se vieron minados por la derrota de Malvinas'.[20] Kohan has since written a book-length essay, *El país de la guerra* (2014), that analyses the centrality of discourses of war to Argentine cultural history.[21] *El informe* parodies the State epic of war in the wake of this hugely significant military defeat, questioning the basis of previously accepted national narratives.

The novel is composed of a peculiar and frustrating correspondence between two men attempting to collaborate in the writing of a 'History of Mendoza' in the present day (1995), interspersed with episodes from the real life of one of the correspondents. Doctor Vicenzi, the principal author of the study based in Mendoza, has contracted Mauricio Miguel Alfano as a research assistant to provide him with material located in archives in Buenos Aires. Their letters form the bulk of the novel: Alfano's exuberant and frustrating 'informes' provide the colourful historical account at the heart of the text, contrasting with Vicenzi's rigid and increasingly exasperated responses that outline precise instructions for how to undertake serious historical research. Reading these conflicting perspectives on what history can mean through specific discourses of independence not only deepens our

20 Kohan, *Narrar a San Martín*, p. 28.
21 Martín Kohan, *El país de la guerra* (Buenos Aires: Eterna Cadencia, 2014).

understanding of the humour generated by the text, but also more clearly exposes the nature of the critique it undertakes.

## Parody and 'Official History'

The successful functioning of parody depends upon the existence of a recognizable model that the text seeks to subvert.[22] In the case of *El informe* this model is provided by the familiar narrative codes of independence as national epic. As I highlighted in my Introduction, the idea of 'la historia oficial' in Argentina refers to the traditional narrative with nineteenth-century origins, enshrined in the national education system by the Nueva Escuela in the first decades of the twentieth century.[23] This model narrates the wars of independence as a tale of military glory, providing detailed technical information about battles and encouraging schoolchildren simply to 'rendir culto a una gran época y a cada uno de sus actores'.[24] As Kohan illustrates in *Narrar a San Martín*, this narrative provides an instantly recognizable portrait of the *padre de la patria*:

> El repertorio de sus virtudes morales forma parte de la 'memoria genética' de cualquier argentino: San Martín es modesto, abnegado, desdeña la popularidad, renuncia a los honores, sacrifica su amor propio en aras de los intereses de la patria, hace donaciones que dan muestra de gran desprendimiento, etcétera.[25]

The familiarity of these narrative motifs ensures that the general target of Kohan's parody is easily apparent to Argentine readers. However, *El informe* interpellates a specific model of the independence tale within this 'official' framework: the writings of Bartolomé Mitre, the founder of the 'official' version of history. Although an Argentine reader may not know Mitre's original writings, the historian's unparalleled influence on the traditional construction of independence means that the text's parodic play is evident to all those who are familiar with the discourses of 'official' history in Argentina.

If we read the text directly in relation to Mitre's *Historia de San Martín y de la emancipación sudamericana*, a cornerstone of the construction of the Argentine soldier as national hero, we can begin to unpick the strategies of subversion at work in Kohan's text. The novel actually produces an alternative account of a minor episode from Mitre's *Historia de San Martín*, entitled 'la conjuración de los prisioneros españoles en San Luis'.[26] This chapter of

22  See Linda Hutcheon, *A Theory of Parody: The Teachings of Twentieth-century Art Forms* (Urbana: University of Illinois Press, 2000).

23  Romero, *La Argentina en la escuela*, pp. 40–41.

24  De Amézola, 'Argentina', pp. 59–60. See also Romero, *La Argentina en la escuela*, p. 64.

25  Kohan, *Narrar a San Martín*, p. 76.

26  Mitre, *Historia de San Martín*, II, pp. 178–85. Kohan has acknowledged that the text uses an episode from Mitre as the starting point for its retelling, but does not give

Mitre's canonical account describes the arrival of a group of Spanish prisoners in Mendoza, their integration into Mendozan society while in captivity and finally their uprising against their gaolers, which is the basic plot used by Kohan. Reading the text as a parody of this specific source offers an opportunity to perceive its direct engagement with the traditional independence tale. It allows us to explore exactly how the text recasts the most canonical version of the founding moments of the nation, considering how its irreverent omissions, additions, and subversion of Mitre's literary style combine to render a 'sacred' narrative ridiculous. It is by tracing the workings of this process of 'desanctification' that the implications of the novel's reflections on history can be reconsidered and its metahistorical play reframed.

*Rewriting Mitre: Epic, Parody, and Emplotment*
The title of the novel promises us a tale about San Martín, and through its tantalizing reference to 'el *otro* cruce de los Andes' (my italics) it suggests its pages will uncover a previously obscured episode involving the nation's foundational historical figure. Hinting at the exposure of hidden information in this way taps into our expectations of commercial historical fiction, which often relies upon a promise of revealing information ignored by 'official' history. Despite the highly literary construction of the text, the novel's dust jacket also explicitly inserts *El informe* within this framework: it features a traditional painting of San Martín and claims that 'esta novela de Martín Kohan revela anécdotas secretas y situaciones desconocidas de la campaña de los Andes y presenta un estilo nuevo, sobrio y preciso de combinar la ficción y los acontecimientos verdaderos'.[27] This positioning of the text (published as part of Sudamericana's commercial *Narrativa histórica* collection) is strikingly at odds with its parodic content. The subversion of national narrative that Kohan undertakes is amplified rather than undermined by this disparity, however. In *Narrar a San Martín*, Kohan notes that 'el héroe nacional consigue siempre mantenerse en pie precisamente porque tambalea [...] Una clave de la persistencia del prestigio del héroe nacional radica justamente en su capacidad de tolerar fisuras.'[28] In a more detailed article on this point, Kohan argues for the reconsideration of the apparent need to 'humanize' the *próceres*:

> Los textos que anuncian el rescate de su dimensión humana se detienen pues en el "pretexto material" del cuerpo del hombre de carne y hueso, para sostener en él la trascendencia desmaterializada de la gloria inmortal;

---

the specific source, which I have traced. Mariana deCió and Enrique Schmukler, 'Entrevista a Martín Kohan', *Letral*, I (2008), 170–77, at p. 175.

27  Martín Kohan, *El informe: San Martín y el otro cruce de los Andes* (Buenos Aires: Sudamericana, 1999). All further references to this edition will be made in the body of the text.

28  Kohan, *Narrar a San Martín*, pp. 13–14.

y se detienen en el relato de los momentos excepcionales de un desborde o de un desequilibrio, para después apuntalar la verticalidad de la figura del héroe, y devolverle su lugar, debidamente equilibrado, entre los símbolos patrios sostenidos por la representación estatal.[29]

Although Kohan here refers to a tendency of historical discourse, when considered in relation to historical fiction, this judgement rejects the idea that the nation's heroes are 'questioned' through the provision of information about their loves and losses. Instead, this introduction of 'fisuras' is interpreted as a means of fuelling interest in the *próceres* without fundamentally altering either their heroic status or importance within the vision of the nation. By presenting *El informe* within this commercial rubric, Kohan performs a destabilizing operation on both the writing of history and the apparent 'challenge' to this vision presumed to exist in conventional historical fiction, which becomes nothing more than a support for the mechanisms of patriotic celebration.

The crossing of the Andes is San Martín's most celebrated heroic military exploit, the core of his fame, and the beating heart of the nation's military epic. The text could not offer a re-telling of a more canonical tale, nor one more closely associated with the *prócer*'s role in representing the nation's greatness. Yet San Martín scarcely makes an appearance in the text. All the familiar battles are absent, and not only does the 'otro cruce' mentioned in the title fail to feature the *prócer*, but it actually refers to a journey undertaken by an insignificant group of enemy soldiers. This frustration of the reader's expectations from the outset is crucial to the functioning of the novel's parody. The text all but erases San Martín, presenting us instead with a romantic tale of love overcoming the divisions wrought by war, a vision impossible to reconcile with the usual tale of independence as a glorious victory over an oppressive enemy. Kohan utilizes this unexpected plot to throw the traditional narrative codes of independence into sharp relief, 'denaturalizing' them in order to expose them to critique.

We might expect this unrecognizable account to be purely invented, but in fact it scarcely departs from the facts presented by Mitre in 'la conjuración de los prisioneros españoles en San Luis'. Only one detail is fundamentally changed: the shifting of the tale's location from San Luis to the province of Mendoza, which comically renders the whole tale useless to Vicenzi's History of Mendoza, and means that all the elaborate story-telling we have witnessed ultimately comes to nothing. Many of the seemingly most unlikely twists and turns of the plot of Alfano's *informes* are, in fact, present in Mitre's account, including the love triangle between Juan Ruiz Ordóñez, Lucía Pringles, and Monteagudo, and a merciful San Martín pardoning Juan Ruiz's life after the Spaniards' bloody uprising. What changes radically is the narrative focus: a

---

29 Martín Kohan, 'La humanización de San Martín: notas sobre un malentendido', *Revista Iberoamericana*, LXXI (2005), 1083–96, at p. 1087.

brief reference to Monteagudo's love for one of the Pringles girls is blown up into a dramatic tale of intrigue and betrayal; San Martín's magnanimity becomes a mere footnote to the whirlwind of emotion surrounding the fate of the tale's 'true' hero. The narrative codes through which this tale is 'emplotted', to use Hayden White's term, therefore take centre stage within the text.

Much of what we could describe as 'metahistorical play' in the text can be reconceptualized as strategies targeted at 'denaturalizing' this particular historical vision. The incongruous high-flown narrative style employed by Alfano in fact draws heavily on the way Mitre's original account is written, and much of what Vicenzi criticizes as not adhering to his notion of historical writing is actually modelled on the style of Argentina's first major historian. Alfano's apparently irrelevant digressions on climate and terrain echo Mitre's scene-setting techniques, and his lack of references to sources mirrors Mitre, who does not interrupt the narrative flow of his tale with footnotes and detailed source indications. Even Alfano's tendency to add to the drama of his tale by directly quoting the words of historical figures, leaving us wondering how he could possibly have access to intimate conversations and thoughts, imitates the dramatic way that Mitre incorporates dialogue into his writing. The historian's account is peppered with apparent quotations from dialogues without a reference to his source, and he even directly invites the reader to join him in 'overhearing' one conversation with the dramatic 'oigámosles'.[30] This 'unobjective' style therefore playfully undermines Vicenzi's idea of traditional historiography as sombre, serious, and primarily factual.

Alfano's narrative imitates the rhetorical strategies of Mitre's account, particularly the use of parallelism and repetition, often in the form of triplets or lengthy listing devices, which give Mitre's account its formal, dramatic style, but are of course completely out of context in what is supposed to be a factual report written in the 1990s. Mitre opens his history of San Martín with a grand statement of the singularity of the powerful historical force behind the struggle for South American independence, describing the continental process as displaying a clear 'unidad de acción', as though he were describing a piece of Classical drama, implying his awareness of the need to construct a compelling dramatic account in order to enthral and inspire his readers. In true Hegelian style, he introduces his *héroe máximo* as the physical embodiment of this driving historical force, portrayed through the highly rhetorical language that characterizes his account of San Martín:

> La unidad de esta acción compacta, persitente, intensa, sin desperdicio de fuerzas, se dibuja netamente en las líneas generales de la vida de San Martín, el libertador del Sud, dando á su figura histórica proporciones continentales, no obstante que sus acciones sean más transcendentales que su genio y sus resultados más latos que sus previsiones. Es una fuerza

---

30 Mitre, *Historia de San Martín*, I, p. 405.

histórica, que como las fuerzas de la naturaleza, obra por sí, obedeciendo á un impulso fatal.[31]

This hyperbolic description of San Martín's importance includes interjection of epithets, listing of adjectives, and a parallel structure celebrating the transcendental quality of the hero's actions and the far-reaching impact of their results. The first sentence illustrates Mitre's characteristic tendency to interrupt the main idea of his sentence with the addition of these rhetorical reminders of the glorious significance of the action he recounts, building an increasingly resplendent and inflated image of the *prócer*. This style reaches its height in Mitre's outline of San Martín's military and political vision, when the historian declares the *prócer*'s aims to be:

> Dar expansión á la revolución de su patria que desentrañaba los destinos de la América, salvándola y americanizándola, y ser a la vez el brazo y la cabeza de la hegemonía argentina en el período de su emancipación : — combinar estratégica y táctictamente el más vasto teatro de operaciones del orbe, el movimiento alternativo ó simultáneo y las evoluciones combinadas de ejércitos ó naciones, marcando cada evolución con un triunfo matemático ó la creación de una nueva república : — obtener resultados fecundos con la menor suma de elementos posibles y sin ningún desperdicio de fuerzas : — y por último, legar á la posteridad el ejemplo de redimir pueblos sin fatigarlos con su ambición ó su orgullo, tal fue la múltiple tarea que llevó a cabo en el espacio de un decenio y la lección que dio este genio positivo, cuya magnitud circunscripta puede medirse con el compás del geómetra dentro de los límites de la moral humana.[32]

This cornucopia of worthy aims and achievements is conveyed through extravagant, superlative imagery and an abundance of parallel structures, from the repeated opening device of each new addition to San Martín's merits to the balance provided by the frequent doubling of nouns or adverbs ('salvándola y americanizándola', 'ejércitos ó naciones', 'su ambición ó su orgullo'). The list concludes with a rather far-fetched metaphor suggesting that our hero's greatness can be precisely measured through the tools of mathematical calculation, a fanciful comparison typical of Mitre's ostentatious embellishments to his prose.

The failure of Alfano to successfully replicate this grandiose, hyperbolic style is integral to the deflation of epic in *El informe*. Alfano's attempts to build drama often fall flat through their ridiculously exaggerated tone and the inept application of the established discursive codes of independence: 'No eran ahora, escribe Alfano, argentinos y españoles, republicanos y monárquicos, idealistas y realistas, tanto como hombres, hombres, doctor Vicenzi' (105). The carefully balanced triplet here disintegrates in the empty banality of its

---

31  *Historia de San Martín*, I, p. 5.
32  Mitre, *Historia de San Martín*, I, pp. 86–87.

conclusion, while the humorous misinterpretation of 'realistas' as the opposite of 'idealistas' (rather than as the royalist enemy of the Argentine 'patriotas') playfully tweaks the well-rehearsed vocabulary surrounding the period. At other points, it is Alfano's overabundance of complex rhetorical strategies that provides the parodic effect. In one of his dizzying statements, he claims that in a sense 'hubo un único cruce de la cordillera de los Andes, uno que de tan glorioso, de tan sublime, de tan puro y eterno, puro y eterno como las nieves puras y eternas que la cresta de esos montes coronan, posterga toda otra travesía' (36). This confused and rambling sentence (which continues in the same vein for several more lines) creates its effect by superimposing one rhetorical convention on top of another. The sentence is essentially a triplet, structured by the repetition of 'de tan', but its resolution is postponed by the insertion of a simile, inspiring the over-repetition of the same acclamatory adjectives. This mechanism of interruption and abundance continues throughout the sentence and is a recurring feature of Alfano's prose: the rhetorical structures used by Mitre to build pride and patriotism are used here to bombard the reader until meaning is all but lost.

Another area of Mitre's discourse subject to parodic play within the text is the way in which he constructs his heroic San Martín, particularly in relation to his 'rival' liberator, Bolívar. Although Mitre celebrates the achievements of both, he takes pains to assert San Martín's superiority, despite his less impressive military record. While recognizing the Argentine's achievements to be slightly inferior to those of America's other great liberator, he insists that San Martín is 'moral y militarmente más grande', contrasting 'el sueño delirante de la ambición de Bolívar' with the modesty that leads San Martín to '[abdicar] en medio de su poderío, cuando comprende que su misión ha terminado'.[33] El informe exposes these long-standing codes by stripping away any subtlety or nuance, such as in the following description of the relationship between San Martín and Bolívar's military endeavours: 'Desde el Norte, escribe Alfano, progresaba en sus victorias don Simón Bolívar, y desde el Sur, incomparable, nuestro sin igual Libertador, paladín de la guerra tanto como del modesto renunciamiento' (155). Bolívar is here comically reduced to nothing but 'don', denying him any military rank whatsoever, while San Martín is covered in glory, his superiority to Bolívar confirmed not only in the pointed insistence that he is 'incomparable', but also in the reminder of his moral advantage over his rival Liberator in the north. Some of Alfano's most hyperbolic praise of San Martín is in fact taken directly from Mitre's account. When his informe lists the achievements of the Argentine hero, stating that 'medio mundo la libertad le debe' (109), he echoes Mitre's claim that San Martín and Bolívar share 'la gloria de la revolución de medio mundo',[34] but again comically ousts Bolívar from his

33 Mitre, *Historia de San Martín*, I, p. 11.
34 Mitre, *Historia de San Martín*, I, p. 11.

role as the 'other' liberator in a playful exaggeration of Mitre's technique. Mitre's comparisons between San Martín and other historical (or Classical) figures, designed to add authority and grandeur to his *historia patria*, also find a misplaced echo in Alfano's tale. When Mitre compares the crossing of the Andes to Hannibal Barca and Napoleon's great military mountain crossings, Alfano follows suit, but disingenuously misses the mark: 'Sólo tres hombres vencieron, en la historia, a las gigantescas montañas: en una misma y eterna gloria, escribe Alfano, brillan, con luz infinita, un cartaginés, un corso y un correntino' (61). Kohan fills Mitre's comparison with bathos by transforming lofty hyperbole into a ridiculous claim that only three men have ever crossed great mountain ranges. This exposes and ridicules the hyperbole behind this rhetorical strategy, deflating its patriotic fervour. Mitre's subtly woven techniques therefore unravel through Alfano's parodically clumsy treatment of the same tools.

*Unveiling the Epic Mode*
The techniques Kohan uses to construct his parody do not merely 'exaggerate' Mitre's strategies in order to make them ridiculous, however. The way that Alfano's tale is constructed relies upon a layering of other literary conventions that combine to produce the text's critique. One strand of this literary encoding is Kohan's use of the epic, the genre *par excellence* that celebrates heroic deeds of battle undertaken as part of a greater cause. By directly employing conventions of this genre, *El informe* teases out the underlying narrative structuring device of Mitre's text, ultimately affirming that San Martín's heroism rests upon its emplotment as epic rather than on the intrinsic value of his acts.

Traces of the epic can be found throughout the whole of Alfano's narrative. Rather than obeying letter-writing conventions, he begins his reports *in medias res*, even opening the whole novel with the incongruous 'voy a retomar' (11), plunging us straight into the action.[35] The hyperbolic adjectives that consistently accompany the Liberator's name (as highlighted above) function as epithets to reinforce the heroism, bravery, and importance of the tale.[36] The language is lofty and formal as we would expect of a tale relating such worthy feats, inverting normal word order to add drama and apparent solemnity ('era ésta una verdadera matanza' (23), or 'para que la memoria histórica ante la posteridad lo preserve' (58), for example). There are also clear traces of the importance of orality, for example in the balance of lines such as 'pura fue su alma como blanco fue su corcel' (42), a pattern that evokes the rhythmic style of the epic as poetry designed to be performed to an audience. Alfano also uses repetition and devices to summarize what

---

35  The *Iliad* is a famous example of the use of *in medias res* as a convention of the epic. Paul Merchant, *The Epic* (London: Methuen, 1971), p. 29.
36  Chibán notes the epic connotation of this particular mechanism in her article 'Vivir, escribir, pensar la histora', p. 84.

has been said in order to keep his audience on track, even though what he is producing is in actual fact a written document designed for the consumption of one person alone. A clear example of this can be seen in the following extract from the dramatic battle scene:

> Cuatro eran los grupos, lo repito a modo de repaso, en que se subdividió la rebelión de los prisioneros españoles; de tres ya nos hemos ocupado, los seguimos, uno por vez, desde su impetuoso primer impulso, hasta el desenlace, parejamente desfavorable hasta aquí, de sus respectivos emprendimientos. (298)

The reminder not only of plot details (the fact that four separate groups are involved in the struggle) but also of the narrative structuring (the fact that we are following each group in turn and have heard about three groups) is typical of the epic's oral narrative, designed to facilitate comprehension in a way that is not required of a written text that can be read and re-read at leisure.

It is significant that such a clear example of this device is found within Alfano's battle scene, as this is the part of the text that most clearly evokes epic convention. This represents a distinct shift from the way this episode is narrated in Mitre's original, where the rebellion of the Spanish prisoners is dispatched in a few brief, fairly matter-of-fact paragraphs. Instead of following this lead, Alfano revels in all the imaginative detail he can muster, describing battle strategies, injuries, and gruesome deaths. While Mitre's version gives a brief and bloodless list of the Spaniards who were killed, Kohan takes each of the soldiers in turn and describes their individual fates with all the attendant blood and gore. This episodic approach to narrating battle scenes – focusing on the fate of one character at a time – and the listing of gruesome injuries are conventions familiar to readers (or rather listeners) of the epic, recalling, for example, *laisses* 38–40 of the *Poema de mío Cid*.[37] Alfano describes how 'sólo unos delgados filamentos pulposos, sólo unos pocos pellejos, mantuvieron a la cabeza de José Ordóñez unida al resto del cuerpo' and how Morgado finds himself 'caído en el suelo en medio de un charco sanguinolento que a laguna parecía querer llegar' (308–9). These bloody descriptions sit deliberately uncomfortably within the contemporary framing of the text. They serve both to extend the parody of the narrative mode underpinning the independence narrative originating with Mitre, and to alienate the reader from these accepted codes by pushing them to their logical narrative extreme, rendering strange what may at first appear 'natural'. The incongruity of this inclusion of the epic is therefore crucial to Kohan's critique of the heroic reading of the military past. It ridicules the possibility of pinning contemporary national constructions on an outdated military epic, first by applying the celebratory rhetoric to the traditional Spanish enemy, revealing glory to be a discursive construction rather than a reflection of the

---

37 Colin Smith (ed.), *Poema de mío Cid* (Madrid: Cátedra, 1976), pp. 171–72.

intrinsic merit of the act itself, and, second, by rendering the traditional codes of independence strange to the reader by pushing them to their extreme.

Alfano's maladroit attempts to praise the liberator often comically 'misfire', ridiculing both the strategies he attempts and the carefully woven narrative that sustains San Martín's status. His *informes* employ a series of formulaic, hyperbolic similes to ensure that no opportunity to praise the *padre de la patria* is missed. Adjectives to describe the liberator within these constructions range from the predictable ('inmortal', 'supremo', 'sin igual', 'glorioso', 'santo', etc.) to the bizarre: San Martín's plans to make use of the sea as well as land earn him the title 'anfibio', while his experience of different weather conditions see him dubbed 'policlimático' (290, 99). Alfano's blend of high-flown language and overly literal images produces consistently incongruous effects, such as: 'nuestro benemérito Libertador, más grande que la catedral de Buenos Aires fue su corazón, aunque la catedral a su vez, y paradójicamente, lo contiene' (63). His rhetorical flourishes are also at times put to inappropriate use, such as in the formula: 'nuestro insigne Libertador, a la Patria dedicó su gloriosa vida y al sangriente tirano su sable corvo' (18). This references perhaps the most controversial detail of San Martín's life (or at least the one that has required the greatest creativity of explanation on the part of his 'liberal' biographers): his bequeathal of his sword to Juan Manuel de Rosas.[38] The clash between form and content here (unquestioning praise versus controversy) provides an ironic comment on the constant tension between the role required of the *padre de la patria* – to embody the nation's purest values – and the inevitable shortcomings and contradictions of a human life. Kohan's ridiculing of these elaborate strategies of praise exposes the rhetorical foundations of an apparently unshakeable foundation of national identity, rendering it a discourse that can be prised apart, subverted, and, crucially, challenged.

Parallel to this deployment of epic convention runs a tale of romance. Kohan 'replots' an insignificant detail of Mitre's account, the mention of two young lovers, as a dramatic reconciliatory national romance. Doris Sommer's analysis of the genre of 'national romance' exposes its fundamental nation-building impulse, allegorically communicated through sexual and romantic union.[39] While *Amalia*, Argentina's national romance *par excellence*, seeks an erotic reconciliation between centre and periphery in the wake of the bitter Unitarian/Federalist conflict, Kohan offers an alliance between Spaniards and *criollos* divided by the wars of independence. This playfully creates an impossible national foundation: José Mármol's text projects a reconciliation essential to the establishment of Argentina as a unified nation, but Kohan's alternative would instead place the very existence of an independent

---

38  For the different explanations of this action offered by prominent historians of San Martín, see Kohan, *Narrar a San Martín*, pp. 140–46.

39  Doris Sommer, *Foundational Fictions: The National Romances of Latin America* (Berkeley: University of California Press, 1991).

Argentina in doubt. An abandonment of hostilities between the Argentine rebels and the colonial enemy is entirely incompatible with the emplotment of independence as a national epic. Reconciliation has no place in a heroic 'fight to the death' that resides in a clear delimitation of good and evil, and to offer a literary romantic fusion of the warring sides is therefore to undermine the validity of war as a desirable national foundation.

*Deciphering Mitre's Codes: Morality and Literary Convention*
It is clear that the target of Kohan's parody extends well beyond a desire to critique Mitre's original text. The use of this original model represents an attempt to isolate the specific values transmitted by the enduring national epic in an implicit contrast with those that characterize contemporary ideas of democracy and equality. This slightly broader intention corresponds to a branch of parody identified by Hutcheon in her analysis of the genre, where the parody of a specific form targets the wider implications and attitudes it presents:

> For instance, in a novel which in many ways is a touchstone for this entire re-evaluation of parody, *The French Lieutenant's Woman*, John Fowles juxtaposes the conventions of the Victorian and the modern novel. The theological and cultural assumptions of both ages – as manifest through their literary forms – are ironically compared by the reader through the medium of formal parody.[40]

The novel performs an ironic inversion of the independence tale's normal pattern through this parodic mould. Alfano's account dwells heavily on judgements inscribed within Mitre's text, exaggerating and juxtaposing them to create critical distance. The novel underscores the assumptions surrounding gender roles in Mitre's narrative, exposing the unavoidably gendered discourse of a foundational national narrative based on war. Mitre frequently uses the idea of masculinity as a form of praise within his text, using 'viril' consistently as a positive descriptor in opposition to negative 'womanly' aspects, such as when he states that 'esta resolución, aunque aconsejada por quien no tenía competencia, era digna de un pueblo viril' (119). Kohan plays on the incongruity of this logic in today's world. Alfano enters wholeheartedly into this praise of the 'varonil', associating any kind of weakness with a negatively cast femininity. The women who populate his letters can generally be found looking beautiful to satisfy the male gaze, waiting obediently for their men at home, or gossiping about appropriate subjects such as sewing. They are subject to the most outrageous sweeping generalizations, for example: 'La irresolución, bien lo sabemos, está en la naturaleza de la condición femenina, queda para el varón el decidir, y para la mujer el vacilar' (206). This deliberately exaggerated, unquestioning

40 Hutcheon, *A Theory of Parody*, p. 31.

celebration of masculinity to the detriment of the constructed female 'other' takes the consequences of this logic to its extreme, excluding women from any active role in an act of aggressive marginalization. From a contemporary perspective, this logic cannot be expected to hold any water, and therefore by pushing the implicit values of this kind of sanctification of the past to their limit, Kohan reveals the inconsistencies in idealizing an ultimately exclusionary concept of liberty. If we continue to conceive of history as a celebration of heroes, it seems, we continue to apply an offensive, outdated logic. Seen from this perspective, the novel demonstrates the schism between contemporary values and the telling of national history, which is portrayed as crystallized and unevolving despite radical shifts in thought.

This is further emphasized through the underscoring of the racial narrative present in the hierarchy of the traditional telling of the tale. We are told:

> El callejón del caserío de Espejo quedó cubierto de cadáveres americanos, o afroamericanos habría que decir tal vez, para ser, como debemos, fieles a los hechos: a los negros solía reservarse este tipo de incursiones para gloria de la patria y de la integración multiétnica. (21–22)

This hypocritical use of the discourse of racial equality exposes both the invisibility of race in standard narratives of independence and the disguised tragedy underlying apparent military glory. The text also makes very direct attacks on racist attitudes held by some of the *próceres*, including Mitre and the *Generación del '37*, whose preoccupation with French Enlightenment culture is crudely parroted by Alfano: 'sabemos [...] que la nación hispánica no era precisamente el exponente más distinguido de la suprema cultura europea' (110–11). 'Más de una vez se ha dicho, y usted lo sabe, que ítalos e íberos más próximos estaban del tosco primitivismo de los africanos que de la altísima cultura de la excelsa Europa' (111). Hearing this attitude retransmitted in such dry, blunt terms leaves the reader no way of denying the prejudice implicit in these ideas. To hear a twentieth-century narrator assuming wholeheartedly this doctrine of cultural supremacy is disquieting, and throws into sharp relief the fact that the nineteenth-century *próceres* contributed to a very different intellectual climate rather than being the bringers of some sort of universal truth. Kohan's play with these outdated values reveals that a critical, reflexive approach to these ideas is incompatible with the over-simplified mode of celebration that patriotism requires. It reveals the internal contradictions of this code (its discrimination despite its discourse of liberty and equality), using a tale from within the independence story to prise apart its own rhetoric.

The same discursive operation is applied to the portrayal of Argentina's relationship with her neighbouring nations, particularly Chile. Alfano dwells on the amicable bond between the two nations, describing Chile as a 'país hermano' and downplaying any idea of division, whereas Vincenzi's militarized view of international relations leads him to treat Argentina's neighbour to the west as a suspicious potential enemy. This tackles a delicate aspect of the narration of independence, particularly for Mitre's construction of San Martín as a national hero on a continental scale: the balance between depicting a continental process and the need to assert the separate and stable nature of the individual nations it produced. Kohan exposes the contradictory nature of this balancing act by pushing different threads of this narrative to their extreme, unveiling their constructed nature and allowing one to undermine the other.

Mitre's account of San Martín relies heavily on the *prócer*'s actions in Chile to justify his depiction of the Argentine as 'el libertador del sur': a hero whose greatness stretches well beyond national borders. The historian therefore takes pains to stress the friendly nature of the relationship between the two *Cono Sur* nations, even dedicating a whole chapter to the praise of 'la alianza argentinochilena'. This focus on cooperation and solidarity is the narrative picked up by Alfano in *El informe*, but his enthusiastic espousal of the rhetoric of fraternity leads him far beyond Mitre's presentation of the alliance, to a point that threatens the division of the two into separate nations. Alfano's constant quibbles over whether Mendoza belongs to Argentina or Chile recalls the fact that the province in fact belonged to the Capitanía General de Chile (as part of the Provincia Transandina de Cuyo) for more than 200 years before becoming part of the Virreinato del Río de la Plata, which completely undermines the supposedly 'natural' division the Andes provides and shatters the illusion that the nation's current territorial configuration is eternal, or rather beyond the reaches of time. Vicenzi reacts angrily to these assertions, insisting on the natural character of the border and claiming that any violation of this principle opens the path for a Chilean invasion of Argentine territory. The humour generated by the vehemence of this response relies upon the fact that Vicenzi is being faithful to two different recognizable narratives communicated to generations of Argentine schoolchildren in history and geography textbooks: the status of the border between Argentina and Chile as a 'natural' rather than political division (due to the presence of the Andes), and the threat posed to the integrity of Argentina's territory by other nations, particularly Chile. Luis Alberto Romero's study of school textbooks insists upon the enduring nature of both of these characterizations, citing the Andean border with Chile as the paradigmatic natural division, and highlighting that 'aun cuando parece evidente que se trata de una relación política, expresada en una configuración espacial, este tema es encarado como un rasgo de la Geografía física del propio país'.[41] Romero also stresses the suspicion cast over Chile, stating that from the late nineteenth century almost to the present day 'la tónica es reiterada y similar: las pretensiones del siempre expansivo Chile sobre territorios indudable e históricamente argentinos'.[42]

By bringing these narratives together, Alfano's open, inclusive attitude exposes the almost hysterical tone of suspicion present in Vincenzi's responses. The juxtaposition of these two positions allows the text to suggest the incompatibility between this militarized, rigid view of relations between neighbouring countries and a discourse of integration. This again shows narratives of national identity failing to keep step with the values of the society around them, as a militarized view of national borders begins to give way to a discourse of integration.[43] The relationship between Vicenzi and Alfano also provides commentary on the internal relations within Argentina itself. The power struggle between Buenos Aires and the provinces is also initiated with the events of 1810. In *El informe*, the 'porteño-central' organization of the country is playfully alluded to by the fact that Vicenzi, who wishes to write a local history of Mendoza, is forced to rely on unreliable accounts sent from the capital as he cannot access the information in his own city. The nation is shown to exist as a political construction, but cracks show in its function as a cohesive and unifying social structure; the idea of the nation as a successful construct is ridiculed by constant reminders of internal divisions, as Alfano 'naively' reveals: 'Que no veo de qué manera va a integrarse Mendoza a la República Argentina, si ni siquiera puede integrarse con la provincia de San Luis' (349). The failure of the nation's founding narrative to provide the harmony and integration it purports to embody is laid bare through this interaction, contributing to the text's questioning of the validity of the current construct of the Argentine nation.

*The Place of Imagination: Surviving the Postmodern Age*
The rewriting of history that I have described above is framed by the sharp contrast of the contemporary urban world that Alfano inhabits, portrayed in terms that seems to consciously dialogue with another dimension of postmodern theory: Fredric Jameson's description of the depthlessness and fragmentation of late capitalist consumer society.[44] This is an atomized, hypermediatized society that sees Alfano accidentally caught up in an absurd court case and sent to jail. The only information the protagonist can glean about his own case comes from a sensationalist report he encounters when flicking through channels on the television, evoking the 'trial by television' that Beatriz Sarlo describes in *Escenas de la vida posmoderna*, whereby a superficial, fragmented media response replaces sluggish state institutions seen to be failing in the provision of justice.[45] The limited human interaction

---

43 Alejandro Grimson, 'Hacia una agenda territorial para un nuevo escenario regional', in *Nación y diversidad: territorios, identidades y federalismo: Debates de Mayo III*, ed. by José Nun, Alejandro Grimson, and Juan Manuel Abal Medina (Buenos Aires: Edhasa, 2008), pp. 87–100.

44 Jameson, Fredric, 'The Cultural Logic of Late Capitalism', in *Postmodernism, or, The Cultural Logic of Late Capitalism* (London: Verso, 1991), pp. 1–54.

45 Beatriz Sarlo, *Escenas de la vida posmoderna: intelectuales, arte y videocultura en la Argentina* (Buenos Aires: Ariel, 1994), p. 66.

that takes place is marked by the impossibility of communication, with conversations consisting of absurd repetition of banalities.

This framing of the exuberant historical narrative that Alfano weaves displays significant parallels with Jameson's description of the waning of historicity.Jameson states that this 'weakening of historicity' exists 'both in our relationship to public history and in the new forms of our private temporality'.[46] The novel's construction of contemporary society depicts Alfano as a 'subject' with no internal consciousness, unable to produce a meaningful narrative of his own experience in the same way as Jameson's 'schizophrenic' subject, who 'is reduced to an experience of pure material signifiers, or, in other words, a series of pure and unrelated presents in time' (27). Significantly, for Jameson, this dissolution of temporality is profoundly related to the question of the place of national historical narrative, whose relationship to late capitalist society he describes in the following terms:

> There no longer does seem to be any organic relationship between the American history we learn from schoolbooks and the lived experience of the current multinational, high-rise, stagflated city of the newspapers and of our own everyday life. (22)

The notion of failed history that Jameson invokes here is the dissolution of a national epic that serves as example and lesson to the present. Kohan's depiction of a postmodern urban world appears to confirm the disintegration of meaningful temporality that can underpin any collective project for the advancement of society through the dissolution of an epic past in the mundanity of an incomprehensible, superficial present.

However, this apparent conclusion is dramatically reversed in the novel's closing pages. The seductive appeal of narrative is confirmed in the final scene of the text, which sees Alfano discovering that his epistolary missives have gained him an admirer in the form of Lili, his employer's secretary. Just at the point that we might be expecting a condemnation of the imaginative narrative impulse that has generated the national myths of origin that the text critiques, Kohan transforms his tale from tragedy to comedy through the romantic union of Alfano and Lili. This declaration of faith in imagination rescues the novel's world from the postmodern abyss that threatens to engulf its characters. Although national history may need to be remodelled for the values of the contemporary age, it is reinstated as part of the need for narrative that counteracts the experiential void threatened by the social atomization of the present. It becomes once again a mechanism through which to establish community, reconfirmed in its traditional role but built anew. This profoundly unpostmodern final manoeuvre reasserts the possibility of historicity, but one that is critically aware of the mechanisms of its own construction and the values it creates.

46 Jameson, 'The Cultural Logic of Late Capitalism', p. 6.

*El informe* therefore not only challenges claims of the capacity of historiography to select the 'relevant' details and present them fairly, but also reconsiders the consequences of continuing to sing a national epic when its values are in many respects out of step with contemporary ways of thinking, particularly about racial and sexual equality. Through parody, therefore, Kohan unstitches the link between Argentina's military heroes and official discourses of 'argentinidad', particularly in relation to what he terms 'el culto militarista del sistema escolar argentino'.[47] His deconstruction of history is grounded in these profoundly national narratives and in a questioning of their legitimizing force, taking Argentina's century-old model of patriotism as his target of attack.

### *El ojo de la patria*: Epistemology and 'Postnational' Dystopia

Osvaldo Soriano's *El ojo de la patria* offers a very different aesthetic mediation of the crisis of patriotic models explored above. The construction of history is not subject to self-reflexive narrative techniques, philosophical musings, or anachronistic tricks. The past is not 'narrated' as such; rather history is incorporated into the present through the figure of a mummified *prócer*, which forms the basis for the intrigue of the plot. This absence of techniques associated with postmodern historical fiction means that the text has not been considered as commenting on the relationship between history and epistemology. Carolina Serapio's discussion of history in the novel does not conclude that it questions what we can know about the past, but that the text offers a nostalgic lament for heroism in relation to Argentine identity.[48] Although Cristián Montés notes the presence of 'el fracaso de los metarrelatos' in Soriano's work, this is not discussed in relation to epistemological questioning through the use of history.[49] My analysis of the questions posed by the text about the mediated nature of knowledge and our relationship with the past is grounded in its interrogation of national identity in a 'postnational' world. The fixed 'values' of independence provide a launchpad for the exploration of the place of value in late capitalist society, portrayed as profoundly connected to the idea of history.

The plot offers a different way of engaging with independence than those of the other texts I have studied so far. By using the body of an unidentified Argentine *prócer* as a symbol of the period, the text's historical figure is neither present as a conventional character nor evoked purely through discourse (whether texts written by himself or others). He is a physical,

47  Kohan, *Narrar a San Martín*, p. 11.
48  Carolina Serapio, '¿Es este el fin? (Acerca de *El ojo de la patria* de Osvaldo Soriano)', in *El archivo de la independencia y la ficción contemporánea*, ed. by Alicia Chibán (Salta: Universidad Nacional de Salta, 2004), pp. 233–45.
49  Cristián Montés, 'La contrautopía en *El ojo de la patria* de Osvaldo Soriano', *Cyber Humanitatis*, 14 (2000), para. 3.

tangible presence, grounded in his own materiality and yet occupying a liminal space between mortality and the eternal through the embalming of his body. In this *prócer*, independence is made flesh, but flesh devoid of subjectivity and agency, physically inert and deprived of the specificity of an identity. By refusing to identify his *prócer*, Soriano detaches the symbolic concept of a national hero from the inevitable negotiations and ambiguity involved in applying this to an individual. Soriano's independence figure, therefore, becomes a cipher for heroism in a purer way than in the texts of my first chapter, while at the same time occupying a physical space that consistently undermines this symbolism. Independence is reduced to its foundational heroic essence, then given a physical form through which to be worshipped, defiled, protected, or transformed.

### The Spy and the State: Genre and Irony

*El ojo de la patria* draws upon the conventions of the spy novel, a popular literary form, but my reading of the text seeks to draw attention to the politicized re-working of the spy genre in this text, resulting in a more complex meditation on the theme of 'patria' than its use of stereotypical national symbols initially appears to convey.[50] The spy can be seen as a popular, contemporary model of the 'national hero': a man who is required to place the needs of the nation before his own personal desires and who fights on the side of 'good', clearly defined as protecting the national interest. The parallel between this contemporary mode of national heroism and the nineteenth-century independence heroes is underlined in the text by the suggestion that the *prócer* was 'nuestro primer confidencial'[51] – an idea to which the protagonist frequently returns, revealing his attempt to trace a link of 'parentage' between the heroes of old and his own situation as a spy in the late twentieth century.

The use of the spy genre in the text is entirely ironic, however, as all the structures it depends upon have fallen away. The model of spy fiction most consciously interpellated is the James Bond series, which is both explicitly referred to and clearly echoed in scenes such as the arrival of a mysterious, gun-laden blonde in Carré's hotel room and the dramatic shoot out on a train towards the end of the novel. The world of Bond is a tale of success, from his lavish lifestyle to his sexual conquests, which Brett Woods describes as

50  Soriano's literary works are often dismissed as 'best-sellers', although his novel, based on events of the 1970s (*No habrá más penas ni olvido*, 1980, first published 1978) has received greater attention and his first novel, *Triste, solitario y final* (1973), is considered a significant example of the detective genre in Argentina. See Amelia S. Simpson, *Detective Fiction from Latin America* (Rutherford: Fairleigh Dickinson University Press, 1990), pp. 59, 61.

51  Osvaldo Soriano, *El ojo de la patria*, 2nd edn (Buenos Aires: Sudamericana, 1992), p. 142. Further references to this edition will be included in the main body of the text.

helping to shape 'the 1960-era male fantasy of the good life being defined by a boundless continuum of sexual endeavour and conspicuous consumption'.[52] This ideal is evoked in *El ojo de la patria* only to portray its demise. The seemingly limitless abundance of wealth provided for Bond to successfully complete his missions is notably absent: Carré lives hand to mouth in run down hotels, and his whole mission almost collapses for the lack of one Swiss franc. His distinct lack of sexual conquests is poignantly underscored in his confession that 'de los hombres como él las mujeres sólo pedían consuelo' (255). The exotic, lavish lifestyle to which Carré seems to aspire appears as a quaint relic from a bygone era, a ridiculous dream in the cold light of reality.

The 'reality' the novel presents is constructed around the disappearance of the raison d'être of figures in the Bond mould. Soriano chooses to produce a spy novel at precisely the moment in which the Cold War era that sustains this figure has come to an end. This disintegration undermines the whole framework upon which much spy fiction is built, where 'good' is taken to have a specific geopolitical meaning:

> During the Cold War, the archetypal spy novel expressed a relatively simplistic view of the world divided between the good – the Western democracies – and the bad – the Soviet Union and its Communist satellite states. It also celebrated man as an individual, with free choice and the ability to change situations.[53]

Throughout the novel, the clearly divided Cold War world, with its Manichean scheme of good versus evil and its faith in the capacity of individual action, is evoked as a fallen *metarrelato*, with Carré telling us that 'la caída del comunismo había borrado los últimos vestigios de certeza' (51). His spy characters are lost souls, reduced to merely exchanging legends about 'los gloriosos tiempos de la Guerra Fría', and unable even to commit acts of betrayal as the webs of allegiance have become so confused.

This provides a significant comment on capitalism, intrinsically bound up with Soriano's use of genre in the text. With the Cold War over and communism seemingly defeated, it would seem that in the world of the spy, 'good' has triumphed over 'evil', leaving capitalism as the only game in town. However, in *El ojo* this apparent triumph ushers in a voracious capitalism that Carré finds bewildering and disorientating. The ideological inflection of the traditional spy novel is therefore overturned, as Carré finds himself fighting market forces and trying to impose the importance of the state over the competing alternative structures that surround him. In fact, his 'spy' figure behaves more like the detective in a Chandlerian hardboiled novel, fighting against the corruption of the world around him. Stephen Knight describes Chandler's Marlowe as 'the model of an adventure hero, an up-to-date

---

52  Brett F. Woods, *Neutral Ground: A Political History of Espionage Fiction* (New York: Algora, 2008), p. 111.

53  Woods, *Neutral Ground*, pp. 107–8.

knight errant', characterized by his 'romantic individualism'.[54] Soriano's Carré attempts to emulate this ideal, struggling to re-assert a Romantic set of values at odds with the degraded world around him, based on heroism, the individual, and an essentialist view of national identity. This evokes both the Romantic idea of nationhood that originated with the *Generación del '37* in Argentina and became key to the function of the independence narrative, as noted in my Introduction, and the Hegelian exaltation of heroic 'representative men' that characterizes Mitre's histories of the period. Independence is therefore invoked as embodying values of transcendence and unity connected through the fading concept of *patria*. It is positioned as a parallel to the clear-cut 'good versus evil' narrative of the Cold War, representing a world unclouded by doubt and uncertainty that the protagonist seeks to restore.

The clear evocation of Chandler's hardboiled detective through Carré's struggle against the corrupt world around him also recalls Ricardo Piglia's well-known theorizing of the genre that asserts that 'el único enigma que proponen —y nunca resuelven— las novelas de la serie negra es el de las relaciones capitalistas'.[55] By transforming his spy into an embodiment of recognizable conventions of the detective genre, Soriano therefore relocates this figure in a universe where the morality of capitalist structures is severely questioned, a playful subversion of a genre usually aligned with capitalist triumph in the Cold War paradigm. The implications of this translation are far from straightforward, however, and Carré is a poor shadow of Chandler's hero. Whereas Marlowe wins battles in his personal quest to restore values to the world around him, Soriano's protagonist is forced to retreat, defeated, at the end of the novel. The brand of utopianism he attempts to embody is dead, consumed by the economic system around him.

The disappearance of this heroic ideal establishes a duality that runs throughout the whole text: an unresolved tension between nostalgia and critique. The *patria* is present both as the location of national identity and as an ideal that is aligned with the state, embodied in the independence figure of the *prócer* within the text. The fading of traditional forms of national identification functions simultaneously as a critique of the rise of the market to replace previous functions of the state, and a problematization of adhering to the *patria* as an unquestionable ideal. Although the novel is predominantly narrated from the protagonist's point of view, the narrative opens up vital moments of critique that provide distance from Carré's perspective. Despite taking his name from spy novelist Le Carré, he is not the self-aware protagonist of this brand of spy fiction, but instead accepts any position sustained by his government as an unflinching guarantee of morality. The ideal of a 'profesional honesto que hace su trabajo y no se contamina', as Piglia

---

54 Stephen Thomas Knight, *Form and Ideology in Crime Fiction* (London: Macmillan, 1980), pp. 137, 149.
55 Ricardo Piglia, 'Sobre el género policial', in *Crítica y ficción* (Buenos Aires: Planeta, 2000), pp. 67–70, at p. 70.

interprets Marlowe, has reached his end point in this text, and Romantic idealism cannot save Carré from ideological complicity, as my discussion of his role in the text will reveal.[56] This reveals a dual function of the national in *El ojo de la patria*: first as a nostalgic lament for lost values that serves as a type of resistance to the aggressively capitalist world portrayed by the novel, but, second, as a problematic construct aligned with a very limited, and potentially dangerous, way of interpreting what the nation can signify.

### Failed Heroism, Capitalism, and the 'Milagro Argentino'

Carré's attempt to re-assert a heroic worldview hinges on the 'milagro argentino' mission he is tasked with completing, in which he is charged with the crucial task of transporting the body of an unidentified Argentine *prócer* across France. Although the mission's ultimate objectives elude Carré's comprehension, its grand title offers a tantalizing possibility of transcendence, surprising in the amorphous and uncertain world he now inhabits: 'le sorprendía que el Presidente planeara un operativo secreto justo en los tiempos en que nadie tenía más misiones que cumplir' (51). Despite Carré's eager acceptance of this renewed possibility of certainty, the mission is presented through layers of irony. The term 'milagro argentino' conjures up associations with the implementation of neoliberal policies in South America: the idea of an economic 'miracle' was applied to both Chile and Brazil when they imposed neoliberal policies under dictatorial regimes, and it was evoked in Argentina during the early presidency of Menem, which directly coincides with the publication of Soriano's text.[57] This connection to a neoliberal context is also accented in the novel through the irony of an explicitly national miracle originating in foreign universities: 'Vienen a limpiar el baño, a tirar la cadena. Tipos de Harvard, de Cambridge. El Milagro Argentino' (204). This reads as a thinly veiled reference to the role of the 'Chicago boys' in Chile, who trained under neoliberal economists at the University of Chicago and went on to define the economic policy of Pinochet's regime.

This context reduces the term 'milagro' from its all-encompassing transcendental potential to a capitalist promise of economic growth, which raises questions about the nature of the project the characters in the novel are supporting (presented in vague terms as a matter of national interest). Carré exhibits a naïve willingness to accept the term at face value with no knowledge of the mission's objectives, a fact that is stressed in an ironic way within the text: '¿Si la Argentina planeaba un milagro, ¿quién podría oponerse?' (119). The 'milagro' reveals itself as a language trap that communicates no real meaning, appealing to the characters' faith in the *patria* as a benevolent force but offering no guarantee that this faith is well placed.

---

56  Piglia, 'Sobre el género policial', p. 70.
57  Ksenija Bilbija references this context in her article '*El ojo de la patria* de Osvaldo Soriano: ¿El milagro (argentino) o la industria (multinacional)?', *Revista Chilena de Literatura*, 59 (2001), 65–79, at p. 70.

This overt critique of the supposedly salvationary powers of neoliberal policies establishes capitalism as the force behind the disintegrating social constructs lamented by the protagonist. The asymmetry between dominant and peripheral national economies is at the heart of the critique of this apparently 'postnational' world, providing ironic commentary on Menem's repeated insistence that his neoliberal project would bring Argentina into the 'First World', finally realizing her glorious economic destiny.[58] *El ojo* repeatedly shows Argentina as a junior partner in the global economy, a fact that is symbolically underscored in the huge disparity between the Bond ideal and the novel's reality as I mentioned above: while British Bond lacks for nothing, the Argentine Carré's heroic potential is severely curtailed by his tendency to end up in ridiculous or even dangerous situations due to lack of economic means. The mismanagement of resources also comes under fire: we are told that the affordable building material Stiller invented for Perón was sold to the Swiss in exchange for a batch of Rolexes, a bitingly ironic take on the nation's economic priorities and the capacity of its political leaders. Argentina is also depicted as out of step with this new world. Tersog has invented a microprocessor, but it is sold to Toshiba after his idea meets with derision in Buenos Aires, a clear indictment of Argentina's ability to keep pace with the global economy. Cultural production is also depicted as a market where Argentina stands to lose rather than gain through the unfettered circulation of capital. The novel's motifs of popular culture are dominated by a stream of imported US cultural products, such as masks of James Dean, Sting, Madonna, and Michael Jackson. The circulation of other US products is also ironically underscored: when Carré finds the message 'en Dios confiamos' engraved on the butt of a gun he is sent, he naively takes it as a friendship sign from the mission, yet this quite obviously reads as a sign of US involvement in producing the weapon (49).

Carré's inability to read the signs of the new order surrounding him demonstrates the extent to which an 'old order' has given way to something new and incomprehensible. Néstor García Canclini's observation that an effect of the globalized economy is 'la sensación de impotencia política en que nos sumerge la experiencia cotidiana de que las decisiones principales son tomadas en lugares inaccesibles y hasta difíciles de identificar' directly parallels the protagonist's experience.[59] Whereas previously the spy defended his state against a clearly defined enemy, the actors in the new world he inhabits are unrecognizable: an amorphous blend of individuals and multinational companies, which Carré consistently fails to fit into his rigid moral framework depending solely on defending the interests of

---

58 Ariel C. Armony and Victor Armony, 'Indictments, Myths, and Citizen Mobilization in Argentina: A Discourse Analysis', *Latin American Politics and Society*, 47 (2005), 27–54, at p. 46.

59 Néstor García Canclini, *Culturas híbridas: estrategias para entrar y salir de la modernidad*, 2nd edn (Buenos Aires: Sudamericana, 1995), p. 13.

the *patria*. States continue to exist – Toshiba is overtly connected with Japan in the text and the cultural dominance of the US also reinforces the importance of national economic power – but the nation-state now competes and collaborates with market interests that are difficult to identify, sharing power in a complex way. While everything around him is permeated by the market ideology of capitalism, Carré attempts to revert to a set of values that transcend the economic and resuscitate a concept of heroism embodied by the figure of the *prócer*.

### The Prócer: Technology and Transcendence

The *prócer* represents a tantalizing possibility of certainty within the disquieting world the rest of the novel presents. As the precious cargo that Carré is charged with transporting, his mummified corpse physically embodies the ambiguous possibility of transcendence encapsulated in the idea of the 'milagro argentino'. As a result, this figure is employed as part of an extended meditation on the meaning of the *patria* and the commitment to a cause, representing a potent intersection of these ideas within the text. The meanderings of a corpse of national importance is recognizable as an Argentine theme, as many of the country's most significant figures were returned to their homeland from abroad, including the bodies of San Martín, Juan Manuel de Rosas, Eva Perón, and Carlos Gardel.[60] The return of another figure would therefore represent a continuation of this tradition and sustain a recognizable thread of Argentine national myth: it would allow Carré to carve out a space for himself within a comfortingly familiar narrative. As a heroic enterprise, however, it captures the sterility presented by the novel in other areas: Carré's potential *hazaña* is the transfer of a corpse, the embodiment of a deceased heroism, rather than the production of a truly new heroic act.

The body of the *prócer*, however, is not simply a corpse or a mummy: an electronic chip has been inserted into his flesh, granting him a shadowy appearance of life by providing him with the power of speech. He is now a fusion of biological matter and human-made technology, a cyborg of sorts. This fact is ironically referenced by the text's allusions to Arnold Schwarzenegger, famous for his role in the *Terminator* films. The text also explicitly casts the *prócer* as a type of Frankenstein's monster, both in Stiller's statement that 'no es Frankenstein pero algo se mueve' and in a brief reference to Mary Shelley's novel towards the end of the text (97). Reading the *prócer* through these overlapping frameworks evokes a context where technology or scientific endeavour promise the transcendence of normal human capacity, creating powerful creatures that threaten our structures and frames of reference. The *prócer* indeed seems destined to fulfil this expectation: the

---

60  This use of the 'itinerant' corpse as a particular component of Argentine national identity could be productively compared to Tomás Eloy Martínez's novel *Santa Evita*, published three years after Soriano's text.

chip he carries gives him an appearance of life (or more specifically, of having been brought back from the dead), which would represent the crossing of a currently impenetrable scientific frontier. Yet his repertoire of human functions is hardly inspiring: we are told that 'cuando está enchufado canta y dice algunas cosas' and that 'se la pasa hablando mal de Rivadavia', which provides an unflattering but accurate summary of the *prócer*'s capacities (97). He responds to sensory stimuli of heat, noise, and light, but in mechanical responses (predominantly expressions of displeasure) that provide no sense of meaningful interaction. His responses occasionally pick up on elements of the surrounding conversation, but never provide a meaningful response; Carré's exclamation of '¡Borrachos!' elicits the response 'Borracho era Rivadavia', an incoherent historical evocation, while his mention of batteries inspires the *prócer* to provide him with a list of battery types. Whereas Mary Shelley's novel explores the consequences of the seemingly limitless potential of human science, Soriano's 'scientist', with all the possibilities of late twentieth-century technology at his fingertips, fails to transcend the boundary that his project touches upon. Technology has neither created earth-shattering disaster nor amazing possibilities; instead, we are left with meaningless, fragmented communication.

The hyper-technological postmodern world the characters now inhabit is encapsulated in Tersog's observation that 'ahora los sueños flotan en un chip' (103), representing the transfer of the subject's desires to the disembodied realm of the virtual, a transition from physical experience to the simulated reality of the hyperreal. Deprived of any active contribution, the *prócer* is defined by the recycled, superficial impressions of the novel's characters, such as Tersog's observation that 'en un prócer lo importante es la mirada' (107) when giving his instructions on how to administer the eye drops the mummy requires: a humorous allusion to the typical depiction of national heroes as staring into the distance with their thoughts on their high-minded purpose. Carré is the only Argentine character who demonstrably cares about the significance of the *prócer* as a heroic figure: Tersog shows interest in the piece of 'art' he has created, but as the only believer in the *patria*, Carré is the only one who can attribute any heroic significance to the corpse. For the others, the value of the mummified body is purely financial: it is nothing more than the vessel that houses the 'life-giving' chip. The literary group Carré encounters is no different: to sustain art they must engage in highly lucrative market transactions and can only see the *prócer* as a vessel to facilitate their economic survival by transporting drugs, overlooking any possible transcendent meaning he might convey. This represents a profana-tion of his role in representing utopia, brought about by the intervention of capitalist, technological structures in the very fabric of his body. The fate of this previously 'sacred' symbol of history indicates a transition from depth to superficiality and a consequent destruction of historicity: any ability to envisage progression or to understand is destroyed as past and future are dissolved in a present engulfed by the hyperreal.

*Patriotic Fragments*

The dissolution of a patriotic model of heroism is echoed in the use of signs and symbols of Argentine national identity in the text. While most characters have abandoned nationalism altogether, epitomized in Stiller's cry of 'la patria, qué boludo!' (121) that echoes in Carré's head, the protagonist attempts to cling to symbolic mechanisms as an anchor for his abiding need for patriotism. He is given a kit to assist him in looking after the *prócer*, including tools and weapons, but underneath these practical and vital objects he finds two packets of *yerba mate*, blue and white rosettes, and a mask of famous tango singer Carlos Gardel. These fragments of a clichéd vision of Argentine identity reduce the idea of the *patria* to a meaningless series of objects, but Carré jumps at the chance to engage with any sense of national belonging. He uses the Gardel mask in the final scenes of the novel, wears an *escarapela* and asks Pavarotti to do the same, despite his self-conscious awareness that others view him as 'un sentimental' as a result (201). Later he attaches a soggy rosette to the T-shirt the *prócer* wears, a pitiful attempt to link disparate patriotic symbols that only serves to confirm its futility through the forlorn image it creates.

Carré's nostalgia also leads him to insist on using a method of identification the other characters find tiresome and out of date: asking questions about the geography of Buenos Aires to determine whether his fellow spies are Argentine or not. This attempt to ground national identity in a physical space fails too, as the spies' condition as exiles means they are disconnected from the living nature of the city, and they remain oblivious as previous landmarks cease to exist. Even the carefully constructed mechanism of teaching patriotism through school history that I described in my Introduction has failed: despite being schooled in Argentina, Carré is unable to recognize the *prócer*, stating only that 'yo lo tengo visto a este hombre' (129), as though he might be someone he had once met in passing rather than a face consciously replicated within the state's symbolic structures.[61]

Famous phrases of independence are echoed as meaningless fragments. Stiller compiles a mocking summary of heroic phrases from independence he suggests Carré may want to use as his last words: '*Ay, patria mía... Se necesitaba tanta agua para apagar tanto fuego... Muero contento, hemos batido al enemigo...*' (103).[62] Although Carré brushes off these taunts, he cannot resist the temptation to cast himself in a heroic mould through imitation: 'Si le preguntan por mí diga que grité *Viva la patria aunque yo perezca* —miró al profesor Tersog como disculpándose—. Ya está usado pero no se me ocurre

---

61  Carré manages to recall Sarmiento's face but fails to picture Moreno's, which could be seen as a comment on the mode of patriotism instilled through the schooling system: the controlled *civilización* that Sarmiento is taken to represent rather than the rebellious Jacobin figure of Moreno.

62  These phrases are famously attributed to Manuel Belgrano, Cornelio Saavedra, and Juan Bautista Cabral, respectively.

otra cosa' (108). His request to use Mariano Moreno's 'last words' presents itself as sterile repetition, indicating a lack of possible heroic originality grounded in the failure of a sense of history as a model to follow. Although the words can be repeated, the impulse behind them is lost. These superficial engagements with a sense of collective identity are all the novel can offer, however, and Carré remains an anachronistic shadow within the bleak landscape the novel depicts.

Within this fragmentation of formal structures, the use of song and ceremony play a particularly significant role. The *prócer's* musical choices are identified as songs with an official role in Argentina, such as the Marcha de San Lorenzo, a military march that has been the official anthem of the Argentine army since 1902, and the 'canción a la bandera'. The national anthem also appears at various points as a symbol that Carré allocates particular importance to and treats with extreme reverence, at one point denying himself the honour of singing it as he feels his actions have made him unworthy. Various patriotic ceremonies are conducted at different points in the novel, from Carré's medal ceremonies in the sewers to the formal ritual conducted for the transfer of the *prócer's* body to a boat towards the end of the text.[63] These rituals are revealed to be false constructions however, designed to flatter Carré's sense of patriotism in order to manipulate him. He is willing to believe anything that conveys a shadow of the patriotism he recognizes, and these trappings of nationalism reveal themselves to be tools for potentially dangerous deception. Nostalgia for patriotism therefore functions as a critique of the dehumanized, valueless neoliberal society the novel presents, but can also provide the potential for deception.

## Patria *and Dictatorship*

While this nostalgia is a real and poignant thread throughout the novel, therefore, it is also undercut by the disquieting assumptions Carré has made about the values he defends when he protects the *patria*. Although he joins the service after the return to democracy in Argentina and the end of the Cold War, we are told that 'se dedicó, como suponía que debía hacerlo cualquier hombre de bien, a proteger al país de las conspiraciones comunistas' (88). This reads as a clear warning flag for the reader, revealing that his understanding of defending the *patria* is conditioned by a specific, historically determined view of the nation that parrots the discourse of the military *junta* during the *proceso*. This fact explodes the discursive system to which Carré clings (the association of capitalism/democracy/good underpinning classic spy fiction), revealing an underlying and omnipresent irony in his longing for a clear superstructure. Defending the *patria* therefore becomes

---

63   This can be seen as a parody of the recognition offered to Malvinas veterans by each of the armed forces in the aftermath of the conflict, which, in the words of Lorenz, were attempts to 'suavizar las rispideces creadas por la derrota entre la sociedad civil y sus fuerzas armadas y al interior de las mismas' (*Las guerras por Malvinas,* p. 174).

an immediately problematic enterprise that no longer provides guarantees
of fighting on the side of right: the concept of the nation is re-politicized
instead of transcending ideological conflict. Carré's inability to move beyond
this framework suggests an end point for the model of patriotism instigated
with the fight for independence, as the *patria* ceases to occupy its role of
transcending the political divide and becomes firmly allied with a rigid
discourse used to underpin state violence in Argentina.

Although Soriano's novel lacks the overt criticism of a militarized discourse
of patriotism present in Kohan's text, it can still be seen as critical of the
Argentine armed forces' monopoly of the idea of 'saving the *patria*' and of the
use of the nation as an apparent guarantee of 'right'. Carré's assumption that
he fights on the side of good because he is contributing to the hyperbolically
titled 'milagro argentino' is provided with no supporting basis in the text.
The heroism he attempts to attribute to his actions is ironically undercut: his
tentative insistence that the people around him 'no imaginaban que hombres
como él arriesgaban la vida para protegerlos' (56) dissolves in the fact that
at the moment of this utterance he is queuing to empty the bank account
of a disabled man who possibly has terminal cancer: an unheroic action in
the extreme.

The undefined nature of the mission's objectives destroys the supposed
moral function of the appeal to the national in its title, and we are left with
the disquieting idea that our spy 'hero' could be providing support for any
kind of power framework. Carré participates because he believes (or wants to
believe) in the *patria*, but, as detailed above, the morally ambiguous world of
the novel consistently exposes the fact that the symbols of patriotic fervour
can be applied to any enterprise and no longer function as a guarantee of
heroic action. The problematic nature of this dynamic is underscored through
explicit references to the *proceso* in the text. We are informed that 'lo que
pasaba durante la dictadura Carré lo ignoraba' (87),[64] which immediately
betrays the underlying threat of his unquestioning attitude towards the *patria*:
if Carré is willing to undertake immoral actions, even kill, for a mission he
does not understand, he could just as easily be sustaining a brutal dictatorship as a heroic national cause. By drawing this implicit parallel between the
*proceso* and the undefined overriding objective of Carré's mission, the novel
elaborates a reflection on the *patria*'s inability to underpin moral certainty,
and the lack of an existing alternative structure to fulfil fantasies of heroism
in the contemporary world.

The novel therefore combines nostalgia for a time of heroic exploits with
a critique of the illusion of moral certainty offered by the figure of the
*patria*. Blind allegiance to a project justified by its 'national' character is

---

64 In an article for Página 12 on 24 March 1996, the 20th anniversary of the coup,
   Soriano wrote: 'No les creo una palabra a los que dicen aún hoy "yo no sabía lo
   que pasaba»' (Osvaldo Soriano, '24 de Marzo'). This underlines the significance of
   Carré's attitude within the text.

problematized, but a need for transcendence beyond the alienating capitalist structures the novel presents remains, and this tension is unresolved within the text. The figure of the *prócer* is not destabilized in the sense that he continues to represent heroic values, but the complete impossibility of realizing these values means he can no longer fulfil his heroic function. While Serapio argues that independence remains intact as a discourse through the text as it functions within its usual symbolic framework of representing heroism and commitment, Soriano introduces a significant variation on this theme by presenting this value system as completely defunct with no way back, despite our continued need for transcendence.[65] Although the protagonist's point of view is predominantly nostalgic, the text undertakes a critique of this longing for an apolitical and unreflexive commitment to the abstract idea of 'the nation'. The result is a conflicting portrait of the place of the national: on the one hand it represents a lost sense of meaning and unity, replaced by ruthless and corrupt market forces, and on the other a dangerous masking of underlying political intent.

## Conclusion: Values Lost and Refounded

The two texts presented in this chapter therefore offer radically different engagements with the political potential of a history constructed in dialogue with the lessons of the postmodern critical turn. Kohan's *El informe* reconfirms an idea of progress and shared values through national belonging, but demonstrates the need to reconstruct the nation's founding narrative to reflect contemporary values rather than those of the nation's nineteenth-century men of letters. Soriano's *El ojo de la patria*, however, portrays a world beyond the end of ideology where nothing is certain and only a tangled web of capitalist plots remains. While this text does not employ the same self-reflexive textual features, it explicitly evokes the idea of fallen metanar-ratives in order to convey the fragmented, uncertain nature of contemporary society, which it seems has left us without a moral compass. In Soriano's novel, no way forward emerges: it performs a lament for a world that is lost and any sense of progress is destroyed. The political critique of the naïve adherence to the *patria* demonstrated in the association between nationalism and authoritarianism in the text does not provide a route to the reconstruction of action. The text remains caught in the suspended anxiety of radicalized uncertainty, unable to draw any new meanings from the ruins of what has been swept away by the voracious, hypertechnological late capitalist world.

Comparing these two novels allows us, therefore, to reconsider the idea of self-reflexive historical fiction as a harmonious fusion of postmodern aesthetics and the wider ideas we associate with the postmodern, particularly their challenge to our methods of producing knowledge. Soriano's text, a subversion of the spy genre that employs a relatively conventional narrative

65  Serapio, '¿Es este el fin?', p. 237.

style and structure, uses the past certainties of history to expose a new and unpredictable present where no judgement can be reliably sustained. By contrast, Kohan's novel exploits both the self-reflexive narrative techniques we associate with 'historiographic metafiction' and engages in overt play with the idea of history as narrative rather than 'fact', but ultimately does not lead us to the type of generalized critique that is often associated with this category. Instead, by tracing the specific historical discourses that are rewritten by Kohan's text, I have drawn the novel's relationship with nation-building to the fore, and therefore isolated a critique of militarism and concern with equality as the thematic driving forces of the text's engagement with this 'myth of origin'. To reduce this complex and politicized critique to a vague 'challenge to liberal humanism' would be to diffuse the power of the text's historical play.

The comparison between these two texts also further illustrates the significance of independence as a historical period attached to a specific set of values through the construction of 'official history'. By exploring a text that cannot be considered to fit within the genre of a historical novel, Soriano's *El ojo de la patria*, I have underscored the idea that these texts' use of history cannot be straightforwardly reduced to engagement with an amorphous order of discourse, as described in my Introduction. Recognizing the discursive function of independence in a novel that escapes definition as 'historical' text aids the separation of this period from more general ideas about history as the recovery of information about the past. In identifying the associations that this text creates between a symbolic representation of the period, the mummified body of the *prócer*, and the novel's reflection on the idea of the *patria*, the specificity of the place occupied by independence in the national imaginary comes more clearly to the fore. Once again, therefore, the rewriting of independence represents a means of addressing the ideas at the heart of this period's association with nation-building in both of these novels, despite their radical stylistic differences. The idea of the *patria* is thrown into crisis by both novels, but Kohan's novel seizes on the opportunity to shape the discursive projections of the nation anew by dismantling this deeply ingrained national narrative. It is by undermining the apparently 'natural' status of this discourse that *El informe* conducts its critique and targeted political intervention, demanding that the reader consider whether these myths of origin fulfil our contemporary needs, or whether we require a new narrative to provide intelligible shared stories for a national community.

# CHAPTER 3

# Peronism and the Popular

## Washington Cucurto's *1810: la Revolución de Mayo vivida por los negros* and Manuel Santos Iñurrieta's *Mariano Moreno y un teatro de operaciones*

My final chapter approaches two texts through their engagement with the popular, locating their rewriting of the independence narrative within fraught contemporary political and cultural debates on historical revisionism.[1] This reading is once again aimed at unearthing the politicized nature of the texts' historical play, and therefore at reconsidering the target of their critique, by recognizing the explicit function of independence as a nation-building discourse. The political force of revisionist history in Argentina demands that we break down our idea of what type of history is being challenged by the rewritings of these texts, as this is the crucial difference between a destabilizing of 'history' and an attack on a version of the past produced as part of a specific political project. In this final chapter, my aim is to show how the texts I will explore employ the techniques we associate with the 'destabilization' of knowledge – self-reflexivity, irony, parody, heteroglossia, etc. – as a means of producing an idea of the political that underpins a different idea of agency: one that relies upon the construction of a self-aware narrative as a means of establishing an ideological resilience that can unravel the workings of hegemonic discourse and assert a political alternative.

My analysis in this chapter also aims to break down another limit imposed by the historical novel framework: that of genre. Reading texts dealing with history as contemporary manifestations of a novelistic form dating back to Walter Scott prescribes a critical focus on how the relationship between history and the novel has changed over time. As a result, this subgenre is taken as the texts' major point of dialogue, and the historical novel is

---

1 A version of this chapter was published in *Modern Languages Open*. Catriona McAllister, 'History and the Popular: Rewriting National Origins at the Argentine Bicentenary'. *Modern Languages Open* (April 2016). DOI: http://doi.org/10.3828/mlo.v0i0.35.

considered almost as an independent literary form, detached from comparison with other contemporary novels and with other cultural products dealing with history. In line with my assertion that specific historical discourses and their political uses are crucial to an understanding of these texts, this chapter challenges the prevailing critical emphasis on defining the characteristics and limits of the postmodern historical novel by straying beyond the novel to the stage, in order to draw out shared thematic concerns across the genre divide. My aim is to demonstrate that these texts are primarily in dialogue with particular constructions of history associated with distinct political projects over the course of the last two centuries in Argentina, rather than with a subgenre of the novel. This chapter will therefore compare a novel – Washington Cucurto's *1810: la Revolución de Mayo vivida por los negros* (2008) – and a play – Manuel Santos Iñurrieta's *Mariano Moreno y un teatro de operaciones* (2010). My analysis will explore the treatment of history in both texts, revealing how comparing works from different literary genres can allow their interactions with politicized historical discourses to come to the fore.

As this chapter focuses on configurations of the popular, it will also centre on the different manifestations of this concept in both texts. The idea of the popular I will deploy encompasses two major threads, both united in the signifier of 'el pueblo'. The first idea of the *pueblo* is a representation of the people as citizens: a united, homogeneous, and patriotic political subject. In Argentina, this idea of the *pueblo* is intrinsically linked to the creation of the independence narrative. The May Revolution gives birth to the idea of the 'pueblo de la plaza pública':[2] a political actor that seemingly embodies the popular will. This *pueblo* unites all individuals under the banner of the nation, ascribing to them a single voice. This vision of the *pueblo* elides people and nation in a seamless enunciative act, becoming an embodiment of what Homi Bhabha terms the 'nation-people'.[3] This is the rhetorical category that allows slippage between the political construct of the nation-state and its apparent unified citizenry: an essential component of the symbolic production of the nation.

In both texts explored in this chapter, this idea of a *pueblo* that is at once historical and timeless, a manifestation of the nation's people, is set against another definition – the idea of the *pueblo* as the 'popular classes' in opposition to a cultural and economic elite. This distinction is presented in two very different ways in the texts I will discuss: one profoundly connected to the construction of the popular classes under Peronism, and the other bound

---

2  Nelda Pilia de Assunção and Aurora Ravina (eds.), *Mayo de 1810: entre la historia y la ficción discursivas* (Buenos Aires: Biblos, 1999), p. 163.

3  Homi Bhabha, 'DissemiNation: Time, Narrative, and the Margins of the Modern Nation', in *Nation and Narration*, ed. by Homi K. Bhabha (London: Routledge, 1990), 291–322, at p. 296. See also Bhabha's concept of the 'double-time of the nation' in the same text.

up with the Marxist idea of the proletariat. My discussion will therefore begin with a consideration of the elaboration of the concept of the *pueblo* under Peronism, and a consideration of how the *pueblo* of independence, both an expression of popular will and the first true historical expression of the 'nation-people', is configured in official history and in the challenges of historical revisionism, which occupied such a visible role in public life in the first decade of this century.

## History, Peronism, the Popular

Within the traditional narrative of independence, the 'pueblo de la plaza pública' plays a crucial role as guarantor of the legitimacy of the new political system ushered in by the May Revolution. The delicate balance of this relationship is essential to the success of the tale as national epic, as the representative quality of the new leadership hinges on the principle of consent that underpins the definition of May 1810 as a revolution. Without popular support, the installation of the *primera junta* would merely represent the tale of the seizing of power by a small group of men intent on imposing their own political vision: more akin to a coup than a revolution.[4] The canonical narrative has therefore insisted on an apparently harmonious relationship between the new political elites and the people they came to govern.[5] A contradiction remains, however, between the crucial role of the 'pueblo' and the focus of the traditional tale of 1810, as Luis Alberto Romero illustrates:

> Aunque la epopeya reconoce un alto grado de popularidad, y por momentos su actor puede ser un genérico 'pueblo', 'criollos', o 'patriotas', por lo general se trata de actores individuales elevados a la categoría de próceres, cuyos actos son gloriosos y transmiten su grandeza al futuro.[6]

This 'pueblo' therefore represents an uncomplicated, united body lending its voice to the clamour for liberation from Spanish rule, while the *próceres* occupy centre stage. It embodies the 'greater good' that justifies the celebration of these events as heroic deeds – a foil to the figures singled out for individual acclaim.

---

4 Halperín Donghi highlights the political function of this assertion at the moment of the Revolution itself, stating that the *primera junta* 'quiere hacer de su legitimidad su carta de triunfo'. *Revolución y guerra*, p. 177.

5 Mitre opens his chapter on 25 May with a direct statement of the *pueblo*'s role as an actor in the newly inaugurated regime: 'Un nuevo actor del drama revolucionario va a presentarse en la escena política: el pueblo de la plaza pública, que no discute, pero que marcha en columna cerrada apoyando y a veces iniciando por instinto los grandes movimientos que deciden de sus destinos'. *Historia de Belgrano*, I, p. 67. Mitre even goes so far as to insist on the intrinsically democratic nature of the Argentine people, whose very nature he claims leads them to aspire to equality. Ibid., pp. 67–68.

6 Romero, *La Argentina en la escuela*, p. 59.

Yet beyond the bounds of this appealingly straightforward school-book depiction, the idea of the *pueblo* is subject to much more complex political projections. Twentieth-century Argentine politics, particularly the emergence of Peronism, brought about tangible redefinition of the signifying potential of this concept within the national context. The Peronist idea of the *pueblo* unites an appeal to the authority of the all-encompassing 'nation-people' with the notion of the popular classes in opposition to 'anti-national' elites. As Sigal and Verón demonstrate, traditional Peronist rhetoric relies upon the fusion of the figure of Perón with the idea of the nation and, therefore, 'siendo la posición de Perón la posición de la Patria, el lugar del Otro es, en definitiva, la anti-Patria'.[7] As these authors highlight, however, the *pueblo* that declares itself Peronist does not in fact incorporate the whole nation (62). It is only Perón's supporters that represent this 'true' *pueblo*, and this is the 'popular' *pueblo* that resists the opposition of the elites. Peronist rhetoric relies on this merging of the Peronist *pueblo* and the nation, using it to underpin the dual concepts that denote Peronist ideas in political rhetoric into the present day: the union of 'nacional y popular'.

It is crucial to draw a distinction between the Peronist idea of the popular and the idea of the popular classes that underpins Marxist thought. While Marxist political traditions conceptualize the proletariat in economic terms focusing on class, Peronism contributes additional cultural implications to its construction of the 'sectores populares'. The 'civilized' working-class revolutionary figure revered by the traditional Left did not correspond to the mass movement unleashed by Peronism, as Maristella Svampa explains: 'Para los socialistas tenía que ver más con la moral y el grado de educación, con la ignorancia y el resentimiento, que con la emergencia de un actor social hasta ahora desplazado de la escena política.'[8] As Svampa describes, an oft-repeated refrain in opposition discourse from both sides of the political spectrum was the threat Peronism apparently posed to 'cultura', which was effectively employed as a synonym of 'civilización' and seen as allied with progress and reason, leaving the Peronist alternative as threatening descent into barbarism and chaos (256). Even as intellectuals criticized Perón and his followers for their 'incultura', however, this rejection of 'civilized' norms was appropriated in Peronist discourse, which adopted what Svampa terms a 'barbarie autorreferencial' (209). An opposition between the Peronist 'pueblo' and 'cultura' was therefore created, becoming a hallmark of Peronism's opposition to the 'civilizing' project of liberalism (259–60). As a result, the idea of barbarism gained new connotations of resistance for Peronist supporters, perceived as freeing the people from the political and social straitjacket of norms imposed by the oligarchy.

This use of the 'civilization/barbarism' dichotomy was translated into historical debates through the connection that developed between Peronism

---

7  Sigal and Verón, pp. 64–65.
8  Svampa, *El dilema argentino*, p. 255. See also pp. 253–55.

and revisionism. Opponents of the charismatic leader likened his hold over the people to the support enjoyed by the 'barbarism' of Rosas's leadership in the nineteenth century. Peronism came to be described as 'la segunda tiranía', the second coming of barbaric authoritarianism first incarnated in Rosas. Although initially resisted by Perón, the parallels drawn between the controversial leader and nineteenth-century *caudillo* figures eventually became not only accepted but a significant feature of Peronist rhetoric.[9] *El Descamisado*, the mouthpiece of the Juventud Peronista, sustained a narrative that celebrated a pantheon of heroes including *caudillos*, and firmly positioned imperialism and the dominant classes as the historical enemy of the people.[10] Peronism's 'incultura' therefore became associated with overthrowing the niceties of liberal historiography: barbarism was celebrated through an alternative historical canon and 'civilization' came to be perceived as part of a liberal project belonging to the anti-national, economically powerful classes.[11]

The historical revisionism associated with Peronism has seen a resurgence in recent decades, initially through Menem (particularly his repatriation of Rosas's body under the banner of 'national reconciliation'), but most significantly throughout the 2000s.[12] Michael Goebel outlines a growing public interest in national history over the course of the decade, citing the popularity of public debates (led by essayists such as Pacho O'Donnell and Felipe Pigna) and the increased use of historical events and figures by political actors over the decade.[13] The prevalence of revisionist historians in these public events and the government's drawing on revisionist history has led Omar Acha to describe the emergence of 'un sentido común histórico "revisionista"' in the lead up to the country's Bicentenary.[14] This claim emphasizes the widespread popularity of a vision that claims that the traditional 'official history' serves the interests of the economic elite and should be replaced by a version with the true 'pueblo' at its heart, as Goebel explains:

> These new historical debates were not dominated by the canonised version of revisionism, with its stock set of heroes and villains, but were nourished by many ideas central to revisionism, such as the notion of two Argentinas, the opinion that Argentina had been pillaged and indebted by a powerful 'oligarchy' in alliance with 'foreign', particularly British, interests or the view that Argentine history had been 'falsified' in order to 'silence' the nation's true soul and interests. (216)

---

9  On how revisionism came to be not only accepted by but instrumental to the Peronist movement see Halperín Donghi, *El revisionismo histórico*, pp. 40–43.

10  Sigal and Verón, *Perón o muerte*, p. 182.

11  Svampa, *El dilema argentino*, pp. 267, 272.

12  Goebel, *Argentina's Partisan Past*, pp. 210–16.

13  Goebel, *Argentina's Partisan Past*, p. 216.

14  Omar Acha, 'Desafíos para la historiografía en el Bicentenario argentino', *PolHis*, 8 (2011), 57–69, at p. 58.

This does not mean that the revisionist concern with *caudillos* and rewriting the liberal pantheon had been erased from national debate, but rather that other aspects of revisionist discourse came to the fore in this contemporary resurgence. Uniting the ideas outlined by Goebel above is the conception of liberal history as anti-popular: a betrayal of the majority by the economically powerful. This neo-revisionist resurgence therefore places significant emphasis on redressing the balance between the 'two Argentinas' – 'pueblo' and 'oligarquía' – in the alternative historical visions it constructs.

The close relationship between the government and revisionist historians culminated in the creation by presidential decree of the Instituto Nacional de Revisionismo Histórico Manuel Dorrego in 2011, which caused a furore among the country's historians, leading to a petition with more than 200 signatories from the profession and denunciations by the Asociación Argentina de Investigadores en Historia, among other public criticisms from the academic community.[15] Their vociferous objections centred on what they perceived as the promotion of a state-sponsored narrative led by historians without sufficient professional training.[16] The Institute (closed in 2015 under Macri's government) used recognizably revisionist rhetoric, promising to counteract the version of history it described as 'liberal y extranjerizante' with an alternative account based on a revised national pantheon. The connection with Peronist revisionist readings was clear in the Institute's professed aim to call attention to the role of the 'sectores populares' and promote a historical vision that is 'nacional y popular'.[17] Its objectives also clearly related to the contemporary political context in a wider sense, in the concern with gender equality (the Institute aimed to '[prestar] especial atención a la reivindicación de la participación femenina'), and its insistence on Argentina's independence struggle as part of a Latin American process, drawing on the increasing focus on integration and solidarity among Latin American nations, particularly in the wake of the 'pink tide'. This represented a conscious move away from the traditional *mitrista* narrative, which singles out Argentina's contribution to independence as an indication of the nation's destiny as leader of the region. In the post-2001 political landscape, this 'destiny' is reconfigured as a contribution to a regional project, reflecting the increasing importance of this narrative of integration. As Grimson describes:

> Después de 2001 [...] nadie cree que la Argentina tenga en su horizonte ser una potencia, ni ingresar al Primer Mundo. Complementariamente, por razones económicas y políticas el país se encuentra más distanciado de Estados Unidos y más cerca de sus vecinos, de quienes ya no tiene certeza

---

15  'Críticas al Instituto Dorrego', *La Nación*, 8 December 2011.

16  'Polémico Instituto de Revisión de la Historia', *La Nación*, 28 November 2011.

17  'Decreto 1880/2011', Boletín Oficial de la República Argentina, 21 November 2011. This was also reproduced as part of the official information on the Instituto Dorrego's website while it was in operation.

de ser superior. [...] En ese marco, la Argentina busca redefinir su lugar en América Latina.[18]

Under *kirchnerismo*, the official representation of the nation's founding narrative was updated to reflect the changing regional dynamic, and this was clearly displayed in the 2010 Bicentenary celebrations, along with the focus on gender mentioned above. The central importance of these themes can be seen in the selection of the two portrait exhibitions displayed in the Casa Rosada for the Bicentenary: the 'Galería de Patriotas Latinoamericanos', an exhibition of portraits of revolutionary figures from across the region, and the 'Salón de las Mujeres Argentinas del Bicentenario'.[19] The historical vision that emerged from this new 'official' panorama brought the combative anti-imperialist rhetoric of left-leaning revisionism together with more contemporary political concerns, redefining what constitutes the 'popular' writing of history from a revisionist viewpoint.

Despite the close relationship between the Kirchner governments and revisionist history, the historical debates of the 2000s retained a complexity that does not merely reduce the concern for the place of the *pueblo* in national history to a pro- or anti-government stance. Although he protests the emergence of an apparent 'nuevo sentido común', Acha concedes that the discourses surrounding the May Revolution in the Bicentenary were not reduced to two easily definable narratives.[20] Not every focus on 'el pueblo' is a revisionist one: for example, the volume *Y el pueblo dónde está? Contribuciones para una historia popular de la revolución de independencia en el Río de la Plata*, edited by Raúl O. Fradkin, situates itself clearly in relation to Social History rather than revisionism, seeking to uncover the role of the *pueblo* as a neglected social actor (overshadowed by the *próceres*) rather than through a rhetoric of combative resistance. There was (and is) a wider concern with re-evaluating the national past that builds upon the changes taking place in the 1990s that I described in my previous chapter, focused on updating a narrative that had 'fossilized' over the course of the twentieth century, re-establishing its connection with the methodological advances of the intervening decades. The *pueblo* therefore ultimately remains a site for contestation and redefinition, rather than an easily attributable cipher.

I have traced both the association between Peronism and a barbaric 'incultura' and the uses of revisionist history in order to provide a framework

18 Alejandro Grimson, 'Nuevas xenofobias, nuevas políticas étnicas en la Argentina', in *Migraciones regionales hacia la Argentina: diferencia, desigualdad y derechos* (Buenos Aires: Prometeo libros, 2006), pp. 69–97, at pp. 93–94.

19 Cristina Kirchner's speech at the launch of the patriots gallery on 25 May 2010 provides a useful example of this connection in the governmental rhetoric surrounding the Bicentenary: Casa Rosada, Presidencia de la Nación Argentina. 'Palabras de la Presidenta en apertura de Galería de Patriotas Latinoamericanos'.

20 Acha, 'Desafíos de la historiografía', p. 57.

for the overtly politicized conception of the 'pueblo' in the texts I will discuss in this chapter and its relation to both the nation and the presentation of the popular classes. *Mariano Moreno y un teatro de operaciones* and *1810: la Revolución de Mayo vivida por los negros* create two very different 'historical' worlds, filtered through the politicized historical debates I have outlined above. By grounding my analysis in this context, I seek to draw out the differing thematic and aesthetic interpretations of the popular in both works, while highlighting the resurgence of revolutionary rhetoric and an emphasis on defining Argentina's relationship to Latin America through this nineteenth-century narrative in both texts. In this way, I aim to add weight to my assertion that these historical rewritings respond first and foremost to the changing political uses of this foundational national narrative, and that their aesthetic mediations of history cannot be meaningfully detached from this context. This final chapter will also allow me to draw comparisons with the other works I have discussed throughout the book, supporting my claim that the shift in historical interpretation they display is both ideologically focused and concerned with providing a politicized response rather than challenging abstract concepts or the possibility of producing reliable historical knowledge.

### *1810: la Revolución de Mayo vivida por los negros*: Carnival and 'Contamination'

The creation of a 'popular' fictional world is a central concern of Washington Cucurto's whole literary output, and his rewriting of the *revolución de mayo* exploits history in order to add another dimension to this enterprise. Cucurto is the literary persona created by Santiago Vega, a poet, writer, and co-founder of publishing house Eloísa Cartonera.[21] While his poetry has attracted critical attention as part of the poetic 'generation' of the 1990s, his prose works have proved more controversial due to their provocative, outrageous content that casts out any idea of political correctness. Beatriz Sarlo, for example, has accused Cucurto of offering a sex- and *cumbia*-infused world with an eye more on the sales-appeal of his literary project than its artistic value, writing rather disdainfully that 'a Cucurto le interesa mucho más mencionar culos y tetas que las vueltas de la subjetividad'. Sarlo argues that the author's writing ultimately appeals to a white, middle-class readership, describing his novels as merely an indulgence of the 'lector culto' grounded in the appeal of 'fantasías de absorbente y exótica vitalidad'.[22] Yet to dismiss Cucurto's writing in these terms is, I will argue, to underestimate the political intent of the highly ironic discourse sustained by the character 'Cucurto'.

---

21  Eloísa Cartonera is a small, independent publisher that binds books in recycled cardboard purchased from the *cartoneros*, workers in the informal sector who collect and sell recyclable material.

22  Beatriz Sarlo, 'Sujetos y tecnologías: la novela después de la historia', *Punto de vista*, 86 (2006), 1–6, p. 5.

With *1810: la Revolución de Mayo vivida por los negros* Cucurto takes the *cumbia*-inspired world that has brought him notoriety and transports it to a reimagined origin of the *patria*. His version all but completely disregards historical fact to take the reader on a chaotic journey through a sex-, alcohol-, and drug-fuelled tale of clandestine homosexual love affairs and self-interested scheming. As in his other prose texts, Cucurto's self-styled 'realismo atolondrado' offers an exuberant fictional world focused on the body, excess, and the popular. The illusion of irreverent playfulness that the text sustains is not a departure from the politicized use of history I have described throughout the book, however, but a deliberate aesthetic of subversion that represents an assault on the 'civilized' literary world.

*History, Power, and the National Narrative*
The rewriting of history that *1810* undertakes is playfully presented as an attempt to recover San Martín, the national hero, from the clutches of power and restore him to his rightful place among the people. The text contains a poetic 'Manifiesto' that outlines this vision, dismissing existing histories as written by and for an economic and cultural elite: 'La historia ha sido por años una actividad / para burgueses adinerados / o vanos intelectuales de cerebro de pajarito'.[23] This reappropriation invokes mechanisms of revisionist history, promising us access to the 'hidden truth' behind the falsified 'official' version. Yet ultimately revisionist history is also rejected as part of the prevailing cultural structures that must be overturned, when the narrator claims that the historical vision he will expose 'no consta ni en un libro de historia de todos esos libros blanquecinos que se dedican a derribar los mitos', a clear reference to revisionist practices (18–19). Through the 'Manifiesto', the text energetically presents itself as a history of the people written by the people, claiming that 'ahora la historia la escribiremos nosotros' and outlining what must be done 'Para que la historia sea del pueblo' (13–14). This declaration therefore presents a writing of history that positions current revisionist 'alternatives' as merely another reincarnation of official discourse due to their adherence to essentially the same aesthetic norms. The popular history advocated by the 'Manifiesto' is one that transgresses all accepted codes for historical writing. It proposes an approach that overturns not only the concrete facts we have been told about the past, but recourse to fact as a valid tool for approaching reality. Instead, the text presents us with the utopian ideal of following 'el camino de la imaginería y el amor' (13): the joyful intrusion of an anti-rational, anti-scientific form of thinking into historical meaning. In claiming to rewrite history through imagination the text presents a broader rejection of the relationship between literature and power embodied by the lettered city: a provocative challenge to all interwoven hegemonic structures rather than a

---

23 Washington Cucurto, *1810: la Revolución de Mayo vivida por los negros* (Buenos Aires: Emecé, 2008), p. 13. The 'Manifiesto' is laid out in the form of a poem on the page. Further references to this edition will be given within the main body of the text.

concern with the stability of historical fact. It is not epistemology that is in doubt, therefore, but the right of the bourgeoisie to define 'culture' and to impose anti-popular values under the label of 'knowledge'.

The connections made between class, power, and control of knowledge in Cucurto's 'Manifiesto' affirm the political potential of challenging values that have been dictated by the cultural standards of the dominant classes. The association between modernity, nation-building, and the power of the lettered city is a connection that is highly visible in Argentina through the history of the 'civilization/barbarism' divide initiated by the *Generación del '37*, as described at the start of this chapter. The way in which *1810*'s 'Manifiesto' positions the text is therefore a radical assertion of a path of 'incultura': a joyful explosion of *barbarie* finally breaking through all limits of *civilización*. an anti-hegemonic challenge presented in recognizably Peronist/anti-Peronist terms. This use of the popular therefore presents itself as a chaotic challenge to bourgeois values of stability, order, and restraint. Cucurto's form of 'incultura' is one that demonstrates knowledge of literary debates, generic codes, and traditional classics, but with the aim of subverting them and subjecting them to his 'alternative'. Seen from this perspective, the 'culos y tetas' that Sarlo dismisses as empty commercial posturing become a deliberate challenge to the limits of 'acceptability' in literature. This is cast into sharper relief through an observation by Santiago Llach, poet and editor of many of Cucurto's works, who states:

> Cucurto es el espejo negro de la literatura pequeñoburguesa. Los críticos, los que lo festejan y los que lo desdeñan, reproducen frente a sus textos las dicotomías sarmiento-peronistas. De las páginas de Cucurto, la literatura pequeñoburguesa sale empetrolada. Lo que ve la pequeña burguesía cuando lee a Cucurto es el vacío de sus propias ilusiones progresistas e ilustradas.[24]

Cucurto's 'historical novel' can therefore be seen as an attempt to strike at a major intersection of power and discourse through its appropriation of national narrative, confronting our ideas about knowledge in order to expose them as a bourgeois construction. Rather than revealing the provisionality of previously solid empirical foundations as we might expect from a historiographic metafiction, the text asserts an alternative ideological worldview that seizes upon this postmodern epistemological uncertainty as a chink in the armour of the lettered city. The wavering of one idea of knowledge, a cultural paradigm devised by the elite, becomes the opportunity for a vibrant popular carnival to burst forth and redefine our processes of meaning-making and our idea of knowledge. The implicit relationship between reader and the values of modernity is reimagined through this aesthetic act: it is no longer *our* understanding of the world that is under attack, but one that has been imposed

---

24  Santiago Llach, 'La cumbia es una metáfora', in Washington Cucurto, *1999: poemas de siempre, poemas nuevos y nuevas versiones* (Buenos Aires: Eloísa Cartonera, 2007), pp. 141–43, at pp. 141–42.

by a powerful 'them', the decline of which represents a tantalizing promise of freedom. The text's concern is therefore not to warn that constructing knowledge is now a problematic enterprise, but to playfully imagine the possibilities of a world completely unfettered by the idea of meaning-making devised by the elite: a world where *barbarie* could reign supreme.

Rather than an attempt to engage with the historical novel as a specific form, therefore, this novel represents a wider challenge to literature's contribution to the maintenance of hegemonic structures through its alliance with the project of 'civilización'. The construction of the text enacts part of this rebellion against convention in its defiantly anti-narrative structure. The text has no discernible linear plot; it follows an episodic structure reminiscent of the picaresque, linked together by the intensely personal narrative voice whose informal, politically incorrect language sets the tone for the text. Details are changed, episodes are re-narrated with different endings and the text warns us against getting carried away by plot: '¡Pero Chichos, léanme bien, esto no es un relato, es un poema de X-504! ¡Basta de narrativa, volvamos de una vez a la poesía!' (229).[25] The narration switches wildly between different literary codes and conventions, from *telenovela*-style romantic melodrama and cliffhangers to parodies of *próceres'* battle speeches, from the grotesque to rare moments of pathos. Characters fail to represent stable entities and behaviour is determined purely by the narrative function they are required to fulfil in a particular moment, allowing San Martín to pass swiftly from Romantic hero to cruel slave master, or devoted father to colonial ruler. Allegories arise and fade throughout the text, forcing the reader to re-establish the positioning of each character with the start of each new scene. The structures of formal historical writing are parodied: a prologue, epilogue, and appendix of newly discovered 'historical documents' are filled with chaotic, outrageous, and often sexually explicit content.

The narrative style is intensively digressive with a strong focus on orality: the narrator constantly addresses his audience, providing exclamations and interjections. At certain points the sonority of his language brings his prose to the border of poetry, to an ambiguous space between the written and the spoken, or even the sung. This oral focus of the text's play with form is crucial to the way it positions literature: it presents itself as the breaking of formal modes by the intrusion of the popular rather than experimentation that seeks to inhibit comprehension and therefore push literature towards an ever more 'culto' audience. By exploring the text's rejection of all cultural norms associated with liberal ideals, we can perceive the significance of the way in which Cucurto's text chooses to overthrow a highly traditional historical narrative. This is not simply a proclamation of history's constructed nature, but an explicitly politicized challenge to the relationship between cultural production and the values of *civilización*.

25  X-504 is the pseudonym of Jaime Jaramillo Escobar, one of Colombia's 'nadaísta' poets (a contestatory vanguardist movement of the late 1950s and early 1960s).

*Defining the Nation: Repositioning the Popular*

The first intrusion of *barbarie* into the traditionally 'civilized' tale of the nation's origin in *1810* comes through the text's inversion of racialized discourses of national identity. The popular world that Cucurto constructs in *1810* presents itself as an attack on the sanctioned discourses of Argentine national identity, particularly the idea of a white, European nation 'descendida de los barcos'. The concept of the *pueblo* as a homogeneous, unified social force is fundamentally challenged by this deliberate process of fragmentation and energetic explosion of heterogeneity into the canonical narrative of the nation's origin. Manuel Chust and José Antonio Serrano note that it is the arrival of independence as a national discourse in Ibero-America that generates the need for this impression of unity as part of the conscious construction of the *patria*: 'Aconteció el concepto "pueblo", a la vez que desaparecieron, o ni siquiera se consideraron, cada uno de los grupos sociales y étnicos existentes.'[26] By using independence as a means of splintering the idea of the homogeneous national population, therefore, *1810* seizes upon and overturns the origin of the idea of the 'nation-people' constructed by the nineteenth-century project of *civilización*. The disruption of the identity codes that underpin the apparently unified national subject forms an integral part of the text's assertion of barbarism and exposure of implicit cultural codes.

Cucurto's revolutionary *pueblo* is a diverse, disorganized force that shatters any attempt to conceive of Argentina as a predominantly 'white' nation. Unlike in other Latin American nations, such as Brazil or Mexico, where the national narrative of *mestizaje* emphasizes the diverse ethnic make-up of the population, Argentina's *crisol de razas* does not follow a similarly pluralist model.[27] Based upon a specific period of immigration, it is implicitly conceived of as a fusion of white, European origins, which ultimately dissolve their differences into the 'Argentine'.[28] Cucurto seizes upon this identity trope in *1810*, providing a radically different racialized narrative of the nation's past. The plot hinges on the arrival to Argentina of a boatload of African slaves, who ultimately become the driving force behind the alternative *revolución de mayo* that the text describes. The arrival of these slaves is, however, recounted through language that evokes the idealized narrative of the immigrant dream: the new city as a land of opportunity, the desire to

---

26  Manuel Chust and José Antonio Serrano, 'Un debate actual, una revisión necesaria', in *Debates sobre las independencias iberoamericanas*, ed. by Manuel Chust and José Antonio Serrano (Madrid: Iberoamericana; Frankfurt: Vervuert, 2007), pp. 9–26, at p. 10.

27  Nicola Miller, *In the Shadow of the State: Intellectuals and the Quest for National Identity in Twentieth-Century Spanish America* (London: Verso, 1999), p. 12.

28  Enrique Garguin, '"Los Argentinos Descendemos de Los Barcos": The Racial Articulation of Middle Class Identity in Argentina (1920–1960)', *Latin American and Caribbean Ethnic Studies*, 2 (2007), pp. 161–84, at p. 165.

work and the promise of freedom and a better life. This description strategically repositions the arrival of Argentina's black population as part of the legitimized immigration narrative, pointedly circumventing the traditional exclusion of black Argentines from the nation's self-representation.[29] By subverting the conventions of this national narrative, the text contravenes the strict historical separation between the arrival of enslaved Africans and twentieth-century European immigrants, aptly described in anthropologist Claudia Briones's observation that 'las poblaciones asociadas a un remoto pasado africano ligado a la esclavitud no encuentran cabida alguna en un "venir de los barcos" que parece acotarse a los siglos XIX y XX'.[30]

Crucially, it is not only the question of race that is highlighted by 'flipping' these roles, however: it is the link between race and economic exclusion. By presenting his black characters in the most economically and politically disenfranchised position possible, that of enslaved workers, Cucurto's chaotic popular world pushes the dual components of the anti-Peronist 'cabecita negra' stereotype (class and race) to their extreme. The racialization of this social category represented a prevalent strategy in the 'othering' of Peronism,[31] and Cucurto's unleashing of his unruly band on the 'orderly' world of Buenos Aires smacks of an overtly Peronist literary revenge. By exposing well-worn discourses of Argentine identity as both limited and exclusionary, therefore, the text paves the way for the creation of its own, new definitions.

This ties in with the dominant themes of Cucurto's other literary works, which are most commonly set in the *barrio* of Constitución and present themselves as a tongue-in-cheek attempt to 'document' Argentina's contemporary immigrant communities. This project is intimately connected with defining the popular and its place in the national political arena. Alejandro Grimson and Elizabeth Jelin argue that the 1990s saw a re-signification of what immigration meant for the country and its economic future, with both mainstream national media and government conceptualizing the phenomenon as a 'social problem' rather than a positive contribution.[32] Although in reality overall immigration from neighbouring countries (including Peru) had not increased, Grimson remarks that more of these arrivals were settling in large urban centres rather than in border regions, and more immigrants were

---

29 On the place of whiteness in Argentina's self-representation see Chapter 2 of Ignacio Aguiló, *The Darkening Nation*.

30 Claudia Briones, 'Formaciones de alteridad: contextos globales, procesos nacionales y provinciales', in *Cartografías argentinas: políticas indigenistas y formaciones provinciales de alteridad*, ed. by Claudia Briones (Buenos Aires: Antropofagia, 2005), pp. 11–43, at p. 25.

31 Garguin, pp. 173–74.

32 Alejandro Grimson and Elizabeth Jelin, 'Introducción', in *Migraciones regionales hacia la Argentina: diferencia, desigualdad y derechos*, p. 9. In the same volume, see also Elizabeth Jelin, 'Migraciones y derechos: instituciones y prácticas sociales en la construcción de la igualdad y la diferencia', p. 48.

arriving from Peru and Bolivia, with fewer Chileans and Uruguayans.[33] In this respect, Grimson and Jelin's observation that early twentieth-century immigration is studied by historians, whereas arrivals of recent decades fall to social scientists is revealing.[34] The heightened visibility of this immigration through increased racial diversity and presence in central, urban areas led to a shift in discourse from both government and the media, and a separation between accepted historic immigration and the contemporary situation took place.

In response to this political context, Cucurto strategically positions himself in relation to the Argentine literary canon, claiming literary parentage in Roberto Arlt's linguistic incorporation of immigrant communities into Argentine literature.[35] This serves to provide a type of 'legitimized marginality' for his presentation of contemporary immigrant communities, establishing a narrative of continuity between today's immigrants and 'historic' immigration. European immigrants, now unquestioningly accepted as part of Argentina's national narrative, are replaced in Cucurto's narrative with arrivals from Bolivia or Paraguay. The illusion of 'newness' of current waves of immigration is therefore broken down, incorporated into a long history that has acquired legitimacy within the national narrative.

In *1810*, Cucurto confronts head-on the implicit narrative of whiteness underpinning this discourse of national identity, which becomes one of the crucial factors in defining 'acceptable' and 'unacceptable' immigration, and the implicit racialization of national identity discourses. This construction draws self-conscious parallels between the response to contemporary immigrants framed as 'threatening' the supposed definition of the nation and the circumstances surrounding the emergence of Peronism. Enrique Garguin argues that with the arrival of Peronism the dominant Argentine national identity narratives expose themselves as representing only a part of the nation – the white, middle-class, porteño vision.[36] Garguin notes that it was immigration from the provinces to Buenos Aires that sparked this recognition of an internal 'other', and that the identification of Perón's supporters as 'cabecitas negras' racialized this social categorization (173). Cucurto's adoption of enslaved black characters as the focus of his text presents this implicit dual narrative of poverty and 'non-whiteness' pushed to its extreme. Garguin illustrates the way that this association was used to protect a limited definition of the nation, claiming that 'this shaped a discursive trend that symbolically denied that Perón's followers were members of the true nation' (174). By re-igniting these familiar discourses, Cucurto exposes the persistence of this restrictive definition of 'los argentinos', translated to the contemporary incarnation of the same debate.

33  Grimson, 'Nuevas xenofobias', p. 77.
34  Grimson and Jelins, 'Introducción', p. 9
35  Alvaro Bernal, 'No saben que yo soy el Rey del realismo atolondrado', Interview with Washington Cucurto, *Destiempos*, 10 (2007).
36  Garguin, '"Los Argentinos Descendemos de Los Barcos"'.

The narrator figure that Cucurto has developed throughout his prose works is integral to deconstructing this narrative of Argentine identity. While Santiago Vega, Cucurto's real-life incarnation, was born in Quilmes in the Buenos Aires province, his alter ego claims a variety of contradictory origins, most often constructing himself as a black Dominican. Cucurto therefore extracts his narrator from the national narrative and embodies the polar opposite to the white, European focus of the dominant Argentine (porteño) identity narratives. There is also another level to this deliberate extraction, as Cucurto explains in an interview:

> Entonces este [personaje] es un poco tucumano, un poco dominicano, un poco paraguayo, un poco de todo según como la gente lo ve. Porque siempre la gente lo ve de manera despectiva. Si sos negro y comés mal y te portás mal, si hacés esas cosas, nunca va a ser argentino, sos paraguayo, peruano.[37]

The figure of 'Cucurto' therefore represents a direct challenge to national identity narratives, highlighting the fusion of racial and class prejudice in the determination of what is accepted within the national.

The racialized dimension of Cucurto's presentation of power structures in *1810* is also invoked in the text's presentation of the ownership of historical knowledge. The close connections between 'official' history and the centres of power are consistently underlined, and whiteness and belonging to the bourgeoisie are used interchangeably: we find recurrent references to 'los libros de historia escritos por la oligarquía blanca', 'los infames historiadores blancos', and the 'historiadores de manos blancos' (12–13). The popular is therefore implicitly redefined as the non-white, directly inverting the hegemonic structures identified within the text. The work *1810* therefore repositions black characters at the heart of the Argentine national narrative, subverting their traditional role in accounts of the independence wars as cannon fodder under the command of heroic white generals. This 'blackening' of Argentina's history is carried through every element of the text. The highly parodic prologue sees Cucurto discover his descendancy from San Martín, thanks to the hero's love affair with Cucurto's great grandmother, Olga. This love affair, the union of the *padre de la patria* with an enslaved black girl, produces a male child who usurps San Martín as the dominant heroic figure in the novel's second half. This re-instates blackness into contemporary Argentine identity, allied with the strongest claim to 'argentinidad' possible: continuing the bloodline of San Martín. This descendancy is given added potency by the invention of a male bloodline: whereas San Martín is only known to have fathered a daughter, Cucurto offers a male heir to continue the heroic virility the *padre de la patria* represents. The illusion of Argentina's

---

37 Timo Berger, '"Yo actualmente soy el mejor escritor dominicano sin duda". Entrevista a Washington Cucurto'.

whiteness is therefore attacked at its core, subverted through a new symbolic line of paternity beginning with the most potent identity symbol of all: the *padre de la patria*.

This 'love story' between Olga and San Martín also furnishes Argentina with another element missing from the past: the creation of a 'national romance' that harmoniously integrates the nation's different races. Sommer suggests that many of Latin America's nineteenth-century 'national romances' used a mixed-race romantic union to project the political harmony that their war-torn incipient nations required.[38] Argentina's most significant national romance, *Amalia*, opts for the union of two white lovers, however, leaving Argentina without this symbolic literary fusion. The love affair between Olga and San Martín provides this absent union, but far from representing a harmonious erotic fusion of racial difference, it blends a pastiche of romantic discourse with biting political critique of social and economic structures. The love story of San Martín and Olga is tinged with the melodramatic clichés of the *folletín*, partly constructed as a 'love against all odds' that ends in tragedy, thwarted by the cruel world surrounding the lovers, but resulting in the potentially redemptive birth of a son.[39] The exaggerated, melodramatic tone of this love affair shrouds it in insincerity, with each affirmation of this supposedly all-conquering love quickly followed by reminders of the power dynamics at work in this relationship. Olga's 'folletinesque' insistence that 'ni siquiera tu ejército, ni mi condición de esclava y la tuya de hombre blanco, nos separará' is followed by the information that '[San Martín] se bajó los pantalones, le subió la trusa y cabalgó, usurpador, todo lo que quiso' (39), a clear-cut reminder of the exploitation that underpins this supposed romance. The love story becomes a foil for hypocrisy and exploitative, unequal relationships of power.

### The Neobarroco/Neobarroso: Argentina se tropicaliza

The text's assault on the traditional idea of 'cultura' is underpinned by an aesthetic of rupture and excess that announces the boisterous intrusion of the popular into the bourgeois form *par excellence*, the novel. Cucurto's model of literary subversion is closely linked to the *neobarroco/neobarroso*: he frequently cites Cuban poets José Lezama Lima, Reinaldo Arenas, and Severo Sarduy as significant influences, alongside Argentines Néstor Perlongher and Osvaldo Lamborghini.[40] What Cucurto draws from these authors is an aesthetic

---

38  Sommer, *Foundational Fictions*, p. 81.

39  The text even hints at the Christ-like significance of this child: '[El general] lo abrazó con el amor más grande del mundo, el de un padre. Un hijo, el hijo, un padre, el padre...' (67). By shifting from the indirect to the direct article, from the idea of a son to the concept of 'the' son, the text instantly evokes the religious connotations of the child and this father–son relationship.

40  See, for example, Bernal, 'No saben que yo soy el Rey'. These authors' names also appear frequently throughout Cucurto's poetry. For a detailed exploration of the

of rupture and excess whose presence is clearly felt in his own writing. The adoption of this current also has strong symbolic importance for the positioning of Cucurto's work. Perlongher, the most prominent theorist of the *neobarroco* within Argentina, has stressed both the lack of baroque tradition in the country and its fundamentally 'un-Argentine' quality as a literary aesthetic, claiming it to be 'out of place' in River Plate literary circles, which he describes as 'desconfiados por principio de toda tropicalidad'.[41]

This idea of an absence of tropicality is closely related to the other national narratives challenged by Cucurto. It goes beyond literature to narratives linking Argentina's geography, climate, and population make-up: the rejection of 'tropicality' again comes at the intersection of Argentina's relationship with a narrative of whiteness, and the vision of the country's position within the region. The rejection of 'tropicality' can be seen in school Geography textbooks, which, like school History, offered a remarkably homogeneous and unchanging vision from the 1940s to the start of the 1990s.[42] These texts helped to establish a narrative of whiteness as Argentina's 'natural' state by presenting it as an inevitable outcome of the country's climate. The textbooks schematically divided Latin American countries into 'andinos', 'templados', and 'tropicales', using this to explain the ethnic composition of each nation. According to this narrative, Argentina is 'templado', and the textbooks therefore 'deducen de manera más o menos explícita una propensión del territorio a mantener un predominio de raza blanca, ya sea por eliminación natural de otras razas o por atracción de una población mayoritariamente blanca'.[43] This conclusion therefore 'explains' the 'absence' of non-white ethnicities and presents this as a natural characteristic of the nation's territory. At the same time, this positioning distances Argentina from other Latin American nations and associates the country with those of Northern Europe.[44] As highlighted in my Introduction, the creation of a racialized national narrative finds its origin in the accounts of independence produced by Mitre, whose celebration of the nation's glory is fundamentally bound up with a depiction of Argentina as an intrinsically white society. This insistence on the 'natural whiteness' of Argentina converts all other ethnicities into 'unnatural abnormalities', beyond the boundaries of

---

neobarroco/neobarroso in Argentina see Ben Bollig, *Néstor Perlongher: The Poetic Search for an Argentine Marginal Voice* (Cardiff: University of Wales Press, 2008).

41  Néstor Perlongher, 'Caribe transplatino: introducción a la poesía neobarroca cubana y rioplatense', in *Prosa plebeya: ensayos, 1980–1992* (Buenos Aires: Colihue, 1997), pp. 93–102, at p. 97.

42  Romero, *La Argentina en la escuela*, pp. 84, 181–82.

43  Romero, *La Argentina en la escuela*, pp. 96–97. Romero also highlights the internal contradictions of this simplistic and deterministic narrative, which positions Chile as a predominantly Andean country, particularly well adapted to 'support' indigenous populations. Ibid.

44  Romero, *La Argentina en la escuela*, p. 98.

the true nation. Indigenous and black Argentines are therefore not simply excluded from any stake in the nation within this narrative, but are actively willed into non-existence to restore the territory's natural balance. In the words of Briones, they are presented as insignificant entities who are 'siempre a punto de terminar de desaparecer por completo'.[45] Argentina's narrative of whiteness is therefore conceived of as a Darwinian tale of evolution towards racial purity, where the nation progresses towards optimum harmony with the natural characteristics of its territory. By positioning himself within a 'tropical' literary current, one associated with Cuba and with little history in Argentine literature, Cucurto declares an aesthetic rupture with the national tradition, and performs a conscious 'Latinamericanization' of the sphere of Argentine cultural reference.

### Dirtying Literature: 'Dama tocada' and 'El Phale'

Also key to Cucurto's use of the *neobarroco* is the idea of 'mal gusto' at the heart of Lezama Lima's baroque: an aesthetic of rule breaking that seeks to fracture accepted forms by contaminating them.[46] Perlongher describes Osvaldo Lamborghini's development of the *neobarroso* as a heightening of this intent, describing it as a 'dirtying' of Argentine literature, a process of contamination and debasement.[47] The intrusion of 'mal gusto' and the 'dirtying' of both literature and history can be seen very clearly in *1810*, linking the promise of a 'popular history' with an assault on accepted cultural forms.

The most direct representation of this 'contamination' of literature in *1810* comes in Cucurto's re-writing of two canonical Argentine short stories. The 'newly discovered' papers presented at the end of the text offer a version of Cortázar's 'Casa tomada', rendered as 'Dama tocada', and Borges's 'El Aleph', inverted to become 'El Phale'. In Cucurto's re-telling, these unconventional versions are the originals, written by the enslaved and used by posterior famous writers in an act of 'infamia' (208). Argentine literature is re-founded in this move, its greatest works stemming from the influence of those far removed from the traditional political and cultural elite. This underscores the significance of the way in which Cucurto represents the independence narrative. These literary inversions form a crucial part of the text's wider attack on the structures of cultural hierarchy that I have been tracing throughout the text, tying history and literature together as part of the same bourgeois construction that represses the 'distasteful' exuberance of the world of *barbarie*.

45  Briones, 'Formaciones de alteridad', p. 25.
46  Significantly, neither Perlongher nor Cucurto cite Carpentier among their *neobarroco* influences. Ben Bollig explains that in Perlongher's construction of the tendency, 'Carpentier is held up as an example of the academic, state-sponsored *barroco*, rather than the rogue spirit found in Góngora and Lezama' (168).
47  Perlongher, p. 97 and Bollig, p. 167.

Some of the play in these parodic stories is a deliberate, tongue-in-cheek insertion of outrageous behaviour and offensive language into the texts (which would make their later versions 'sanitized' re-writings by white, well-to-do authors). The sedate daily activities of knitting and cooking described in Cortázar's opening sequence are replaced by a decadent, sex-driven existence in Cucurto. As the title 'Dama tocada' suggests, the tale is irreverent in the extreme: Victoria Ocampo appears as 'Victrola', part of her name replaced by a derogatory slang term, and we learn that she and her sister 'tenían de noviecitos a dos boludos que se pasaban el día leyendo literatura francesa' (211).[48] 'El Phale' openly declares its sexualization of Borges's story from the title itself, and the story's content does not disappoint this expectation. Graphic sexual descriptions open the text, expressed in extremely colloquial terms and evoking the (female) body's most taboo physical processes: menstruation and defecation. These transform Borges's narrator's wistful longing for a decorporalized woman, the deceased Beatriz Viterbo, into an extremely bodily representation of the female engaged in sexual acts. Significantly, these descriptions are brought into relationship with the act of writing: 'Con la punta de mi pija, con sangre y puntitos de mierda en un acto cucurtiano escribo' (220). Writing is also contaminated, made physical and sexualized, rather than remaining on the plane of philosophical ideas that Borges's story inhabits. The text revels in the inclusion of language that defies any definition of 'lo culto': the slang terms used to convey the graphic sexual acts are as much an assault on the carefully constructed literary masterpieces as the content of the acts themselves.

These linguistic intrusions are accompanied by explicitly political inversions that reinforce the link between a 'popular aesthetic' and the socio-political dimension of the text's challenge to the lettered city. The supposed banality of the daily existence presented in the first paragraphs of 'Casa tomada' is revealed as a privileged lifestyle by transposing the scene of the action to an entirely different type of housing: the large colonial house becomes a 'yotibenco', a slang term for tenement-style immigrant housing derived by reversing 'conventillo'.[49] Whereas Cortázar's fantastic story takes life in the house as the recognized point from which the strange events will depart, Cucurto de-naturalizes the ownership of the house in an overtly political statement: 'La casa es el tema nuestro y de 40 millones de argentinos. La casa siempre imposible, el sueño eterno, lejano impróspero para nuestra pobreza' (213). Owning property is transported to the realm of the fantastic, exposing the class implications of the serene normality the opening of Cortázar's story presents.

---

48  The word 'victrola' can also refer to a type of phonograph often sold in the San Telmo market of Buenos Aires, a play on words that recalls the *porteño* setting.

49  *Conventillos* are associated with the wave of European immigration to Argentina in the late nineteenth century and early twentieth. This anachronistic use of this type of housing again serves to underline the links Cucurto is making between different periods of immigration and their widely differing place in the national narrative.

These subversions culminate in a final twist on Cortázar's plot that emphasizes the political implications of the original tale and asserts an alternative allegiance with popular values. At the conclusion of 'Dama tocada', we discover that each locked room in the house contains a family who will be trapped in the isolated space forever, cut off from the vibrancy and the community surrounding them. Whereas in the original tale the anxiety focuses on who might get *into* the house, here the final anxiety revolves around being able to get *out* and into a space of community that is taken to define popular life. The colonial mansion transforms from a longed-for space of protection into a suffocating, restrictive trap as Cortázar's nightmare is turned on its head. In dragging this story through the 'mud', Cucurto re-positions the popular as the side of right in the battle between *civilización* and *barbarie*, aiming to position the reader's loyalty on the same side.

In the re-writing of 'El Aleph' Cucurto also translates Borges's story to a different social milieu, which is again used to create an energetic and chaotic retelling as well as provide a political moral, serving almost as a fable. He adds a Borgesian layer by constructing his tale as a parodic detectivesque search for the meaning of the 'Phale', which has many incarnations throughout the story, from a dead woman whose body is stuffed with drugs, to '[el] gran Phale yanqui que es el ciberespacio de yahoo', which receives the following description: 'En estas épocas ya ni soñar maravillas se puede, pues tú tienes tu Phale en cada locutorio coreano al alcance de la mano' (221). All the wonder and amazement of Borges's story is deflated out of it, transformed into the banality of daily existence and corrupted through its use in the seedy underworld in which the story is located.

The translation of the story's setting is shown most clearly in the manifestation of the Phale as the name of a business fronting a drugs and prostitution operation: '*El Phale, ornamentación y festejos*'. While initially this baffles the narrator, he comes to see the sense in expressing something that contains all points of the universe in these terms: 'ornamentación, festejos, Phale, con el correr de las horas ya no me parecían palabras tan extrañas, sino palabras justas, lamborghinianas' (233). The exuberant sexualization of the Aleph shifts from seeming an incongruent distraction from the search for meaning to becoming the centre of meaning itself; Cucurto places his own literary aesthetic in the position of being capable of explaining reality to the same extent as any serious, philosophical text.

In a similar way to 'Dama tocada', the text engages in further forms of contamination that challenge the function of the original story. Borges sets his tale in the *barrio* of Constitución, which is now the hub of Cucurto's fictional world. Cucurto takes advantage to drag Borges's philosophical construction to the level of the exuberance of daily reality. The setting here is once again the vitality of an immigrant community, and Cucurto's narrator announces: '*lo que debería yo estar haciendo es escribiendo el Bolialef!*' (219). This statement combines the title of Borges's story with *boliviano* or even *bolita*, a common derogatory term for Bolivian immigrants also used for others who conform to the physical and socio-economic stereotype that the term implies. The text 'contaminates' the canonical version of the story by again aggressively redefining the national narrative of whiteness; the eruption of contemporary immigrant communities into the tale re-configures Borges's original as a silencing of this vitality in favour of a world of lofty ideas. Cucurto's re-definition of the canon violently exposes 'silences' unimagined by the originals, questioning the definition of culture that this literature has helped to create.

The 'contamination' of literature Cucurto engages in here therefore employs two interrelated strategies: it incorporates the intrusion of popular language and graphic sexual acts into the texts, along with challenges to the implicit class and racial assumptions that underpin canonical texts and interact with the national construct. It is an aggressive 'contamination' of the bourgeois by the popular, of the philosophical by the sexual, of the national with the outside, of the acceptable with the obscene. This process provides a drastic rewriting of the Argentine literary canon, but it is an operation with far wider implications in Cucurto, which can be expressed as the rejection of the 'correct'.

### Overturning the Bourgeois: Rebellion and Provocation

While Cucurto's exuberant inversion of canonical tales generates a radical and energetic rebellion against narrative forms of *civilización*, the text's rejection of any imposition of 'correctness' results in some textual strategies likely to sit uncomfortably with the reader. In abandoning the tried and tested literary codes of the lettered city, *1810* also casts out any idea of political correctness, and the text is replete with exaggeratedly stereotypical characterizations of race, gender, and sexuality that transgress contemporary ideas of acceptability. The most evident of these is the portrayal of the black characters within the text, which mercilessly evokes racial stereotypes of eroticized black females and well-endowed black men who are only interested in dancing, sex, and having a good time. Doris Sommer goes as far as to wonder whether *1810*'s 'sexist, racist and just plain smutty language' is designed just 'to get a rise out of readers whose liberalism he strains to the breaking point with elaborately staged bad taste'.[50] This 'bad taste' is certainly a defining feature of *1810*, and its role within the text requires careful consideration, demanding that we decide how to respond to these clear transgressions of any idea of political correctness.

If we choose to condemn the text for its deliberately insensitive portrayal of race and gender, we are refusing to enter into the challenge it presents: to abandon *civilización* in favour of an energetic embracing of *barbarie*. This can be perceived as a game created by the text, or perhaps more usefully as a 'carnivalesque' temporary inversion of the status quo. Cucurto evokes a carnivalesque spirit in his references to Armando Discépolo and his

---

50  Doris Sommer, 'Cucurto's Cardboard Coloring Book: Argentine Independence and Other Stories to Recycle', *Perífrasis*, 1(1) (2010), 7–15, at p. 8.

*grotesco criollo*, and even directly alludes to Rabelais in his description of the 'pantagruélica' living conditions of immigrants in one of the episodes he recounts (219). Mikhail Bakhtin stresses the overturning of societal hierarchies and norms as a defining feature of carnival, which becomes a 'temporary liberation from the prevailing truth and from the established order' (9–10). The raucous appropriation of the most solemn and official of all Argentina's national commemorations in *1810* can be interpreted as a direct inversion along these carnivalesque lines: it is a defiant interpellation of the most institutionalized national event in order to resignify its potential.

Seen from this perspective, the text's provocative 'bad taste' becomes an integral part of its extreme embracing of the chaotic and the carefree, presented as an invigorated alternative to the sterility of more controlled cultural forms. The reinsertion of the body into sanitized official spaces and insistence on its materiality become significant reintegrations of a 'folk culture' in Bakhtin's terms, perhaps more widely definable as 'the popular' for Cucurto in the sense of barbaric 'incultura' outlined above. Interpreting this integration in terms of a carnivalesque spirit reveals the relationship between the rejection of traditional, more sober literary form and the inclusion of the body with greater intention than merely to titillate or provoke the reader, as Sarlo's and Sommer's comments above respectively suggest. This is crucial to the anti-canonical rewriting of independence that Cucurto's text undertakes, as it is this subversion of the sobriety of independence that underpins its aggressive insertion of *barbarie* into one of the pillars of *civilización*.

The carnivalesque also encompasses an idea of laughter that demands a particular relationship between reader and text. The laughter of carnival, for Bakhtin, is a utopian laughter of the people, both mocking and joyful, as opposed to either the 'negative satire' or 'recreational drollery' of contemporary understanding.[51] Within *1810*, therefore, this laughter requires us to enter into the popular universe created by the text, rather than either remaining outside its reach or dismissing its mechanisms as empty entertainment. In order to embrace the text's universe of *barbarie*, we must participate in its all-encompassing, subversive carnivalesque laughter. Cucurto's text challenges the reader to abandon the 'straitjacket' of liberal discourse and take the alternative he creates on its own terms, as an unleashing of an exaggerated *barbarie* that underscores stereotypes ultimately emerging from the discourse of *civilización*, and his appropriation of these stereotypes forms part of this challenge.

By conducting this game of inversion through independence, the text engages with the status of this period as a focal point for projections of the nation, and employs this to target the intersection of cultural norms, exclusionary discourses of national identity, and the distribution of political and economic power associated with the liberal project. If we wish to enter

---

51 Bakhtin, Mikhail. M., *Rabelais and His World* (Bloomington: Indiana University Press, 1984), pp. 11–12.

the text's world of *barbarie*, however, we must be prepared to temporarily abandon the literary expectations of *civilización*.

## *Mariano Moreno y un teatro de operaciones*: Democracy and Revolution

Santos Iñurrieta's *Mariano Moreno y un teatro de operaciones* represents a very different engagement with the idea of the popular in both aesthetic and political terms. The play is directly connected with the cultural context of the Bicentenary, being first performed in 2010 as part of the Bicentenary programme of the left-leaning Centro Cultural de la Cooperación Floreal Gorini (CCC) in the heart of the Corrientes theatre district in Buenos Aires. Its self-categorization as a 'seria comedia política' and première by 'el bachín teatro', the company directed by Santos Iñurrieta and renowned for its Brechtian performance style, stress the political intent behind the work.[52] *Moreno* depicts a cast attempting to rehearse a play about the eponymous *prócer*, thwarted in their theatrical endeavours by the absence of the actor playing the lead role, discontent within the company towards the increasingly authoritarian and self-important director, and the presence of a threatening mob outside the theatre door. Combining a 'play within a play' mechanism and a *Waiting for Godot*-esque structure, the text is both intensely metatheatrical and resolutely non-naturalistic. Its self-reflexive style draws heavily on Brechtian theatrical conventions, producing a questioning of historical narrative that demonstrates clear affinities with the other texts in my corpus.

The construction of history is at the forefront of the text's metatheatrical games. The play's action follows a rehearsal process, allowing for much discussion of what should be included and excluded from the final stage version. This is given a metahistorical focus through the constant debates about the relative significance of each historical event and the different political framing that will be given to the work through the choices the company make. A reference to the arrival of the 'actor oficial' sparks an instant self-reflexive digression into the implications of 'official history':

Asistente: (amenazante) ¿A qué se refiere con "el actor oficial..."?
Actriz: (violenta) ¡Conteste!
Moreno: Al actor que ustedes esperan que interprete a Moreno.
Director: No se referirá a un actor que interprete a Moreno según los intereses de la clase dominante, ¿no?[53]

---

52 The company writes its name in lowercase, as reproduced here. For further information on the bachín teatro's formation see Jorge Dubatti, 'Manuel Santos Iñurrieta y "el bachín teatro": post-neoliberalismo, arte y política', in *Mariano Moreno y un teatro de operaciones; La gracia de tener*, by Manuel Santos Iñurrieta (Buenos Aires: Ediciones del CCC Centro Cultural de Cooperación Floreal Gorini, 2012), pp. 11–18; and Raúl Serrano, 'El bachín: teatro militante', *La revista del CCC*, 11 (2011).

53 Manuel Santos Iñurrieta, *Mariano Moreno y un teatro de operaciones*, Scene 4, pp. 24–25.

This humorous misinterpretation portrays history as an ideological battle-ground, with each member of the cast ready to pounce on any indication that one in their midst supports interpretations associated with the elite. As the play progresses, the director's attempts to suppress uncomfortable facts or skim over ideologically complex issues become increasingly obvious, and he is held to account by his rebellious troupe of actors. His dismissal of Santiago de Liniers's counterrevolutionary uprising in the wake of the May Revolution as 'un hecho menor' is immediately seized upon by the company, who weave this event into contemporary ideological frameworks by positioning it as the nation's first coup. Similarly, the director's assertion that the alleged murder of statesman Moreno is an insignificant detail generates outrage, as the company perceive this as 'un asesinato político, fundante de nuestra historia más oscura'.[54] This therefore underscores the ideological urgency of selecting material for a narrative of the past, with different framings and omissions taken as direct indications of the speaker's political leanings.

As well as underscoring the process of selection implicit in the construc-tion of historical narrative, the text engages in questioning the boundaries of what constitutes historical fact. The director criticizes his cast for their 'erroneous' version of history when 'Actriz' pronounces a speech supposedly by Juana Azurduy, a *mestiza* guerrilla leader in the independence wars who, the director insists, left no written records.[55] The words Actriz attributes to Azurduy are actually taken from a speech given by Eva Perón on 1 May 1952.[56] This deliberate use of anachronism therefore establishes a pattern of ideological affinity across distinct historical periods, translating the conflicts of the past into politically relevant fables for the present, and discarding chronology as a valid tool for understanding the past. It disputes the assump-tion that 'good' history depends upon the accurate transmission of dates and facts, presenting its alternative vision as containing more truth than a strictly factual account.

This challenge to traditional historiography therefore displays significant shared concerns with texts that could be approached through the postmodern historical novel framework. The explicit insistence on the ideological shaping of history in *Moreno* places constant emphasis on the question of who writes history, and to what intent. Crucially, however, this game takes the fact that knowledge is constructed as its starting point rather than its final conclusion, and proudly presents its own ideologically determined reading of the past. Postmodern lessons of history's narrative shaping are applied in order to warn the spectator of the political undertones of particular readings, but this is

---

54  Iñurrieta, *Mariano Moreno*, Scene 25, p. 56.

55  As a lower-class *mestiza*, Azurduy received little education, learning only basic literacy. Catherine Davies, *South American Independence: Gender, Politics, Text* (Liverpool: Liverpool University Press, 2006), pp. 137, 162.

56  'Discurso de Evita en el Día del Trabajador – Plaza de Mayo (1952)', reproduced online by *El historiador*.

framed as a tool that enables us to destabilize the narrative of the dominant classes, rather than relativizing interpretations of the past. When we read *Moreno* in this light, this distinction means that history can be reconfirmed in a traditional didactic role: it encourages us to unravel the underlying ideological codes behind narratives in order to insert them into a politicized historical scheme with a clearly defined ideological 'truth' at its heart.

*Pluralism and Didacticism: Brecht and* el bachín
This politicized focus is underpinned in *Mariano Moreno y un teatro de operaciones* by the play's use of Brechtian conventions. Brecht's 'epic theatre', which aims to produce the famous *verfremdungseffekt*, is defined by practices now familiar to a theatre-going public: an episodic dramatic structure, destruction of the 'fourth wall' by drawing our attention to the mechanics of stagecraft before us, and a didactic focus throughout the work. Santos Iñurrieta's *Moreno* offers an accomplished contemporary rendering of many aspects of Brechtian technique. The application of these dramatic conventions to such a familiar narrative is designed to provide a 'jolt' distancing us from the events presented, rather than allowing them to wash over us as a reassuring retelling of a story known by heart, and therefore endows this familiar narrative with a distinctly political mission.

The original production, which I saw in September 2010 at the CCC, was unmistakeably Brechtian in style.[57] The audience were transported to the world of epic theatre from the very first scene: a sonorous, lyrical speech entitled 'Quién es el que regresa'. The monologue, performed as a voice-over by renowned actor Patricio Contreras, was accompanied by a simple melody for guitar and one voice performed live on stage, overlaid with the occasional tapping of typewriter keys, struck one at a time in an irregular, disjointed rhythm. The contrasting layers of this opening soundscape provided a Brechtian 'distancing' from the action on stage. The seductive appeal of Contreras's measured, almost hypnotic delivery, mirroring the film of gently breaking waves projected onto the cyclorama (the white gauze at the back of the stage), was disrupted by the contrasting simplicity of the live musical performance. The jarring rhythms of the recorded voice, live music, and disjointed non-musical sound therefore prevented the audience from surrendering fully to the rhetorical eloquence of Contreras's words, seemingly fulfilling the Brechtian intention that artistic beauty should not create an 'illusion' masking its own status as performance. The allusion to the crafting of the play present in the incorporation of typewriter sounds provided a further reminder of the constructed nature of the action before us, asserting from the outset that we are expected to perform the role of Brechtian critical spectator.

---

57 Santos Iñurrieta, *Mariano Moreno y un teatro de operaciones*, dir. by Manuel Santos Iñurrieta.

The technical aspects of staging in the original production also reflected familiar principles of Brechtian technique. Stark, white lighting complemented a simple, non-representational set composed of three adjoining platforms and a moveable freestanding block, more akin to a makeshift arrangement for rehearsals than a fully finished set. The actors' heavy make-up reinforced their status as performers, their faces painted white with thick black eyebrows and a smudged grey circle in the hollow of their cheeks. Costume once again corresponded to the restricted colour palette present in the other technical aspects of staging, combining to create an entirely monochrome setting. Fused with the exaggerated physicality of the performers on stage, the black and white hues hinted at cinematic influences, evoking the era of silent film. Harshly juxtaposed tones, reminiscent of the heightened contrasts employed by German expressionist cinema, contributed an eerie unreality, while the actors' exaggerated comic gesticulation evinced Charlie Chaplin's distinctive physical comedy.[58] This incorporation of allusions to highly stylized cinematic technique contributed to the rupture with naturalistic approaches, perhaps recalling Brecht's own enthusiasm for cinema's 'epic' potential.[59]

Although most of these aspects of staging are not prescribed in the printed edition of the play, its intended Brechtian performance style is carefully built into the work. By eschewing traditional character names in favour of generic denominations such as 'Actor' and 'Actriz' (with the exception of Moreno, who is still clearly denoted as an actor) the rejection of conventional characterization is clear and the self-reflexive emphasis on theatricality reinforced, complemented by the fact that the setting of the action within a theatre is specified in the stage directions. Brechtian performance style is also continually alluded to throughout the work, which contains frequent self-reflexive references to its dramatic techniques. In Scene 4, which introduces us to the rehearsal process that structures the play, the director lectures his cast on the conventions of epic theatre in a bombastic style that is undermined by the more practical and immediate concerns of his cast. This serves as a reminder of the work's self-presentation as political theatre, but more significantly it ridicules the temptation to treat epic theatre in reverential terms that would position it as part of a bourgeois cultural repertoire rather than as a disruptive

---

58  Clowning motifs recur in the aesthetic of Santos Iñurrieta's work as playwright/director, from *Mientras cuido de Carmela* (2013) to *La gracia de tener* (2011–12 production). An interest in cinema, and Chaplin in particular, is displayed in his 2004 production, *Charly (detrás de la sonrisa)*, which depicts a group of early film stars who unite behind the figure of Charly, and in his Chaplin inspired one-man play, *Crónicas de un comediante* (published 2009).

59  Brecht saw cinema as an ideal vehicle for the impact he wished to have on audiences, arguing, 'For the film the principles of non-Aristotelian drama (a type of drama not dependent on empathy, mimesis) are immediately acceptable.' Bertolt Brecht, *Brecht on Theatre: The Development of an Aesthetic*, ed. and trans. by John Willet (London: Eyre Methuen, 1973), p. 50.

force. The episodic structure of the text ensures a constant shifting in pace and movement between different types of discourse, allowing the audience very little time to adjust to any one style. Highly comic interactions give way to scenes of poetic solemnity, only to return almost immediately to frustratingly circular discussions among the cast over how they should proceed in their dramatic endeavours. The actual historical narration is primarily undertaken by comical puppets representing Domingo French and Antonio Luis Beruti, revolutionary figures most famous for distributing rosettes to the crowd gathered on 25 May, who offer a radically condensed overview of hundreds of years of history in a series of brief exchanges (Scenes 2, 9, 11, and 22), employing simple, almost childlike language entirely at odds with the serious political denunciations behind their words. They describe the Spanish arriving 'con barquitos muy bonitos' and their rapid dialogue revolves around the simple but ideologically loaded question '¿todo bien con los españoles?', which receives a damning response: 'Sí, todo bien. Excepto por la espada, la cruz y los espejitos de colores. Excepto por la forma de adornar a los nativos con cadenas, grilletes y latigazos.'[60] The inappropriately childish language is maintained in the diminutive 'espejitos', while the euphemistic choice of 'adornar' to describe chains and physical punishments is imbued with intense irony. The incongruity at the heart of this scene is essential to the destabilizing of the audience's perspective the play seeks to produce, and is consistently exploited as a comic mechanism throughout the rest of the work.

The departure from linear narrative created by this constant shifting between types of discourse is self-reflexively acknowledged as a way of engaging the audience's critical potential, as expressed in a metatheatrical aside spoken by Actriz:

> Este texto que digo ahora es otra interrupción, porque si siempre procedemos conforme a la forma, y a la estructura dramática, comenzamos a pareceremos tanto a las bestias, puro impulso y sin razón.[61]

In rejecting linear progress through a theatrical work, this statement divorces the concepts of order and reason so firmly wedded in positivist thought (a significant influence on the Argentine liberal political tradition). 'Order' is instead taken to mean blind conformity, and departure from this established path becomes the means to achieve true, reasoned, engaged thought. This inverts the civilization/barbarism paradigm, presenting order as mere base instinct, the antithesis to thought, while creativity and disorder are placed in the positive pole of the binary. This forms part of a wider commentary throughout the work on the workings of hegemonic discourse and its normalizing impulse. This critique is focused on the concept of 'el sentido común', which is heavily satirized throughout the play, particularly in Scenes 16 and 24.

---

60  Santos Iñurrieta, *Mariano Moreno*, Scene 2, p. 21.
61  Santos Iñurrieta, *Mariano Moreno*, Scene 5, p. 28.

Scene 16, entitled 'Sobre un sentido común', follows on from the director's attempts to impose his own artistic vision as an example of 'common sense'. His egotistic and self-important approach to artistic creation sees him in raptures over a scene of his own devising, which consists of a piano hanging from a thread, spinning and dripping water with a voice-over stating 'si los pueblos no se ilustran'.[62] The cast seize upon the assertion that this patronizing and paternalistic imposition of bourgeois cultural values represents 'common sense' and immediately engage in a parodic quick-fire illustration of the unspoken implications of the concept. Their dialogue fills the ambiguous signifier with a damning portrayal of bourgeois commonplaces, structured absurdly around the motif of the piano:

> *Todos: (A público. Uno a la vez)* ¡Cómo están robando pianos últimamente! ¿No? - A un amigo mío ya le robaron dos pianos en lo que va del año. Antes los dejabas abiertos en la vereda y no pasaba nada. - Es la juventud que está enajenada, todo el día con el rock sinfónico, ven un piano, te pegan un tiro sin preguntar. [...] - Y uno pasa por las villas y están llenas de televisores y pianos - No quieren trabajar, con la cantidad de pozos que hay para hacer... [...] Yo solo pido memoria completa - Y yo exportar libremente.[63]

This fear of crime and youth subcultures, combined with the presentation of the poor as lazy and feckless, form a recognizable portrait of hostile responses to both 'el pueblo' and popular culture. The incongruous intrusion of the motif of the piano into this tirade renders this discourse ridiculous, but most significantly, the concluding utterances of the sequence portray these attitudes as explicitly linked to support for neoliberal economics and a questionable position on the atrocities of the 1976–83 military dictatorship. The scene therefore weaves a set of cultural attitudes together with a specific political position, ultimately associating capitalist practice with a willingness to support brutal military regimes. These attitudes are torn down from their self-allocated position of 'el sentido común', common knowledge shared by 'right-minded' people, and revealed instead as discourses sustaining class inequality and state violence. The 'normality' that this combination of political and cultural attitudes supports is therefore exposed as a system that functions to suppress the popular alternative. By providing an intensely ironic depiction of this 'common sense', made ridiculous through incongruous elements in the dialogue and by placing these words in the mouths of the cast (who represent the *pueblo* throughout), *Moreno* destroys the illusion of shared values upon which this discourse depends, paving the way for the popular

---

62  Santos Iñurrieta, *Mariano Moreno*, Scene 15, p. 42. This echoes Brecht's vision of the status of the artist when he states, 'The "poet's words" are only sacred in so far as they are true; the theatre is the handmaiden not of the poet but of society' ('Masterful Treatment of a Model', 213).

63  *Moreno*, Scene 16, pp. 43–44.

vision constructed throughout the play to assert an alternative political and cultural structure.

### Revolution and Pueblo

The choice of Mariano Moreno as the play's focus is inseparable from the way the *pueblo* is constructed and thus from the work's political intent. Moreno featured in the revisionist resurgence primarily as the victim of a political assassination (such as in Pacho O'Donnell's *El águila guerrera*), or celebrated for his revolutionary fervour in opposition to the more conservative Saavedra, as in Felipe Pigna's best-selling *Mitos de la historia argentina*.[64] It is this second vision of Moreno that most closely parallels Santos Iñurrieta's narrative on the *prócer*, with Felipe Pigna even obtaining a mention in the text.[65] Moreno's revolutionary commitment was an important contemporary narrative at about the time of the Bicentenary, as highlighted in Jorge Dubatti's summary of a pre-show discussion for Santos Iñurrieta's *Moreno* in 2010. The discussants included Juan Carlos Junio, the director of the CCC and Horacio González, then director of Argentina's National Library, and Dubatti notes that 'para Juan Carlos Junio en la revisión actual de Moreno se rescatan su pensamiento revolucionario y su sentido americanista', and cites González's observation that 'la memoria pública popular reconoce en Moreno la imagen de lo que fue: un militante'.[66] This second description in particular illustrates the 'updating' of the independence narrative in popular history to reflect twentieth-century definitions of revolution, evoking the militant experience of 1960s and 1970s Argentina that played such a crucial role in *kirchnerista* political discourse at this time. The presentation of Moreno as Jacobin has been transformed from character flaw into his most valuable legacy through this reconsideration, couched in the rhetoric of a left-wing revisionist narrative. Santos Iñurrieta's play combines a discourse of democracy and revolutionary militancy that overtly embraces this contemporary politicized rendering of the idea of left-wing political commitment. Significantly, this is explicitly tied into ideas of a class-based revolutionary struggle, retaining the ideological inflections of the 'traditional Left' while participating in a much broader contemporary left-wing discursive context.

Comparing this presentation of Moreno with the despotic, authoritarian figure depicted by Caparrós in *Ansay* reveals a resurgence in revolutionary rhetoric that is intricately linked to changing discourses surrounding left-wing

---

64  Pacho O'Donnell, *El águila guerrera: la historia argentina que no nos contaron*, pp. 11–13; Felipe Pigna, *Los mitos de la historia argentina: la construcción de un pasado como justificación del presente: del 'descubrimiento' de América a la 'independencia'*, I, p. 322. Moreno can also be presented as an 'extranjerizante' liberal enthralled to the needs of foreign investment, but this has not been a prominent neorevisionist trope.

65  Santos Iñurrieta, *Mariano Moreno*, Scene 7, p. 31.

66  Dubatti, 'Manuel Santos Iñurrieta', pp. 13–14.

political violence in Argentina. I have described in Chapter 1 how, from the late 1990s, a new discourse on the violent militancy of the 1970s emerged, which sought to re-inject agency into the actions of those who became victims of the military regime. However, the opposition between revolution and liberal democracy that prevailed in the discourse of the militant Left in the 1970s (both Montoneros and beyond) was gradually overturned, replaced with a discourse of democracy and human rights after the horror of the outcome of the political violence.[67] In a study of intellectual discourse in the Bicentenary, Graciana Vázquez Villanueva argues that 'el discurso intelectual, en la pluralidad de sujetos y problemáticas focalizados, hace de una serie de conceptos políticos —"memoria", "revolución", "violencia"— los ejes a partir de los cuales evoca e intenta recomponer el sistema que rigió en aquellos años'.[68]

Santos Iñurrieta's play combines a discourse of democracy and revolutionary militancy that reflects these changes since *Ansay* was published. The play's title puns on that of the controversial work attributed to Mariano Moreno, the *Plan de operaciones*, with none of the denunciations of authoritarianism present in Caparrós's text. Instead, the commitment to a cause is once more returned to centre-stage in its traditional role as inspiration, re-imbued with utopian potential. The celebration of the 'Jacobin' wing of the May Revolution is constructed as an ongoing commitment to revolutionary change, which echoes the use of this historical period in *La revolución es un sueño eterno*. Yet while Rivera's 1980s text longingly asks whether a new generation will come to take on the revolutionary mantle, Santos Iñurrieta's text is imbued with confidence in the possibility of change. If Rivera's novel asks who will build the revolution, Santos Iñurrieta's *Moreno* confidently answers: we will. This emphasizes both how sensitive this founding narrative is to the constantly shifting political landscape and how significant these political reshapings of the independence narrative are for an interpretation of the texts that rewrite it.

The idea of popular revolution that emerges from the text is fundamentally linked to the shifting definition of independence over the late 1990s and 2000s that I outlined in the early part of this chapter. The inclusion of Juana Azurduy, speaking through the words of Eva Perón, reflects the tendency in contemporary neo-revisionist discourse to carve out a space for female historical protagonists as one of the groups 'excluded' by the traditional liberal narrative. The insistence on the solidarity between Latin American nations through their shared independence history is also key to the discourse of inclusion that permeates the

---

67  See the discussion at the opening of Chapter 1 of this book.

68  Graciana Vázquez Villanueva, 'Discurso intelectual y Bicentenario: memorias y utopías', in *Memorias del Bicentenario: discursos e ideologías*, ed. by Graciana Vázquez Villanueva (Buenos Aires: Facultad de Filosofía y Letras, Universidad de Buenos Aires, 2010), pp. 209–34, at p. 211.

text.[69] One of the most solemn moments of the piece, the moving monologue delivered by Actriz in Scene 18, charts the significance of history for the present by weaving together significant Latin American events and figures from the past two centuries around variations of the refrain 'tiene que ver conmigo'. The individual who inherits the legacy of May 1810 is portrayed as equally indebted to Bernard O'Higgins and Salvador Allende, to the defence of human rights undertaken by the Madres and Abuelas of the Plaza de Mayo, and to the rich multi-cultural heritage of the region as a whole. The incantatory effect of the listing of these events, often alluded to through oblique references appealing to the complicity of the audience as a knowing 'owner' of these shared cultural references ('Salvador y la Moneda' for the overthrowing of Allende in Chile's 1973 coup, or 'el cáncer en la lengua' to refer to revolutionary leader Juan José Castelli, for example), builds a tender portrait of an inspiring and painful past to be honoured by those in the present. History has been adapted to reflect contemporary values, but it retains the ability to envisage steady progression towards a glorious future.

The text employs these recognizable contemporary historical discourses to foreground ideas of solidarity and equality in its narration of independence. Yet it does not lambast the traditional tale as 'liberal y extranjerizante' as we find in much contemporary neo-revisionist discourse. The concept of popular revolution that underpins the work evidently draws on Marxist theory, stressing the fundamentally economic nature of the class relations in the text. The *próceres* that populate its pages are cast as pioneers of this vision, primarily through citation of excerpts from their written works, such as this statement from Belgrano published in the *Gazeta de Buenos Aires* in 1813 and reproduced in Scene 10 of *Moreno*:

> Se han elevado entre los hombres dos clases muy distintas; la una dispone de los frutos de la tierra, y la otra es llamada solamente a ayudar por su trabajo. Los unos se someten invariablemente a las leyes impuestas por los otros. El imperio de la propiedad es el que reduce a la mayor parte de los hombres a lo más estrechamente necesario.[70]

In this sense, the traditional balance of a 'pueblo' led by an 'enlightened' class of ideological visionaries is undisturbed, but the radical quality of the May Revolution is drawn to the fore.

Over the course of the play, however, a gradual transfer of power from Moreno to 'pueblo' takes place. The boundaries between the present and

---

69 Juan Carlos Junio makes the connection between Independence and contemporary discourses of Latin American integration explicit in his prologue to *Moreno*, emphasizing the significance of this context for an interpretation of the play: 'Aquellas ideales de libertad continental que encarnara Moreno y tantos otros, hoy se ven plasmados en los logros de la integración, de Unasur, del Banco del Sur, etc.'. 'Presentación', *Mariano Moreno*, p. 9.

70 Santos Iñurrieta, *Mariano Moreno*, p. 35.

the historical narrative the company seeks to represent become increasingly blurred. The director adopts the persona of Cornelio Saavedra, sending Moreno to his death among the baying mob outside the theatre door in a clear parallel of Saavedra's alleged assassination of the young revolutionary. The action also depicts a symbolic takeover of the creative process by the company, positioned as a popular collective. As mentioned above, the director lectures his cast on the conventions of epic theatre in Scene 4, attempting to impart his dramatic wisdom to those under his authority. By Scene 18, however, the director's control has disintegrated, and the actors repeat the Brechtian lessons of the earlier scene for the audience, but this time performed as a collective, ensemble piece rather than dictated by a controlling authority figure. This symbolic appropriation of power by the 'workers', the cast, is a metatheatrical reproduction of the revolution the company seek to depict. As the 'dictatorial' director emerges, the collectivized 'pueblo' joins together in resistance. Artistic praxis is therefore transformed into a site for the dispute of cultural ownership and performance becomes a means of challenging ingrained class and social relations. This also evokes the working practices of el bachín: although Santos Iñurrieta is straightforwardly acknowledged in the roles of author and director in the production credits for the 2010 staging of *Moreno*, el bachín functions as a company with a more collaborative approach than this indicates.[71] The desire to realize an individual creative vision is parodied in *Moreno* as a reminder of the urgent need for alternative theatrical practice, which replaces the Romantic view of individual genius with a collective approach, insisting that our role in responding to art is not to 'admire' but to engage.

The individual therefore gradually gives way to a powerful collective force, encapsulated in the transfer of revolutionary potential from Moreno to the company of actors at the text's end. After Moreno is shot, the rest of the cast walk towards the front of the stage as the lights fade. The continuation of a truly popular uprising is therefore expressed through this striking stage picture, echoed in the words of the poem that closes the piece:

Y otra vez la imagen, del hecho, del acontecimiento.
Y otra vez mi voz, jugando entre mil voces.
Y otra vez, allí los rostros, del rostro,
Del protagonista multiplicado, multiforme.
—¿Y Mariano Moreno?
—Mariano Moreno ganando nombres.[72]

---

71  Describing the writing process for another of the company's productions, *La gracia de tener*, Santos Iñurrieta details his sketching of an initial draft with fellow director Claudio García before entering a collaborative process with the company: 'Luego continuamos con el grupo del laboratorio-taller del bachín en 2009, y finalmente con el grupo logramos una primera versión escénica "definitiva".' Dubatti, 'Manuel Santos Iñurrieta', p 16.

72  Santos Iñurrieta, *Mariano Moreno*, Scene 28, p. 62.

The name of Moreno is repositioned as a collective force embodied in the 'protagonista multiplicado, multiforme' of the people. The revolutionary-democratic spirit he is depicted as representing throughout the work is transformed into an active, living political force, inciting us to believe in a new period of change. The traditional narrative is therefore not overthrown but subtly rewritten for contemporary times: a carefully selected *prócer* leads the charge, but no longer as a hymn to a glorious past, confirming the legitimacy of the state engendered by this period. Instead, *Moreno* carries forward a recurring Marxist interpretation of the independence tale in Argentina by celebrating its revolutionary example, but the play's specific presentation also reflects salient elements of contemporary discourse on the period as outlined in the introduction to this chapter. *Moreno*'s independence narrative is therefore primarily a didactic exploration of the tale, reconfirmed in its role as pedagogical tool, reconfirming rather than negating the potential of history as a tool for forging meaning about both the present and the past.

## Conclusion: Owning the Past

The clear affinity between the thematic concerns of *Mariano Moreno y un teatro de operaciones* and the other texts of my corpus, particularly those that also deal with Moreno (*Ansay* and *La revolución es un sueño eterno*), reveal the need to broaden analysis beyond a concern with the historical novel as subgenre. Equally, the intrusion of the poetic in *1810: la Revolución de Mayo vivida por los negros* demonstrates the text's play with the genres of poetry and prose, rather than specifically with a limited category of narrative.

By analysing a play and a novel through their depiction of a particular historical moment, their different constructions of the contemporary concern with the role of the *pueblo* in the nation's past come to the fore. *Moreno*'s retelling emphasizes the people as political actor and social force, capable of bringing about revolutionary change. The play's wider construction of the popular is centred on the democratization of culture, no longer separated into revered 'elite' and discarded 'popular' forms, and on the destruction of bourgeois pretensions to determine cultural norms. Whilst *1810* demonstrates an equally self-aware exploitation of the freedom to redefine the cultural sphere, its aesthetic approach asserts a very different idea of the *pueblo*. Marxist constructions of the proletariat are entirely absent, replaced by a raucous, exuberant popular world that embraces the hierarchical inversion of the carnivalesque. Despite *Moreno*'s nod to the association between 'civilización' and political control of the popular classes, 'barbarie' is not embraced as an anti-hegemonic alternative. In Cucurto's text the concept of the people as a political actor is absent, the battleground transferred instead entirely to the cultural realm. Revelling in the traditionally Peronist concept of 'incultura', the text imagines a world free of any form of restraint, uninhibited by order, political correctness, or traditional ideas of what constitutes 'literature'.

The interplay between these contemporary rewritings of Argentina's founding revolution and ideologically bound public discourses of history highlights a dimension of the relationship between literature and history that is often ignored. In reimagining this tried and tested national tale, these texts engage with historical versions that have played a visible role in public life and have functioned as a political tool, being rewritten to suit the aims of competing projects and ideologies. The self-reflexive play with history in these texts therefore goes beyond an ambiguous blurring of 'fact' and 'fiction' to become a self-conscious engagement with the political traditions that have shaped Argentina's past and present. They do not merely dismantle epistemological certainties, but instead engage in constructing alternatives that imagine a different vision of the nation, built upon a self-aware foundation. Rather than dismissing meaning as an elusive impossibility, therefore, they present meanings that acknowledge their own ideological positioning, transcending false claims to 'neutrality' or 'objectivity' and clamouring to fill the vacant space left by the demise of the status of 'official' history.

# Conclusion

## Fiction and the Political Uses of History

Throughout the book I have sought to demonstrate the crucial importance of locating texts that rewrite history not only within their contemporary context, but also in relation to the politicized history of the discourses they imaginatively reconfigure. This mode of analysis provides the opportunity to break down the generalizations, highlighted in my Introduction, about the relationship between the political and the historical in these texts, construed as either grounded in a vague 'critique' (Hutcheon) or in an equally ambiguous idea of 'resistance' (Pons; Colás; Perkowska). Specifically, I have targeted the assumption that the political power of self-reflexive historical fiction lies in its interrogation of epistemology, a dominant conclusion due to the influence of Hutcheon's configuration of the relationship between postmodernism, politics, and history. Using the words of Jacques Ehrmann, Hutcheon tells us that the 'teaching' of historiographic metafiction is that 'history and literature have no existence in and of themselves. It is we who constitute them as the object of our understanding'.[1]

I have argued, however, that the postmodern perspective that history is formed of a series of constructed narratives is the starting point for these texts, not their final conclusion. By accepting and revelling in this awareness of history's inherent narrativity, this self-reflexive historical fiction seizes the opportunity to offer us a historical account that does not take as its starting point the referent, the events themselves, but the discourses that have been generated in order to weave that past into a meaningful tale.

Delving more deeply into the political configuration of specific historical narratives, by which I mean the ways in which historical events have been signified as part of distinct political projects, can therefore help tease out a much more purposeful critique within this disruption of traditional narratives. In the case of independence, recognizing the nation-building purpose allocated to this discourse since its inception is crucial to understanding the ways in which this narrative has been reconfigured in literature. Texts that

---

1 *A Poetics of Postmodernism*, p. 111.

rewrite this period engage with an area of history that has occupied a public role in the life of the nation, and that has been used as a 'morality tale' to teach citizens how to belong to the *patria*. By approaching literary uses of history in this way, we acknowledge history as a public discourse, moving us beyond considering challenges to historical discourse exclusively as interrogations of the mechanisms of knowledge creation or abstract concepts. It is this consideration that can open up engagements with 'official history' to meaningful exploration, particularly in terms of their potential political critique. Throughout the book, I have sought to demonstrate that it is not the viability of history as a synonym for knowledge that is at stake here, but an examination of the political articulations of Argentina's past in hegemonic discourse throughout much of the twentieth century and the challenges it has received.

By identifying independence as a discourse associated with nation-building rather than merely an abstract idea of 'historical truth', I have isolated the particular myths at the heart of the independence tale that are picked up and reworked by the texts of my corpus. The combination of the 'epic of democracy' and the 'military epic' encompassed in the traditional vision of the events of May 1810 and the wars of independence presents a series of basic narrative units: the ideas of revolution, democracy, heroism, and nation. The 'official' narrative is constructed as a celebration of each of these elements, drawn together as part of a harmonious patriotic tale. In the reworkings undertaken by the texts of my corpus, these assertions are reconfigured as questions, reflecting on the place of revolution, the viability and desirability of heroism, the fate of democracy and its promise of equality, and the self-representations present in the idea of the nation. Each of the texts I have discussed employs independence as a means of confronting some or all of these themes, offering a different reconfiguration of patriotic discourse.

These reconfigurations are closely tied in with specific national political circumstances, reflecting and contributing to an evolving intellectual, cultural, and ideological climate. The shifting presentation of the relationship between revolution and democracy in the texts of my corpus is particularly illuminating in this sense. While the 'official' independence narrative depicts a seamless fusion of the two, with the May Revolution presented as driven by democratic values and giving birth to liberal democracy, militant discourse on the Left in Argentina in the 1960s and early 1970s celebrated revolution as the means of bringing about equality in opposition to 'bourgeois' liberal democracy, as I discussed in my first chapter. The brutal defeat and repression of the militant organizations in the mid- to late 1970s sparked a profound reconsideration of this combative discourse, and both Rivera's and Caparrós's texts invoke this point of radical transformation in the discourse and praxis of the Argentine Left. As exiled Argentines began to construct their resistance to the military dictatorship through the discourse of human rights, democracy gradually transformed itself into the new rallying cry for justice, ushering in a new paradigm for the self-representation of the Left in Argentina. In these two novels, independence offers the opportunity to 'denaturalize' deeply ingrained ideas of the relationship between revolution and democracy, both in the traditional narrative and Marxist-inspired discourse.

Democracy is profoundly linked to the idea of the nation in the texts that I have explored in my second chapter. Encapsulating a different type of crisis, one that is much more closely bound up with the direct challenges to some of Argentina's most pervasive narratives of national identity produced by the military dictatorship and defeat in the Falklands/Malvinas conflict, both *El informe: San Martín y el otro cruce de los Andes* and *El ojo de la patria* reflect on the values at the heart of the definition of the nation. Revolution retreats from centre stage in these novels; instead, it is the chasm between democratic ideals and the reality of the nation that is explored and critiqued.

In the cultural context within which I situate the texts of my third chapter, the political configurations of national history in the build-up to the May 1810 Bicentenary, the characterization of democracy as the means of guaranteeing human rights has realized its maximum expression in the discourse of *kirchnerismo*, which structured a large part of its political identity around the defence of human rights in this period. Here, the idea of bringing about profound change through the mechanisms of conventional representative democracy has performed a reconciliation of the concepts of revolution and democracy that tallies neatly with the original presentation of the independence tale. Despite the growing importance of historical revisionism as a possible new 'sentido común', independence is not cast aside as a remnant of 'liberal' history within this changing context, but instead is adjusted to match the dominant concerns of current political circumstances, as has occurred at other moments in the past. This reconciliation of revolution and democracy is fundamental to Santos Iñurrieta's representation of the independence period as laying the foundations for a glorious new national future that will deepen and consolidate these foundational revolutionary aims. The idea of democracy that Cucurto's novel explores is fundamentally bound up with the discourse of equality and representation that also characterizes this recent period, provocatively asserting a popular world of *barbarie* in the place of the orderly *pueblo* of the traditional independence tale.

By tracing these dramatic shifts in the presentation of revolution and democracy across the texts of my corpus, the radically different political engagements of each act of rewriting independence come to the fore, and particularly the crucial significance of the changing national political context for the specific reconfigurations that they produce. Significantly, in each of the cultural contexts I have discussed, independence has played its role as a 'political actor', from the celebration of the ideal of the revolutionary hero in the discourse of left-wing militancy to the appeal to the *patria* as the ultimate good by the discourse of the military dictatorship of 1976 to 1983. This foundational narrative therefore remains a site for the symbolic production of political meaning, and it is with full awareness of this fact that the texts of my corpus appropriate, reconfigure, and challenge particular aspects of this inescapable tale.

The 'ideological mapping' of independence that I have undertaken offers a means of drawing together different threads of the national past, particularly surrounding the experiences of the most recent military dictatorship. By approaching these texts through their reworking of independence, a complex presentation of this context has emerged, which brings the trauma of state terror into dialogue with the experience of defeat suffered by the guerrilla organizations of the 1970s, the impact of the Falklands/Malvinas conflict, and the implications of all of these elements for existing narratives of national identity. As highlighted in Chapter 1, the recovery of the militant experience is now a prominent focal point within the exploration of the period prior to and during the dictatorship of 1976 to 1983. My examination of Caparrós's and Rivera's novels positions these texts at this intersection of the defeat of the revolutionary ideal and the trauma of state violence, tracing their literary configuration of the internal critique within the Argentine Left. The significance of the Falklands/Malvinas conflict as an assault on deeply rooted ideas of Argentine national identity represents a crucial component in understanding the post-dictatorship context. In a meeting with Martín Kohan during the writing of this book, I was struck by his description of his generation as the 'post-Malvinas' generation rather than that of the 'post-dictatorship'. This characterization emphasizes the profound impact of this event on the 'national imaginary', fundamentally destabilizing deeply ingrained narratives of national identity, many of which stem from the ideas of the indivisibility of national territory and the military as the saviours of the nation that find their root in the 'official' telling of independence. The cultural context addressed by my final chapter is profoundly informed by these radical political shifts and traumatic events in the last decades of the twentieth century, representing a political landscape in which these different threads of national experience are interwoven and reconfigured. By tracing the theme of independence over a corpus that spans this whole period, my discussion has emphasized the reshaping of identity narratives that has taken place in response to both political events and changing attitudes, particularly concerning the place of the military in the idea of the nation and fluctuating ideas of the meaning of democracy. Through this approach, I have also highlighted the shifting dynamics of regional power and national population that have rendered some of Argentina's most cherished identity narratives all but obsolete.

This does not mean, however, that there is no relationship between these texts and the climate of ideas associated with postmodernism that have shaped our understandings of Latin American historical fiction. My contention is that the indisputable relevance of postmodern ideas of history to the construction of these texts, particularly the consideration of history as a series of discursive constructions, means that it is more productive to reflect differently upon how these ideas are being applied, than to simply dismiss this context. Crucially, we must recognize the ways in which these texts self-consciously exploit ideas associated with the postmodern in order to produce their own targeted critique. This enables us to move forward *with* the texts, to recognize their own responses to the particular circumstances of each era, rather than becoming bogged down in questions of genre or concern over whether we can (or should) apply the label 'postmodern' to the texts themselves. My analysis has instead underscored a more complex interplay between the freedom offered by postmodernism's insistence on narrativity and the constructed nature of history, and the role of history as a public discourse that intervenes directly in the political sphere. The rewritings undertaken by the texts in my corpus are inseparable from the educational purpose of the original historical narrative that they dismantle and re-imagine. Some of these texts are overtly didactic, particularly Rivera's *La revolución es un sueño eterno* and Santos Iñurrieta's *Mariano Moreno y un teatro de operaciones*, which, significantly, are the two works that draw explicitly on Marxist approaches to the national past. Both Kohan's *El informe* and Caparrós's *Ansay* can be considered as interventions with a didactic purpose, although more obliquely so. Even the least overtly didactic of the texts discussed here, Cucurto's *1810: la Revolución de Mayo vivida por los negros*, adopts a ludic approach that nonetheless starkly confronts Argentina's self-construction as a nation, particularly in terms of class and race.

The assertion that postmodernism undermines our ability to produce stable knowledge suggests that these self-reflexive historical texts view their own narrative as inconclusive. These texts, however, are constructed as responses to the overtly politicized debates of the cultural climate within which they act, representing interventions into this politicized cultural terrain. If not attempts to construct the nation anew, they can certainly be perceived as a form of open dialogue with the concrete political realities that stem from the narratives upon which the nation has been built. In these texts, the focus on discursivity functions as a reminder that the stories we tell about our past and our identity shape the political reality of the present day. By recognizing the constructed nature of this national discourse, they offer the opportunity to detach these historically determined narratives from the essentialist idea of the 'people' and the 'nation' harboured in nationalist discourse. Their rewritings assert the 'chance' of historical events rather than a national 'destiny', and therefore open possibilities for alternative constructions to be established under different rules.

Through the readings undertaken in this book, I have proposed a reconsideration of this limited range of political options in relation to self-reflexive Latin American historical fiction. My contextualized reading of a corpus structured around the theme of independence has enabled me to reassess the place of both politics and history in these texts and the implications of this positioning for the readings we can generate. The individual texts present a range of specific political engagements that cannot be accounted for purely in terms of a 'cultural resistance', which overlooks the implications of which narratives are being reconfigured and to what purpose they are being reshaped. These texts employ a postmodernist emphasis on narrativity to outline distinct political visions, tracing the 'emplotment' of specific ideological narratives as a means of underpinning our ability to generate any meaningful political engagement. Their self-aware manipulations of history are an attack on political naivety, a warning to use postmodern awareness to learn the lessons of an all-consuming, utopian political faith, and an attempt to reconfigure a narrative so important to nation building as a means of looking to a political future. Theirs is a constructed vision of the world, and proudly so.

# Bibliography

Acha, Omar, *Historia crítica de la historiografía argentina: Vol 1: Las izquierdas en el siglo XX* (Buenos Aires: Prometeo Libros, 2009)

—, 'Desafíos para la historiografía en el Bicentenario argentino', *PolHis*, 8 (2011), 57–69 <http://historiapolitica.com/datos/boletin/polhis8_ACHA.pdf> [accessed 15 October 2019]

Aguiló, Ignacio, *The Darkening Nation: Race, Neoliberalism and Crisis in Argentina* (Cardiff: University of Wales Press, 2018)

Aínsa, Fernando, *Reescribir el pasado: historia y ficción en América Latina* (Mérida Venezuela: CELARG; El otro el mismo, 2003)

Altuna, Elena, 'Las gestas imaginarias: Ansay revisitado', in *El archivo de la independencia y la ficción contemporánea*, ed. by Alicia Chibán (Salta: Universidad Nacional de Salta, 2004), pp. 263–76

Anderson, Benedict, *Imagined Communities: Reflections on the Origin and Spread of Nationalism* (London: Verso, 2006)

Anguita, Eduardo, and Martín Caparrós, *La voluntad: una historia de la militancia revolucionaria en la Argentina*, 3rd edn, 3 vols (Buenos Aires: Norma, 1997)

Ansay, Faustino, 'Relación de los acontecimientos ocurridos en la ciudad de Mendoza en los meses de junio y julio de 1810', in *Biblioteca de Mayo, Tomo IV: Diarios y Crónicas* (Buenos Aires: Senado de la Nación, 1960), pp. 3314–64

—, 'Relación de los padecimientos y ocurrencias acaecidas al coronel de caballería don Faustino Ansay desde el mes de mayo de 1810, que se hallaba en la ciudad de Mendoza en la América del Sud hasta el 23 de octubre de 1822 que llegó a Zaragoza, su patria, escrita por él mismo, año de 1822', in *Biblioteca de Mayo, Tomo IV: Diarios y Crónicas* (Buenos Aires: Senado de la Nación, 1960), pp. 3365–94

Armony, Ariel C., and Victor Armony, 'Indictments, Myths, and Citizen Mobilization in Argentina: A Discourse Analysis', *Latin American Politics and Society*, 47 (2005), 27–54

Bacarisse, Pamela, 'The Projection of Peronism in the Novels of Manuel Puig', in *The Historical Novel in Latin America: A Symposium*, ed. by Daniel Balderston (Gaithersburg: Hispamérica, 1986), pp. 185–99

Bakhtin, Mikhail M., *Rabelais and His World* (Bloomington: Indiana University Press, 1984)

Balderston, Daniel, 'Introduction', in *The Historical Novel in Latin America: A Symposium*, ed. by Daniel Balderston (Gaithersburg: Hispamérica, 1986), pp. 9–12

Ballesteros Rosas, Luisa (ed.), *Representaciones literarias de las independencias iberoamericanas* (Madrid: SIAL Ediciones, 2018)

Barboza, Martha, 'La escritura como desplazamiento de la oralidad en *La revolución es un sueño eterno*, de Andrés Rivera', *Espéculo*, 42 (2009) <http://www.ucm.es/info/especulo/numero42/desplaza.html> [accessed 17 October 2019]

Barrientos, Juan, *Ficción-historia: la nueva novela histórica hispanoamericana* (Mexico City: Universidad Nacional Autónoma de México, 2001)

Berg, Edgardo, *Poéticas en suspenso: migraciones narrativas en Ricardo Piglia, Andrés Rivera y Juan José Saer* (Buenos Aires: Biblos, 2002)

Berger, Timo, '"Yo actualmente soy el mejor escritor dominicano sin duda". Entrevista a Washington Cucurto', Proyecto Patrimonio 2010, *letras.s5.com* <http://letras.mysite.com/tb060710.html> [accessed 1 September 2020]

Bernal, Alvaro, 'No saben que yo soy el Rey del realismo atolondrado', Interview with Washington Cucurto, *Destiempos*, 10 (2007) <http://www.destiempos.com/n10/alvarobernal_n10.htm> [accessed 15 November 2019]

Bertoni, Lilia Ana, *Patriotas, cosmopolitas y nacionalistas: la construcción de la nacionalidad argentina a fines del siglo XIX* (Buenos Aires: Fondo de cultura económica, 2001)

Betancourt Mendieta, Alexander (ed.), *Escritura de la historia y política: el sesquicentenario de la Independencia en América Latina* (Lima: IFEA, Instituto Francés de Estudios Andinos, 2016)

Bhabha, Homi K., 'DissemiNation: Time, Narrative, and the Margins of the Modern Nation', in *Nation and Narration*, ed. by Homi K. Bhabha (London: Routledge, 1990), pp. 291–322

Bilbija, Ksenija, '*El ojo de la patria* de Osvaldo Soriano: ¿El milagro (argentino) o la industria (multinacional)?', *Revista Chilena de Literatura*, 59 (2001), 65–79

Bollig, Ben, *Néstor Perlongher: The Poetic Search for an Argentine Marginal Voice* (Cardiff: University of Wales Press, 2008)

Brecht, Bertolt, *Brecht on Theatre: The Development of an Aesthetic*, ed. and trans. by John Willet (London: Eyre Methuen, 1973)

Briones, Claudia, 'Formaciones de alteridad: contextos globales, procesos nacionales y provinciales', in *Cartografías argentinas: políticas indigenistas y formaciones provinciales de alteridad*, ed. by Claudia Briones (Buenos Aires: Antropofagia, 2005), pp. 11–43

Buch, Esteban, *O juremos con gloria morir: historia de una épica de estado* (Buenos Aires: Sudamericana, 1994)

Calveiro, Pilar, *Política y/o violencia: una aproximación a la guerrilla de los años 70* (Buenos Aires: Norma, 2005)

Campos, Victoria E., 'Toward a New History: Twentieth-Century Debates in Mexico on Narrating the National Past', in *A Twice-told Tale: Reinventing the Encounter in Iberian American Literature and Film* (Newark, DE: University of Delaware Press; London: Associated University Press, 2001), pp. 47–62

Canale, Florencia, *Pasión y traición* (Buenos Aires: Editorial Planeta, 2011)

Caparrós, Martín, *Ansay ó los infortunios de la gloria* (Buenos Aires: Seix Barral, 2005)

Carpenter, Victoria (ed.), *(Re)Collecting the Past: History and Collective Memory in Latin American Narrative* (Oxford: Peter Lang, 2010)

Casa Rosada. Presidencia de la Nación Argentina. 'Palabras de la Presidenta en apertura de Galería de Patriotas Latinoamericanos', 25 May 2010 <https://www.casarosada.gob.ar/informacion/archivo/22233-blank-31757128> [accessed 1 September 2020]

Cattarulla, Camilla, and Ilaria Magnani (eds.). *Escrituras y reescrituras de la independencia* (Buenos Aires: Corregidor, 2012)

Chibán, Alicia (ed.), *El archivo de la independencia y la ficción contemporánea* (Salta: Universidad Nacional de Salta, 2004)

—, 'Vivir, escribir, pensar la historia: *El informe: San Martín y el otro cruce de los Andes*, de Martín Kohan', in *El archivo de la independencia y la ficción contemporánea*, ed. by Alicia Chibán (Salta: Universidad Nacional de Salta, 2004), pp. 81–90

Chust, Manuel, and José Antonio Serrano, 'Un debate actual, una revisión necesaria', in *Debates sobre las independencias iberoamericanas*, ed. by Manuel Chust and José Antonio Serrano (Madrid: Iberoamericana; Frankfurt: Vervuert, 2007), pp. 9–26

Colás, Santiago, *Postmodernity in Latin America: The Argentine Paradigm* (Durham, NC: Duke University Press, 1994)

'Críticas al Instituto Dorrego', *La Nación*, 8 December 2011 <http://www.lanacion. com.ar/1431129-criticas-al-instituto-dorrego> [accessed 15 November 2019]

Cucurto, Washington, *1810: la Revolución de Mayo vivida por los negros* (Buenos Aires: Emecé, 2008)

Davies, Catherine, *South American Independence: Gender, Politics, Text* (Liverpool: Liverpool University Press, 2006)

Davies, Lloyd Hughes, 'Portraits of a Lady: Postmodern Readings of Tomas Eloy Martinez's "Santa Evita"', *The Modern Language Review*, 95 (2000), 415–23

De Amézola, Gonzalo, 'Argentina', in *Los procesos independentistas iberoamericanos en los manuales de historia*, 3 vols (Madrid: Organización de Estados Iberoamericanos para la Educación, la Ciencia y la Cultura, 2005), I, pp. 17–80

De Ció, Mariana, and Enrique Schmukler, 'Entrevista a Martín Kohan', *Letral*, 1 (2008), 170–77. DOI: https://doi.org/10.30827/rl.v0i1.3567 [accessed 1 September 2020]

'Decreto 1880/2011', Boletín Oficial de la República Argentina, 21 November 2011 <https://www.boletinoficial.gob.ar/detalleAviso/primera/61096/20111121? busqueda=1> [accessed 1 September 2020]

Delaney, Jean H., 'Imagining "El Ser Argentino": Cultural Nationalism and Romantic Concepts of Nationhood in Early Twentieth-Century Argentina', *Journal of Latin American Studies*, 34 (2002), 625–58

Di Meglio, Gabriel, 'La guerra de independencia en la historiografía argentina', in *Debates sobre las independencias iberoamericanas*, ed. by Manuel Chust and José Antonio Serrano (Madrid: Iberoamericana; Frankfurt: Vervuert, 2007), pp. 27–44

Dubatti, Jorge, 'Manuel Santos Iñurrieta y "el bachín teatro": post-neoliberal-ismo, arte y política', in *Mariano Moreno y un teatro de operaciones; La gracia de tener*, by Manuel Santos Iñurrieta (Buenos Aires: Ediciones del CCC Centro Cultural de Cooperación Floreal Gorini, 2012), pp. 11–18

Earle, Rebecca, '"Padres de La Patria" and the Ancestral Past: Commemorations of Independence in Nineteenth-Century Spanish America', *Journal of Latin American Studies*, 34(4) (November 2002), 775–805. DOI:10.1017/S0022216X02006557

Echevarría, Roberto González, 'Lezama, Góngora y la poética del mal gusto', *Hispania*, 84 (2001), 428–40

Edwards, Erika Denise, *Hiding in Plain Sight: Black Women, the Law, and the Making of a White Argentine Republic* (Tuscaloosa, AL: The University of Alabama Press, 2020)

Feinmann, José Pablo, *La sangre derramada: ensayo sobre la violencia política* (Buenos Aires: Ariel, 1998)

Franco, Marina, and Pilar González Bernaldo, 'Cuando el sujeto deviene objeto: la construcción del exilio argentino en Francia', in *Represión y destierro: itiner-arios del exilio argentino*, ed. by Pablo Yankelevich (La Plata: Al Margen, 2004), pp. 17–48

García Canclini, Néstor, *Culturas híbridas: estrategias para entrar y salir de la modernidad*, 2nd edn (Buenos Aires: Sudamericana, 1995)

Garguin, Enrique, '"Los Argentinos Descendemos de Los Barcos": The Racial Articulation of Middle Class Identity in Argentina (1920–1960)', *Latin American and Caribbean Ethnic Studies*, 2 (2007), 161–84

Gillespie, Richard, *Soldiers of Peron: Argentina's Montoneros* (Oxford: Clarendon, 1982)

Gilman, Claudia, 'Historia, poder y poética del padecimiento en las novelas de Andrés Rivera', in *La novela argentina de los años 80*, ed. by Roland Spiller (Frankfurt: Vervuert, 1991), pp. 47–64

Goebel, Michael, *Argentina's Partisan Past: Nationalism and the Politics of History* (Liverpool: Liverpool University Press, 2011)

Grimson, Alejandro, 'Nuevas xenofobias, nuevas políticas étnicas en la Argentina', in *Migraciones regionales hacia la Argentina: diferencia, desigualdad y derechos* (Buenos Aires: Prometeo libros, 2006), pp. 69–97

—, 'Hacia una agenda territorial para un nuevo escenario regional', in *Nación y diversidad: territorios, identidades y federalismo: Debates de Mayo III*, ed. by José Nun, Alejandro Grimson, and Juan Manuel Abal Medina (Buenos Aires: Edhasa, 2008), pp. 87–100

Grimson, Alejandro, Mirta Amati, and Kaori Kodama, 'La nación escenificada por el Estado: una comparación de rituales patrios', in *Pasiones nacionales: política y cultura en Brasil y Argentina*, ed. by Alejandro Grimson, Mirta Amati, and José Nun (Buenos Aires: Edhasa, 2007), pp. 413–502

Grimson, Alejandro, and Elizabeth Jelin, 'Introducción', in *Migraciones regionales hacia la Argentina: diferencia, desigualdad y derechos* (Buenos Aires: Prometeo libros, 2006), pp. 9–15

Gúber, Rosana, *Por qué Malvinas?: de la causa nacional a la guerra absurda* (Buenos Aires: Antropofagia, 2004)

Halperín Donghi, Tulio, *El revisionismo histórico argentino* (Mexico City: Siglo Veintiuno, 1970)

—, *Revolución y guerra: formación de una élite dirigente en la Argentina criolla* (Buenos Aires: Siglo Veintiuno, 1972)

Hernández, Mark. *Figural Conquistadors: Rewriting the New World's Discovery and Conquest in Mexican and River Plate Novels of the 1980s and 1990s* (Lewisburg: Bucknell University Press, 2006)

Hobsbawm, E. J, *Nations and Nationalism since 1780: Programme, Myth, Reality* (Cambridge: Cambridge University Press, 1992)

Hutcheon, Linda, *A Poetics of Postmodernism: History, Theory, Fiction* (New York: Routledge, 1988)

—, *A Theory of Parody: The Teachings of Twentieth-century Art Forms* (Urbana: University of Illinois Press, 2000)

—, *The Politics of Postmodernism* (New York: Routledge, 2002)

Jameson, Fredric, 'The Cultural Logic of Late Capitalism', in *Postmodernism, or, The Cultural Logic of Late Capitalism* (London: Verso, 1991), pp. 1–54

Jelin, Elizabeth, 'Migraciones y derechos: instituciones y prácticas sociales en la construcción de la igualdad y la diferencia', in *Migraciones regionales hacia la Argentina: diferencia, desigualdad y derechos* (Buenos Aires: Prometeo libros, 2006), pp. 47–68

Jelin, Elizabeth, and Federico Lorenz (comps.), *Educación y memoria: la escuela elabora el pasado* (Madrid: Siglo XXI: Social Science Research Council, 2004)

Jitrik, Noé, *Historia e imaginación literaria: las posibilidades de un género* (Buenos Aires: Editorial Biblos, 1995)

Juan-Navarro, Santiago, *Archival Reflections: Postmodern Fiction of the Americas (Self-reflexivity, Historical Revisionism, Utopia)* (Lewisburg: Bucknell University Press; London: Associated University Presses, 1999)

—, *A Twice-told Tale: Reinventing the Encounter in Iberian American Literature and Film* (Newark: University of Delaware Press; London: Associated University Press, 2001)

Knight, Stephen Thomas, *Form and Ideology in Crime Fiction* (London: Macmillan, 1980)

Kohan, Martín, *El Informe: San Martín y el otro cruce de los Andes* (Buenos Aires: Sudamericana, 1999)

—, 'La humanización de San Martín: notas sobre un malentendido', *Revista Iberoamericana*, LXXI (2005), 1083–96

—, *Narrar a San Martín* (Buenos Aires: Adriana Hidalgo, 2005)

—, *Ciencias morales* (Barcelona: Anagrama, 2007)

—, *Dos veces junio* (Buenos Aires: Debolsillo, 2013)

—, *El país de la guerra* (Buenos Aires: Eterna Cadencia, 2014)

Kohut, Karl, 'Introducción', in *La invención del pasado: la novela histórica en el marco de la posmodernidad*, ed. by Karl Kohut (Frankfurt: Vervuert; Madrid: Iberoamericana, 1997), pp. 9–26

Llach, Santiago, 'La cumbia es una metáfora', in Washington Cucurto, *1999: poemas de siempre, poemas nuevos y nuevas versiones* (Buenos Aires: Eloísa Cartonera, 2007), pp. 141–43

López, Kimberle S., *Latin American Novels of the Conquest: Reinventing the New World* (Columbia: University of Missouri Press, 2002)

Lorenz, Federico, *Las guerras por Malvinas* (Buenos Aires: Edhasa, 2006)

—, '¿Sueñan las ovejas con bicentenarios?', *El Monitor*, 23 (November 2009), 32–34   <http://www.me.gov.ar/monitor/nr00/pdf/monitor23.pdf> [accessed 28 August 2013]

Lukács, Georg, *The Historical Novel* (London: Merlin Press, 1962)

Lyotard, Jean-François, *The Postmodern Condition: A Report on Knowledge*, trans. by Geoff Bennington and Brian Massumi (Minneapolis: University of Minnesota Press, 1984)

Malaver Cruz, Nancy, *Ficción y realidad: retos de la novela histórica (1992–2010)* (Bogotá: Universidad Central, 2018)

McAllister, Catriona, 'History and the Popular: Rewriting National Origins at the Argentine Bicentenary'. *Modern Languages Open* (April 2016). DOI: http://doi.org/10.3828/mlo.v0i0.35

—, 'Borders Inscribed on the Body: Geopolitics and the Everyday in the Work of Martín Kohan', *Bulletin of Latin American Research*, 39(4) (2020), 453–65 DOI: http://dx.doi.org/10.1111/blar.13089

—, 'Flying the Flag: Questions of Patriotism and the Malvinas Conflict', in *Revisiting the Falklands-Malvinas Question: Transnational and Interdisciplinary Perspectives*, ed. by G. Mira and F. Pedrosa (London: Institute of Latin American Studies, 2021), pp. 161–71

McHale, Brian, *Postmodernist Fiction* (New York: Methuen, 1987)

Menton, Seymour, *Latin America's New Historical Novel* (Austin: University of Texas Press, 1993)

Merchant, Paul, *The Epic* (London: Methuen, 1971)

Miguens, Silvia, *Lupe, después del viaje* (Buenos Aires: Tusquets Editores, 1997)

Miller, Nicola, *In the Shadow of the State: Intellectuals and the Quest for National Identity in Twentieth-Century Spanish America*, Critical Studies in Latin American and Iberian Cultures (London: Verso, 1999)

Mira Delli-Zotti, Guillermo, 'La singularidad del exilio argentino en Madrid: entre las respuestas a la represión de los '70 y la interpelación a la Argentina postdictatorial', in *Represión y destierro: itinerarios del exilio argentino*, ed. by Pablo Yankelevich (La Plata: Al Margen, 2004), pp. 87–112

Mitre, Bartolomé, *Historia de Belgrano y de la independencia argentina*, Biblioteca argentina, 23–26, 4 vols (Buenos Aires: J. Roldan y C.a, 1927)

—, *Historia de San Martín y de la emancipación sudamericana*, 3 vols (Buenos Aires: Diario La Nación, 1950)

Monsiváis, Carlos, 'Pero ¿Hubo alguna vez once mil héroes?: "Si desenvainas, ¿por qué no posas de una vez para el escultor?"', in *Aires de familia: cultura y sociedad en América Latina* (Barcelona: Anagrama, 2000), pp. 79–112

Montés, Cristián, 'La contrautopía en *El ojo de la patria* de Osvaldo Soriano', *Cyber Humanitatis*, 14 (2000) <http://www.cyberhumanitatis.uchile.cl/index.php/RCH/article/viewFile/9112/9105> [accessed 10 October 2019]

Morello-Frosch, Marta, 'La ficción de la historia en la narrativa argentina reciente', in *The Historical Novel in Latin America: A Symposium*, ed. by Daniel Balderston (Gaithersburg: Hispamérica, 1986), pp. 201–8

O'Donnell, Pacho, *El águila guerrera: la historia argentina que no nos contaron*, 5th edn (Buenos Aires: Sudamericana, 1999)

Ollier, María Matilde, *De la revolución a la democracia: cambios privados, públicos y políticos de la izquierda argentina* (Buenos Aires: Siglo Veintiuno, 2009)

Paasi, Anssi, 'Dancing on the Graves: Independence, Hot/Banal Nationalism and the Mobilization of Memory', *Political Geography*, 54 (2016), 21–31

Palermo, Vicente, *Sal en las heridas: las Malvinas en la cultura argentina contemporánea* (Buenos Aires: Sudamericana, 2007)

Perkowska, Magdalena, *Historias híbridas: La nueva novela histórica latinoamericana (1985–2000) ante las teorías posmodernas de la historia* (Madrid: Iberoamericana, 2008)

Perlongher, Néstor, 'Caribe transplatino: Introducción a la poesía neobarroca cubana y rioplatense', in *Prosa plebeya: ensayos, 1980–1992* (Buenos Aires: Colihue, 1997), pp. 93–102

Perón, Eva, 'Discurso de Evita en el Día del Trabajador – Plaza de Mayo (1952)', *El historiador* <https://www.elhistoriador.com.ar/discurso-de-evita-en-el-dia-del-trabajador-plaza-de-mayo-1952/> [accessed 31 March 2021]

Piglia, Ricardo, 'Sobre el género político', in *Crítica y ficción* (Buenos Aires: Planeta, 2000), pp. 67–70

Pigna, Felipe, *Los mitos de la historia argentina: la construcción de un pasado como justificación del presente: del 'descubrimiento' de América a la 'independencia'* (Buenos Aires: Norma, 2004)

Pilia de Assunção, Nelda and Aurora Ravina (eds.), *Mayo de 1810: entre la historia y la ficción discursivas* (Buenos Aires: Biblos, 1999)

Pizarro Cortés, Carolina, 'The Decentring of the Historical Subject in the Contemporary Imaginary of the Independence Process', *Journal of Latin American Cultural Studies*, 20 (2011), 323–42

'Polémico Instituto de Revisión de la Historia', *La Nación*, 28 November 2011 <http://www.lanacion.com.ar/1427023-impulsa-el-gobierno-una-revision-de-la-historia> [accessed 18 November 2019]

Pons, María Cristina, *Memorias del olvido: Del Paso, García Márquez, Saer y la novela histórica de fines del siglo XX* (Mexico City: Siglo Veintiuno, 1996)

—, 'El secreto de la historia y el regreso de la novela histórica', in *Historia crítica de la literatura argentina Vol. 11, La narración gana la partida*, ed. by Elsa Drucaroff (Buenos Aires: Emecé, 2000), pp. 97–116

Portal Oficial del Gobierno de la República Argentina, 'Sistema educativo', <http://www.argentina.gob.ar/informacion/educacion/129-sistema-educativo. php> [accessed 3 June 2013].

Price, Brian L. (ed.), *Asaltos a la historia: reimaginando la ficción histórica hispanoamericana* (México DF, CP: Ediciones Eón, 2014)

República Argentina, Junta Militar, *Documentos básicos y bases políticas de las Fuerzas Armadas para el Proceso de Reorganización Nacional* (Buenos Aires: Imprenta del Congreso de la Nación, 1980)

Riva, Sabrina, '*La revolución es un sueño eterno*, de Andrés Rivera: una subjetiva genealogía del poder', *Espéculo*, 37 (2007) <http://www.ucm.es/info/especulo/ numero37/suetern.html> [accessed 26 September 2019]

Rivera, Andrés, *La revolución es un sueño eterno* (Buenos Aires: Alfaguara, 2000)

Romero, José Luis, *El desarrollo de las ideas en la sociedad argentina del siglo XX* (México: Fondo de Cultura Económica, 1965)

Romero, Luis Alberto, *La Argentina en la escuela: la idea de nación en los textos escolares* (Buenos Aires: Siglo Veintiuno, 2004)

Rouquié, Alain, *Poder militar y sociedad política en la Argentina* (Buenos Aires: Emecé, 1981)

Santos Iñurrieta, Manuel, *Mariano Moreno y un teatro de operaciones; La gracia de tener* (Buenos Aires: Ediciones del CCC Centro Cultural de Cooperación Floreal Gorini, 2012)

Sarlo, Beatriz, *Escenas de la vida posmoderna: intelectuales, arte y videocultura en la Argentina* (Buenos Aires: Ariel, 1994)

—, 'Sujetos y tecnologías: la novela después de la historia', *Punto de vista*, 86 (2006), 1–6

Serapio, Carolina, '¿Es este el fin? (Acerca de *El ojo de la patria* de Osvaldo Soriano)', in *El archivo de la independencia y la ficción contemporánea*, ed. by Alicia Chibán (Salta: Universidad Nacional de Salta, 2004), pp. 233–45

Serrano, Raúl, 'El bachín: teatro militante', *La revista del CCC*, 11 (2011) <http://www.centrocultural.coop/revista/articulo/198/> [accessed 21 September 2013]

Shumway, Nicolas, *The Invention of Argentina* (Berkeley: University of California Press, 1991)

Sigal, Silvia, and Eliseo Verón, *Perón o muerte: los fundamentos discursivos del fenómeno peronista* (Buenos Aires: Legasa, 1986)

Simpson, Amelia S., *Detective Fiction from Latin America* (Rutherford: Fairleigh Dickinson University Press, 1990)

Smith, Colin (ed.), *Poema de mío Cid* (Madrid: Cátedra, 1976)

Sommer, Doris, *Foundational Fictions: The National Romances of Latin America* (Berkeley: University of California Press, 1991)

—, 'Cucurto's Cardboard Coloring Book: Argentine Independence and Other Stories to Recycle', *Perífrasis*, 1(1) (2010), 7–15

Soriano, Osvaldo, *No habrá más penas ni olvido* (Barcelona: Bruguera, 1980)

—, *El ojo de la patria*, 2nd edn (Buenos Aires: Sudamericana, 1992)

—, *Cuentos de los años felices*, 6th edn (Buenos Aires: Sudamericana, 1994)

—, '24 de Marzo', *Página 12*, 24 March 1996, reproduced at <http://www.elortiba.org/soriano.html> [accessed 30 August 2013]

Svampa, Maristella, *El dilema argentino: civilización o barbarie: de Sarmiento al revisionismo peronista* (Buenos Aires: El cielo por asalto, 1994)

—, *La sociedad excluyente: la Argentina bajo el signo del neoliberalismo* (Buenos Aires: Taurus, 2005)

Varela, Mirta, *Los hombres ilustres del Billiken: héroes en los medios y en la escuela* (Buenos Aires: Colihue, 1994)

Vázquez Villanueva, Graciana, 'Discurso intelectual y Bicentenario: memorias y utopías', in *Memorias del Bicentenario: discursos e ideologías*, ed. by Graciana Vázquez Villanueva (Buenos Aires: Facultad de Filosofía y Letras, Universidad de Buenos Aires, 2010), pp. 209–34

Vezzetti, Hugo, *Sobre la violencia revolucionaria: memorias y olvidos* (Buenos Aires: Siglo Veintiuno, 2009)

Vila, Pablo, *Troubling Gender: Youth and Cumbia in Argentina's Music Scene* (Philadelphia: Temple University Press, 2011)

Weldt-Basson, Helene Carol (ed.), *Redefining the Latin American Historical Novel: The Impact of Feminism and Postcolonialism* (Basingstoke: Palgrave Macmillan, 2013)

White, Hayden V., *Metahistory: The Historical Imagination in Nineteenth-century Europe* (Baltimore: Johns Hopkins University Press, 1973)

Woods, Brett F., *Neutral Ground: A Political History of Espionage Fiction* (New York: Algora, 2008)

Yankelevich, Pablo, 'Tras las huellas del exilio: a manera de presentación', in *Represión y destierro: itinerarios del exilio argentino*, ed. by Pablo Yankelevich (La Plata: Al Margen, 2004), pp. 9–16

Zipes, Jack, *Fairy Tales and the Art of Subversion: The Classical Genre for Children and the Process of Civilization* (London: Heinemann, 1983)

# Index